DawnKing

Janalyn Voigt

DawnKing
COPYRIGHT 2019 by Janalyn Voigt

All scripture quotations, unless otherwise indicated, are taken from the Holy Bible, New International Version(R), NIV(R), Copyright 1973, 1978, 1984, 2011 by Biblica, Inc.™ Used by permission of Zondervan. All rights reserved worldwide. www.zondervan.com

The Author is represented by and this book is published in association with the literary agency of WordServe Literary Group, Ltd., www.wordserveliterary.com.

Harbourlight Books, a division of Pelican Ventures, LLC
www.pelicanbookgroup.com PO Box 1738 *Aztec, NM * 87410

Harbourlight Books sail and mast logo is a trademark of Pelican Ventures, LLC

Publishing History
First Harbourlight Edition, 2020
Paperback Edition ISBN 978-1-5223-0207-0
Electronic Edition ISBN 978-1-5223-0205-6
Published in the United States of America

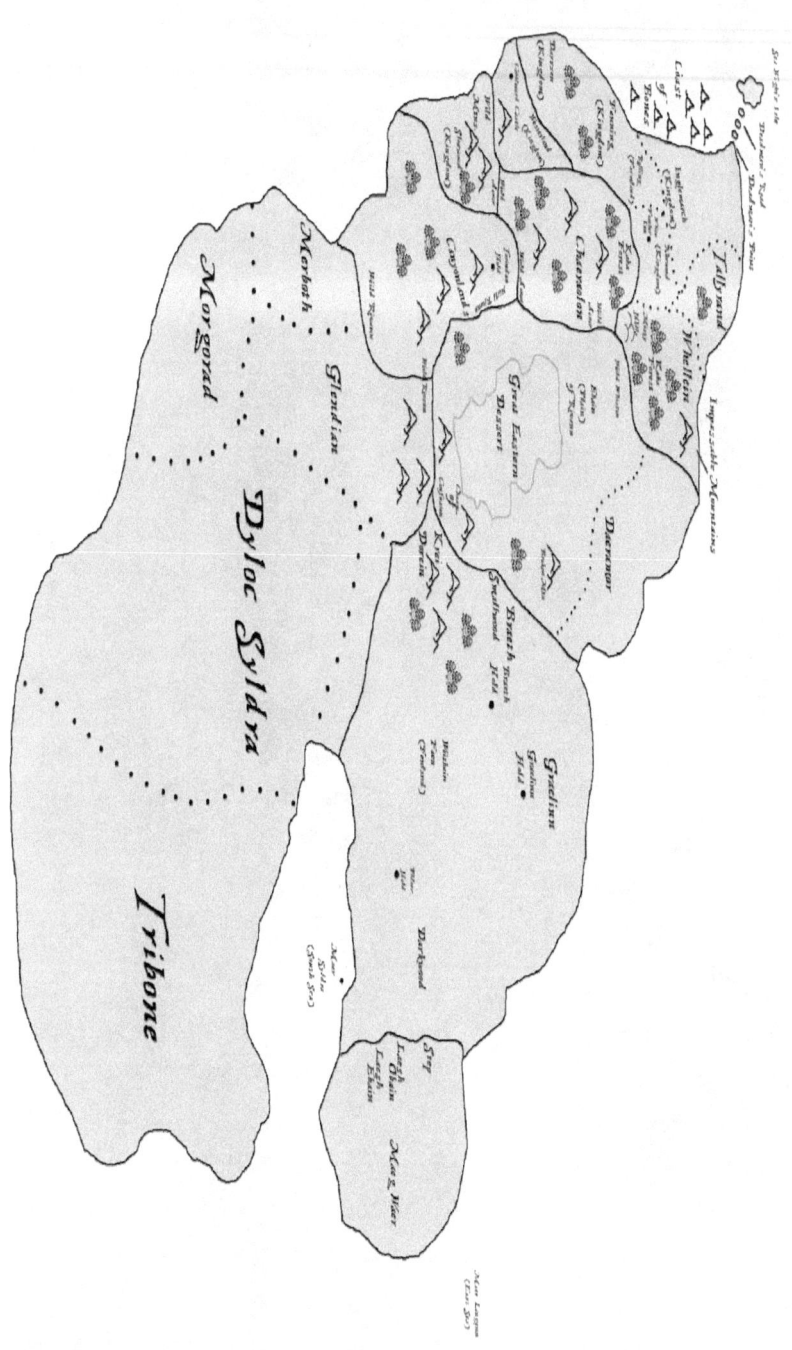

Janalyn Voigt is a fresh voice in the realm of fantasy. Her writing is crisp, her verbs muscular, and it's all wrapped up in a lyrical style. Blending action and romance, DawnSinger is a journey through fear, failure, and faith, and I look forward to its sequel. Eric Wilson, NY Times bestselling author of Valley of Bones and One Step Away

In DawnSinger, Janalyn Voigt has penned a novel full of surprises. With adventure, mystery, and an unlikely romance, this beautiful, epic fantasy debut will leave you scrambling for the next book in the trilogy. Jill Williamson, Christy Award-winning author of By Darkness Hid

DawnSinger is a delightful fantasy spun with bardic prose and threaded with danger and intrigue. Linda Windsor, author of Healer, Thief and Rebel, Brides of Alba Historical Trilogy

Janalyn Voigt builds an exciting world, tranquil on the surface but filled with danger, ancient enemies, and a prophecy yet to be fulfilled. DawnSinger leads you into a land only imagined in dreams. I can't wait to read the second book in the Tales of Faeraven trilogy. Lisa Grace, bestselling author of the Angel in the Shadows series.

Part 1
Treacherous Journey

1

"Easy now." The wind buffeted Kai's face as he leaned forward to put a hand on his winged horse's shoulder. Battle cries, explosions, and screams littered the air. Repressing his own urge to bolt, he turned Flecht to meet the welke riders approaching from Torindan. Regret flooded him. Both he and his wingabeast would die. Torindan would fall this day, thrusting the once-united Kindren kingdoms into confusion.

Conquering the high hold of Faeraven would not appease Freaer's blood lust. A stronghold could fall and be rebuilt, as Freaer himself had proven at Pilaer. Ah, but a heart, once silenced, would never beat again. While the Lof Shraen of Faeraven and the daughter he'd named his heir remained alive, Freaer would not rest.

Elcon and Mara had been among those who'd

escaped with him from Torindan. If he had anything to say in the matter, they would yet avoid capture. Surviving a clash with two of Freaer's finest seemed unlikely, but Kai could delay the assassins.

The giant raptor birds flapped their ragged wings and snapped the air with pointed beaks in a display of ferocity. Sunlight gleamed along their rider's swords, no doubt honed to wicked sharpness.

Kai's skin crawled. Garbed in the red of Freaer's elite assassins, the welke riders glared at him across the intervening distance, a space closing with alarming speed.

Kai touched the reins against his wingabeast's neck, all it took to tilt Flecht sideways and away. The wind snatched at Kai's breath, and he turned his face to breathe. Silver wings fanned around him and stroked downward. The wingabeast leveled in flight.

Bloodcurdling shrieks rent the air, the welkes' hunting cry.

Kai's heart raced, and he looked back. Both riders were following, one pulling ahead of the other. Flecht's course carried them above the forest that stretched across Elder lands to the sea. He guided Flecht lower, ready to duck beneath the tree canopy. Tiny, flitling birds darted through kaba leaves so thick they left no gap. If he tried to break through the screen of leaves and branches here, Flecht's feathers would shred. Only one choice remained.

He drew his sword and turned to meet the attack. The hiss of flight feathers reached him along with the stench of the assassin's sweat. Flecht shuddered but held. Metal grated against metal with jarring force. The assassin grunted and fell back.

His arm numbed by the blow, Kai retreated.

The second welke rider bore down on Kai.

With his good arm, Kai deflected the assassin's blows.

The welkes hovered abreast. The first assassin showed gapped teeth in a malevolent grin. "Want to fight, do you? Well then, Kindren, let's see what you're made of." The two circled him.

"What's that smell?" The first asked.

The second, smaller in stature, made an exaggerated sniffing sound. "Stinks like fear to me."

"You're not so brave." The gap-toothed smile mocked him again.

Ignoring the obvious ploy to break his concentration, Kai gritted his teeth and ran at the smaller of the two. The rider met his blow with stunning force. Kai fell back. The first rider set upon him at once. Kai shifted, but the blow caught his chest, the sword tip penetrating his surcoat and chain mail. Warmth ran down his side.

Shrilling, Flecht carried him backward.

The assassins took turns punishing Kai, allowing him no rest.

Flecht's sides heaved but bore Kai without balking. Kai faced his tormentors, panting like an old man. Neither he nor his wingabeast could go on like this. If the assassins took his life they might spare Flecht.

Kai bowed his head and waited for the end to come.

Riffling followed by a thump brought his head up. An arrow protruded from one of the welke's chests. Its gap-toothed rider widened his eyes. Shrieking, the raptor bird slipped from the sky.

An expression of terror spread across the smaller

rider's face. A bowstring sang somewhere below, and a second arrow planted itself in the remaining welke's chest. The raptor bird must have died on the instant, for it made no sound as it hurtled downward, carrying its screaming rider to his doom.

A wingabeast erupted into the air beside Kai.

Flecht shrilled and backed.

"Steady!" Kai called.

Aerlic, his bow slung behind him, perched on his silver wingabeast.

Kai gave him a nod. "I'm glad to see you."

"I can well imagine."

"Thank you for saving my life."

Aerlic nodded. "You shouldn't have tried to fight alone. Next time take me along."

Kai smiled at the flame-haired archer, the best shot among the guardians of Rivenn. "I'll bear that in mind."

"We should go." Aerlic gestured with his head. "Unless you want to take on more welke riders."

Kai followed the archer's gaze.

Above the pyres of smoke spiraling into the air behind Torindan's curtain wall rose a flock of welke riders.

"You're bleeding!"

Remembering the prick of pain from the assassin's sword tip, Kai looked down to the blood oozing through his surcoat. "I don't think it's much."

"We need to tend your wound."

"That's not exactly convenient right now."

"Your dying from blood loss would be less so."

Kai's lips twisted in a smile. "You have a point."

"There's a cave I know nearby where we can hide. Can you make it there?"

Weakness assailed Kai, but he had to continue. "Lead on."

The archer sent his wingabeast south and west, traveling low. Kai kept pace, forcing himself to remain upright in the saddle. They scaled the west side of a peak and slipped around to a ledge facing east. The wingabeasts touched down behind a screen of plume trees.

Kai held back a gasp while Aerlic helped him out of his surcoat and chain mail.

Examining the gash in Kai's side, Aerlic hissed in air. "That must be painful." Aerlic cleansed the wound with water from his drinking supply and rubbed ointment at its edges before binding it with bandages.

Kai pulled on his surcoat. "We should leave." He crept outside to look through the plume trees' white foliage.

Aerlic came up beside him. "I don't think that's a good idea."

Kai winced at the truth of this. Welke riders dotted the sky, clearly searching. "I hope the others hide well."

ભ

Alongside the crossroads before Mara, a weilo drooped its branches. The tree's curling leaves rustled as if whispering secrets, but she knew it for a trick of the wind. If only a tree could tell Rand and her which way led to Cobbleford. The main road bent back upon itself to run south and east, but a fork turned north in the direction they wanted to travel. Taking it meant fording the river near the remnant of a washed-out bridge. Either that or they would have to fly across on the wingabeast, not a reassuring thought. Rand's lack of skill riding a winged horse nearly matched her own. After such a promising start, the path faded into thorny underbrush where blackened spars pointed skyward. A fire had once raged through here. The path reappeared at the mouth of a gloomy stand of keirken trees. "Why is there no sign to mark the paths?"

"Don't worry, Mara." Rand's smile bolstered her. "The way seems clear."

Mara's skin crawled at the thought of entering that tunnel of trees. All sorts of creatures could jump out at them from the heavy shadows. "I don't like the look of that forest."

Rand glanced into the distance. "I'll confess it seems unwelcoming, but you can't always choose your path."

"The main road might reverse itself and lead north."

His forehead creased. "I doubt that will happen."

"Are you certain?" Mara couldn't help but ask. "I think we should find out for sure before going the other way. That fork isn't well traveled. What if it's a dead end?"

"I'm certain that is the path we should take." He nodded as if that settled it.

Mara crossed her arms. "Taking it upon yourself to escort me to Cobbleford does not give you permission to make every choice for us both."

His gaze searched her face. "I'm sorry, Mara, but I know more about finding my way in the woods than you do."

She gritted her teeth. "Don't forget that I grew up at the White Feather Inn. While gathering wild foods for our guests I learned my share of woodcraft."

"Why do you want to go the wrong way, then?"

"You can't know it's the wrong way for certain."

His jaw firmed. "Look, we're wasting time. Why don't we talk by the water? The wingabeast needs to drink."

Mara stuck out her chin. "I'd rather be alone right now."

"Lof Raena, may I remind you—"

"No you may not." She arched an eyebrow for emphasis. "I don't want to hear anything you have to tell the high princess of Faeraven." Tears clogged the back of her throat, and she turned her head to keep him from seeing them fall. A lof raena usually had a kingdom to serve, but hers had fallen and might never rise again. That mattered to her more than she'd realized.

He blew out a breath. "Will you see reason? I can't go off and leave you alone."

She stopped herself from reminding him that he'd done just that without hesitating when he'd abandoned her in the wilderness. Bringing up something he'd apologized for wouldn't be fair. Trusting him again would take time, and his trampling her emotions didn't help. On impulse, she pushed through the weilo's trailing branches into the shade beneath the tree. In its privacy, she dried her cheeks on her sleeve before pushing aside the screening leaves to look out at him. "I prefer to wait here."

Rand opened his mouth but shut it again. "Suit yourself." He stomped off toward the river, the wingabeast following him with graceful steps.

Mara let the leaves fall back into place. The green shade beneath the tree embraced her. A flaemling landed on a branch above her and flicked its red feathers. The bird opened its throat and voiced an aching lament that resounded deep within her. Her father might be dead or dying. If he passed into the Land Beyond, her life would change forever. How could she disappoint the hope he'd placed in her? She would have to ascend to the high throne of Faeraven.

Mara peered out from the screen of leaves. The lonely road ran straight then disappeared around a bend. That it might curve back around the right direction seemed possible. Rand should be more reasonable. If he was wrong about the fork he wanted to follow, they would lose time retracing their footsteps. They really should make sure the main road didn't bend northward before taking that derelict track. She left her hiding place and stepped onto the road. Her feet made little sound as she hurried along. Fading sunlight slanted through the trees that lined the road, casting long shadows. She went around the bend and stopped, undecided. The road curved westward just ahead. If she didn't start back, Rand might return and find her gone. She didn't want to worry him, but how could she give up without going just a little farther? And yet…

Something felt wrong.

A grove of strongwoods lifted twisted branches against the deepening sky. The trees bordered a meadow thick with undergrowth. Anything could be hiding in there.

She should go back. Curiosity lured her onward. The bend wasn't far. She started forward, darting glances into the shadows. The sensation of someone watching crawled over her skin. Mara's steps slowed. She should persuade Rand to come back with her.

Movement flickered at the edge of her vision.

A grey wolf loped out of the underbrush and halted a small distance away. A black one joined the first, then another grey. Dying sunlight glossed the wolves' coats as they watched her with piercing gazes.

Mara turned to leave.

More wolves stood between her and escape. She darted glances behind her. The beasts ringed her about on every side. Tongues lolling and saliva dripping, they stalked closer.

Mara's mouth went dry. With shaking hands, she unsheathed the dagger from the belt at her waist. Its weight in her hand comforted her, but the blade wouldn't offer much help against so many. She picked up a rock at her feet and flung it at one of the wolves, her arm good from long practice. Da had taught her in childhood to fell birds for the pot with a well-aimed stone. The wolf yelped and bolted into the meadow. Mara threw a second rock. Another went running. A rangy white wolf, the largest of them all, fixed her with an unwavering stare.

Never taking her eyes from the beast, she reached for another rock.

The white wolf crouched, ready to spring.

Mara straightened slowly. She hauled back her arm.

The wolf sprang for her throat.

CR

Rand cupped the back of his neck with his hand and drew a deep breath of the moist air flowing above the White Feather River. He didn't understand Mara's stubborn insistence on traveling the opposite direction of her destination. She seemed to enjoy countering him. Either that or she felt reluctant to arrive at Cobbleford Castle. Could that be the trouble? Cast upon the wild lands after the fall of Torindan, she had little choice but to seek asylum with her grandfather. Rand could hope that her father would not die of the wounds his brother had inflicted on him. If he did, Rand's father would have assured the demise of the Alliance of Faeraven. The only thing that could stop that happening would be if Mara took her place as the new Lof Raelein, ruler of Faeraven. She would need to gather the scattered Kindren and call for help from the Elder nation. She could no more escape her duty than Rand could his father's wrath for keeping her alive to perform it.

The wingabeast waded into a shallow place up to its forelegs and lipped the water. Sunlight gilded the surface while blue and green lights gleamed in the currents, reflections of the sky and the weilos that leaned from the banks. Something boomed downstream, no doubt a log crashing against a boulder. He sampled the air and let out his breath in a sigh.

The way north did look rough, but the fact that neither Kindren nor Elder willingly entered the wild lands explained the road's neglect.

Rand squared his shoulders. He refused to let Mara stop him from delivering her into her grandfather's safekeeping.

He shouldn't have left her alone back there. The thought presented itself, impossible to ignore. He wouldn't have done it if she hadn't irked him, but he counted that no excuse. Irritation had clouded his judgment. The woods held perils from which the dagger at her belt would not protect her. *Time to go.*

He whistled for the wingabeast. The graceful creature lifted its head and waded back to him, shedding water. Rand patted its arched neck and took up the reins. With a growing sense of urgency, he led the animal from the bank toward the weilo where he'd left Mara. A glance into the hiding place at the heart of the tree did not ease him. Light filtering through the screen of leaves revealed her absence. He peered down the road and caught sight of Mara hurrying along the road. Her strong mind left her vulnerable, as now. Protecting such a spirited woman wasn't easy, but for her sake and his own he must learn. He started after her.

Mara rounded the bend, never looking back, and moved out of sight. Rand ran to catch up but slowed as he approached the bend. He didn't want to startle her, although a fright might teach her not to wander off alone. Mara came into view, surrounded by wolves at the edge of a grove of keirkens. Rand halted in the road to gauge the situation. Before he could decide what to do, Mara hurtled a rock into the pack. It made a dull thud. A wolf yelped and fled. Mara fobbed a rock at a second wolf. The creature streaked away behind the first.

Rand pulled the knife from his boot and crept closer. Mara was doing well on her own, but she couldn't fend off so many.

She bent to pick up another rock.

A white wolf snarled and gathered for a leap.

Rand's heart thudded. He would never reach Mara in time. He hauled back his arm.

The white wolf leaped.

Rand hurled his knife.

Time slowed. The blade sang, joined by the whoosh of an arrow. Rand's blade embedded in the wolf's throat in the instant a feathered shaft penetrated it's side. The beast dropped to the forest floor, eyes staring.

Arrows pelted the pack. Several of the lanky creatures fell. The wolves scattered across the meadow.

Rand rushed to the white wolf and retrieved his blade from its throat.

The rock fell from Mara's grasp. She swayed on her feet.

Rand stepped between her and the grove. The arrows had come from above. He scanned the trees, weighted by shadow, although here and there golden light filtered through. In several of those places the leaves moved more than the light breeze would warrant.

"Who's there?" His challenge rang out. "Show yourself!"

"Says who?" a gruff voice asked. An arrow pierced the ground at Rand's feet. Laughter rang through the trees.

"Hold your fire!" A second voice thundered the command. The merriment died away.

Rand squinted, trying to see. "Whoever you are, thank you for protecting my companion from the wolves."

"Filthy beasts." The gruff voice spoke again.

"Why would such a tender maiden walk alone in these woods?" The leader called in a voice bearing the stamp of the southern kingdoms.

Rand pinpointed his location in one of the darker patches of shadow. "Only the maiden can answer that question."

"She will have that chance, but not in your presence."

Rand tightened his grip on his knife. "I am her protector."

"We have seen how well you perform that duty." The leader retorted.

Heat rushed through Rand at the truth of this observation. He had let his emotions rule him and utterly failed Mara.

"My guardian and I must continue our journey without delay," Mara spoke from behind Rand.

"I am not so certain of that, fair maiden." The leader's tone softened.

"We are on an errand of utmost importance!" Mara's voice shook.

"Be careful what you say to strangers, Mara." Rand warned her without turning his head.

"Do you silence her now? I have heard enough. Drop your blade and step away from the maid."

The hilt of Rand's knife pressed his palm. How could he do anything of the sort? He would die for Mara if the need arose. And yet...he could never hope to defeat them all. If he tried, Mara might be injured. Throwing his life away would do nothing to protect her, but as long as he remained alive, he might find a way to help her.

He laid his weapon on the ground and stepped away from Mara.

2

THE OUTLAW LEADER

Mara wanted to weep at how quickly Rand moved away from her. When her father had commanded him to leave her alone, he had given up easily then too. And yet, what else could he do? She would not want him to die for her.

"Bind his hands," the leader snarled.

Several men dropped from the trees and thudded to the ground. Dressed in rough garb and wearing masks and hoods in the manner of outlaws, they surrounded Rand.

With her view cut off, Mara strained to see. "Don't harm him!"

"Will you defend him?" The leader's query wafted from the trees.

"Are you a coward to speak from hiding?" She provoked him. "Show yourself."

"You remind me of a maid I once knew. Her temper often bested her."

His voice seemed familiar, somehow. She scowled, trying to place it.

"But since you insist..." With a rustling of leaves he swung down, a dark figure hanging by a branch. He dropped and strode to her. A mask covered most of his face, and a cap covered his head. The leather jerkin of a hunter stretched across his broad shoulders. "Never let it be said I denied a maiden's request."

"Who are you?" she asked, overcome by the sensation that she knew him.

"A man living out his days in the wild."

"Why do you conceal your face behind a mask?"

He flashed a smile. "Perhaps I do not wish to offend those forced to gaze upon it."

Most of the men left Rand and came to stand behind their leader. They had bound Rand's hands behind his back.

"What shall we do with him?" A burly man, one of several who remained beside Rand, asked in gruff tones.

"Blindfold him." The outlaw leader gestured with his head. "Take him to camp."

"Must we?" the burly man screwed up an eye. "I've an idea he's trouble."

"You're probably right, Trader, but he and I need to finish our talk." He circled Rand, looking him up and down. "Something tells me he's not who he seems."

Rand glared at the leader but said nothing.

Trader untied the strip of cloth that bound his sleeve at the cuff and knotted it around Rand's head.

Flanked by two of the band with one following and another before him, Rand disappeared into the darkness of the keirken grove.

"Where are you taking him?" Mara asked in sharp tones.

"Does it matter that much to you?" The leader spoke in the accent of the north.

"Your voice…" She trailed off, trying again to place him.

"Never mind me. I want to help you. Tell me, has

your companion harmed you?"

Why should an odd tremor run through his voice? It reminded her of other words spoken long ago, when she'd taken her leave from a friend. Her eyes narrowed. "If I didn't know better..."

"Will you answer my question?"

He'd thrown her by disguising his voice and hiding his face but she knew him now. "Tell me your name."

"What does it matter? They call me Searcher. That is who I am, with my domain the wild lands and my heritage the wind."

"Why did you leave your job in the stables, Hael? You should be home at the inn."

He took her arm and pulled her away from the others. "Mara —"

She leaned closer and lowered her voice. "Tell me what happened."

"I couldn't stay after—well, everything. Your father understood and released me from my pledge of service."

Mara understood what he hadn't said, that she had broken his heart. Guilt stabbed her once again, but she couldn't change her feelings. "But surely your skill with horses would bring you another job."

"I was on my way to promise myself to the king of Norwood for a life of service and fell in with the wrong traveling companions. They stole my horse and, when I tried to reclaim him, accused me of thievery."

The injustice of being charged in the theft of one's own horse bore in on her. "Couldn't you prove your innocence?"

"They'd taken my horse's papers and forged a sale, but I couldn't prove the lie."

"But horse theft! That's punishable by—"

"Death." He gave a quick nod. "That's why I've lived as a fugitive ever since."

She touched his sleeve. "Oh, Hael. I'm sorry."

He smiled. "I've survived well enough, thanks to my grandfather, Taels."

"I remember you speaking of the things he showed you."

Hael smiled. "He taught me how to survive in the forest." A gust of wind rustled the trees at their tops but left them untouched below. He glanced up. "It's growing dark. We should go. You'll be safe in our camp tonight."

"That's where you sent Rand."

"Don't worry. I won't allow him near you."

"I'm not afraid of Rand." She released her breath. "He hasn't harmed me, at least not in body."

His fingers trailed across her cheek. "Has he hurt you in other ways?"

"He's made me cry." She shook her head, unable to explain her relationship with Rand to a man who might still be in love with her.

"Back at the inn, when he first came, something seemed strange about him."

Mara thought back to how quickly Rand had agreed to help her run away from home, how he had taken her knife and held it to her throat in the burned-out homefarm that hid them. Later, he'd forsaken her in the wilderness. But Hael knew nothing of that. "What do you mean?"

"Don't trust him, Mara." Hael gritted out the words. "I'm certain he means you ill."

The blindfold came away from Mara's eyes. She took an uncertain step.

Hael grasped her arm. "Steady there."

"My eyes are blurry from that blindfold."

"Sorry, Mara, but it protects you as well as my band. After you leave, you can tell anyone who might question you that you don't know the camp's location."

Mara's vision cleared just as Hael removed the mask from his face. In the wavering light from a campfire at the center of the small clearing where they stood, he looked unchanged from the friend she remembered. A ragtag group of men lounged about the fire with tin plates of stew. A few women sat among the men or helped with the cooking. Weathered by life outdoors, they appeared, at least in firelight, to retain a certain beauty. One with a smile that flashed often caught Mara's attention. She gave orders to the others preparing the food, obviously in charge. Her colorful skirts flowed with her mincing step, while the dark tangle that rippled down her back swayed in rhythm.

At the edge of the firelight huddled a group of wagons with rounded tops. Mara had seen wanderers' wagons often at the inn. Travelers of the open road, the owners made their way through Norwood, parting with their wares in exchange for a meal, a brace of pheasants, or crocks of jam. On summer nights their stirring music would drift through the open window of her bedchamber. She'd sneak out and glimpse them dancing in their camps. The sight had awakened an ache within her.

Wanderers lived with a freedom that she, bound

to her chores at the inn, could not fathom. Aunt Brynn had nothing good to say about them. Beggars and thieves, she'd called them. Ma'am had been more charitable, naming them lost souls. Only Da seemed to understand their chosen way of life. It was not for him, he said, to drift about the world, but — and his eyes gleamed — he admired those who did.

The gruff-voiced man named Trader stopped to speak with the woman in colorful skirts. She gave him a plate and a lanthorn, which he lifted before him. Mara watched it swaying in the darkness until it stopped at the edge of the clearing.

The lanthorn light picked out a figure seated on the ground and leaning against a keirken. The leather jerkin he wore looked like Rand's. Trader lowered the horn lamp to a boulder and set the plate beside it. The square of light it cast picked out the sitting man's features and showed the rope around his waist that tethered him to the trunk behind him. Trader crouched and untied Rand's hands, leaving his legs bound.

Mara laid a hand on Hael's arm. "You must free Rand. It's not fair to keep him tied like a beast."

Hael bent his head to her. "Don't ask this of me."

Mara shifted away from him. "You seem a stranger to me now, someone to fear."

"Because I will not free a man I distrust? I'm sorry, Mara. I won't do that even for you."

"But I need him to guide my path."

"I'll do that instead. Where was he taking you?"

"To Cobbleford." Could she trust Hael? She had once thought so. Now she wasn't sure.

"You mentioned an urgent errand."

She gazed into the fire, where flames wrapped hungrily around the logs. She pulled in a breath and told the simple truth. "I don't wish to talk any more. I'm weary."

"I should have realized that. Come with me." Hael led her to the colorful woman she had admired. "Nadya, please care for my friend."

The woman looked her over with dark eyes while firelight cast a golden sheen over her skin. "What is her name?" Nadya spoke in the heavy accent of her people.

"I'm Mara."

"Oh, ho! You have brought home a wild dove who speaks for herself." She gave a quick nod, and the chains about her neck jangled. "Leave her to me."

Hael's gaze rested on Mara. "She escaped an attack by wolves this day and needs a quiet place to rest."

"Trader told me what happened." Nadya frowned. "Were you hurt?"

Mara shook her head.

"Thank you, Nadya." Hael touched Mara's hand in parting.

"You are hungry?" Nadya asked.

"Whatever you have in that pot smells delicious."

"You like bruin stew?" Nadya bent to fill a plate. "Sit and eat." She gestured with her hands as if to make her accented words more understandable.

"Thank you." Mara accepted the food and sank onto the stool Nadya had indicated. It had no padding, but after spending so long on her feet she welcomed the chance to sit down. She applied herself to her meal, the warm stew comforting both stomach and soul.

"So hungry." Nadya perched on a nearby stool.

"We've eaten mostly trail food for days. My guide hunts well, and I can net fish, but we couldn't take the time to do either."

"Why your hurry?"

Nadya's sympathy tempted Mara to broach the subject she'd avoided with Hael. Caution held her back. She shrugged. "We did not wish to linger in the wild lands."

"You are a long way from home, I think."

The truth struck Mara with unexpected force. "I have no home."

Nadya shook her head. "I am sorry for you."

"But you don't have a home either."

Nadya gestured with her head toward the wagons. "Mine goes along with me. I would not like to lose it."

Understanding dawned on Mara. She'd never considered how wanderers felt about their movable homes. "Have you always lived in a wagon?"

"Of course." Nadya looked at her as if she'd taken leave of her senses. "I am a wanderer."

"Why do you live in a camp of outlaws then?" At the thought she might have been too personal, Mara's face warmed. "If you don't mind my asking."

"My husband and I would have brought sorrow to our people if we had stayed with them. We had to leave, for their sakes." Nadya picked up a stick and poked at the fire, a moody expression on her face. Curious but unwilling to ask another nosy question, Mara waited for her to speak again. A log fell in the fire, sending sparks flying. Nadya roused and looked at Mara. "Tell me, have you ever been in love?"

"I—I'm not sure."

"With love, you should be sure. I welcomed my parents' choice for my husband. Trader and I understood one another. How should we not when we grew up together? I told myself I loved him when we married, but I didn't know what that meant until later, when I almost lost him."

"Trader is your husband?" Mara tried to imagine the burly man married to Nadya and couldn't.

Nadya smiled. "You have met Trader? My husband talks rough, I know, but he is very kind. We sold our wares enough to keep body and soul together, but Trader sometimes gave away as much as he sold. Too bad he cannot trade anymore."

"What happened?" Engrossed by the story, Mara lost her shyness.

Nadya shook her head. "If only we had not stopped at Darksea, we might still be found on the road among our people. I danced to draw a crowd for trading. It always worked." She spoke with honesty rather than pride. Mara could imagine that a beautiful and graceful woman like Nadya would have no trouble drawing a crowd. "Raefe, the prince of Darksea, watched me dance on the shore of the Western Sea. He called for me afterward to warm his bed, but Trader and I left Darksea by the old roads. The prince could not follow us. My escape shamed him, and he claimed that I had snared him by dark arts. No matter where we went after that, we were driven away along with anyone who dared travel with us."

"I'm sorry."

Nadya nodded. "I miss my family, but Trader and I are happy here. It's nice to live in peace."

"Do you all live in wagons?"

"Some sleep there." Nadya gestured upward.

A raft of stars drifted in the sky above the clearing. "I don't understand…"

"Not there." Nadya grinned. "Darkness hides the bluff behind us. Those without a wagon make their home in caves. Why do you have no home?"

Rand would warn her to guard her tongue. "That's too long a tale, I'm afraid."

"And you are ready for sleep? Never mind, little dove. In my wagon tonight, you will find a home."

A second lanthorn floated across the clearing. Hael's face stood out above the light, which soon reached to Rand and Trader. Hael spoke to Rand with tension in his posture. Whatever he had to say, Mara had an idea Rand wouldn't enjoy hearing it.

ભ

Rand looked up from his plate at the crunch of footsteps.

The outlaw leader approached with a lanthorn. The impulse to push to his feet and wait for the man in a fighting stance surged over Rand. He fisted his hands, but then sagged in helplessness.. He could do nothing to defend himself or Mara while tied to this accursed tree.

"Searcher honors you with his presence." The burly man proclaimed.

Rand bit back the sarcastic retort that pressed his lips. Reviling the outlaw leader might make him feel better but it wouldn't help free him. Searcher still wore his mask and dark, tousled hair sprang from beneath his cap. He lowered his lanthorn and peered at Rand. "Well, now. You look a mite more subdued."

Rand glared at him but gave no other response. A lifetime of enduring his older half-brother's beatings had taught him to avoid being baited. He had learned that a clear head with no blade made a better weapon than a sword in angry hands. Rand didn't miss the tension in the outlaw leader's shoulders or the way he balled his hands into fists. His own unwillingness to be drawn had found its mark.

"State your name and raven," the leader snapped.

"I am Rand of...Daeramor," he spat out the name of the first Kindren kingdom that crossed his mind. If he said he came from Pilaer, they'd string him up at once. Even in the lanthorn light, Rand could tell by the leader's frown that he'd caught his hesitation.

"*Where* in Daeramor Raven?"

"Arramondan." Rand brought out the name of the raven's stronghold. "Do you know of it?"

"I'll say that I do." A smile covered Searcher's face. "I hid in caves within the graystone cliffs before coming here. I don't recall hearing of a *Rand* in town. Is the name short for anything?"

Rand didn't want to admit that it stood for Randolph. Most Kindren had not heard of Randolph of Pilaer, the Contender's illegitimate son, and the Elder were even less likely to know of him. In the present circumstances, revealing secrets to his captor seemed a bad idea. "It's just Rand."

The leader pressed his lips together but, if he had doubts, did not comment on them. "Rand of Daeramor, what is your occupation?"

"I am but a tracker who supplies game for the shraen's table."

Searcher stood over him menacingly. "And how did you come into the company of Mara of Norwood?"

Rand hesitated again. He couldn't tell the whole truth about that either. If he revealed that his father had sent him to the White Feather Inn to kill Mara, he might never see the light of morning. He shrugged.

"She hired me to take her to relatives in Westerland."

"Oh?" the outlaw leader's voice trembled with an emotion Rand could not identify. "Whereabouts did this happen?"

"In Rivenn." Rand volunteered no other information, hoping that the leader would not question Mara and discover the falsehood in what he had already said. What would Mara say of him? Rand could only hope that in some small way he had begun to earn her trust.

The leader leaned closer. "You are lying. I know it."

"Why would you say that?" Rand shot back. "I'm certain you are mistaken."

"Don't play with me. I know when and where you met Mara, and it wasn't in Rivenn. Mara told me that you made her cry. I'll see you hanged before I ever let you near her again." He strode off with his lanthorn jerking from side to side.

Rand whistled under his breath.

"It's best not to anger Searcher." Trader, who had stood quietly by throughout the confrontation, took Rand's plate from his unresisting hands. "Your stew's gone cold. Shall I fetch more?"

Rand shook his head, no longer hungry. While Trader tied his hands again, Rand leaned his head against the tree and closed his eyes. If he'd learned anything from the conversation it was that Searcher's interest in Mara was intense for a stranger. Almost, it could be that of a lover. At that thought, all clear-mindedness forsook him.

3

THE HIDING PLACE

Kai parted the brush at the edge of the cliff and looked out over a landscape where welkes flapped their ragged wings and warriors garbed in red and gold crowded the open spaces. Stands of strongwoods and keirkens offered the illusion of refuge to those still fleeing from Torindan. In the distance, kaba trees wove their tops into a canopy that stretched westward. To the east, smoke choked the air above the ruins of Torindan. He looked away with a lump in his throat.

Warriors rushed into a stand of strongwoods, wreaking havoc. Cries carried to him, cutting in and out of hearing, a trick of the wind. A lock of hair whipped his eyes, and he lifted a shaking hand to claw it back. Stranded here on the mountain, he could do nothing to help the victims. If he tried to fly to them, the hovering welke riders would swoop down to attack him. Against so many, he would die for nothing.

If he could have remained with Elcon, he wouldn't now worry that the cries he heard belonged to him. He shook his head to dispel his uneasy thoughts. With the welke riders in pursuit, those who had escaped Torindan with him had needed to scatter. The tracker had wanted to go with Elcon, but had yielded to Dorann, who knew how to heal with herbs, when he'd chosen to follow Anders and Elcon. Kai had no doubt that Elcon's servant would fight to the death for his master. Arillia, on Eathnor's wingabeast, went with with her husband.

Stepping back, Kai let the brush fall into place.

Aerlic kept the wick of his lanthorn low while carving a notch into one of the wooden shafts in the pile beside him. He had used his slingshot to fell a whirlight for their supper and now used the large white bird's feathers to fletch new arrows. He looked up when Kai entered the cave that had become their temporary home. "More deaths?"

Kai grimaced. "I have seen more than enough of Freaer's forces running down refugees from Torindan."

"I cannot bear to stand by and watch their plight. Trying to help might be suicide, but I'm beginning to think death a better fate than this eating away of the soul."

"Believe me, I know how you feel, but we serve the Lof Shraen before any other. We must survive and reach the Lof Raena in Cobbleford. The welke riders have eased off their night patrols. That gives us a window of time to escape."

Aerlic nodded. "Anything is better than this."

"Then we agree."

"Which route should we take?"

"Those who hide themselves in the forest flanking the road to Norwood have the best chance to survive. We should follow their example."

"Traveling north will take longer, but under the circumstances it might be safer than taking our chances in the wild lands."

"We should leave under cover of darkness, and the sooner, the better. If Freaer's armies press on to

Westerland through the wild lands, we'll be completely trapped."

"I'd better finish these, then." Aerlic bent once more to his task. "I suspect they'll come in handy."

CR

Arillia touched her husband's burning forehead. She winced when Elcon muttered gibberish she could not understand, the ravings of a feverish mind. In the far reaches of the cave where he lay, she could see his face only in dimness. Elcon's servant hovered by her side, ready to help tend him. She could not move aside easily to let him, however. She trusted Anders, but her husband's care seemed best left to the one who would suffer most if he died.

Bringing Elcon from Torindan while wounded had risked his life, but with warriors from Pilaer breaking into their hiding place, they'd had little choice. Thinking back to that awful day, she shuddered. She had known the attack would come, but its arrival had shocked her regardless.

She brushed her husband's brow with a kiss. If only he would wake, she could tell him her secret. She didn't want to face that he might die, but she would hate for him to leave her without knowing the truth.

The guardian, Eathnor, kept watch at the entrance of the cave where they sheltered. He and Anders had switched off on this duty since they'd hidden here. The vigil had taken its toll on them all. Strain marked Eathnor's face, Anders looked ready to drop from exhaustion, and she felt ready to jump at the slightest sound. How much longer could they endure being trapped here? If only Elcon had not suffered a sword driven into his side, they could have escaped into the wild lands and would not need to huddle in this dank place.

Eathnor tensed and leaned toward the opening that gave onto a ledge. "It's Dorann." He said his brother's name with marked relief and went outside. She could understand Eathnor's feeling. After welke riders followed them from Torindan, Kai had directed them to scatter. That had probably saved them, but it had also left them without knowing the whereabouts of the others or whether they even lived.

She wondered often about Syl Marinda, or Mara, as Elcon's daughter preferred to be called. Arillia couldn't deny that she had at first resented the girl. Accepting another woman's child was not easy, but she had begun to do it. She would never deny Elcon the right to pass the rulership of Faeraven to whomever he chose, but she'd once hoped to give him that heir. Her womb had betrayed her, refusing to carry a baby to birth. She had continued to hope until Elcon's daughter had turned up alive. Even then, it had seemed possible her husband would not name the half-caste girl as heir of Faeraven when many of the Kindren had rejected her Elder mother as their Lof Raelein. She wondered, not for the first time, if Elcon's feeling for the girl's dead mother had inhibited his judgment.

Arillia sighed. What good were such thoughts? Giving in to jealousy only brought pain. She must accept Elcon's choice of an heir or go mad wishing for what could never be.

Eathnor had gone out of the cave and now returned with his brother behind him. The two shared similar features and a certain sturdiness, but their coloring differed. The scant beams penetrating the opening made Dorann's hair and eyes glow with amber light, while Eathnor gazed at his brother from pale eyes, and the locks of hair that fell onto his forehead were streaked in shades of brown.

Eathnor grinned at his brother. "I thought you might find your way here."

"I couldn't leave the Lof Shraen." Dorann advanced into the cave. "Once I was certain the welke riders hadn't followed me, I circled back. I searched for days before finding your marker."

"Which one?" Eathnor remained at his post. "I left several in the hope you would return, but I couldn't make them obvious."

"Three stones laid alongside the path," Dorann looked back to answer him. "They formed roughly a half circle with the open end pointing toward a deer trail. Once I saw it, I knew where you'd gone."

"Ah, yes. I thought you'd remember this cave."

"How could I not? You and I spent more than a few days snowed in here once while hunting. We were glad to find shelter from the storm that blew in."

Eathnor laughed. "Ah, yes."

Dorann nodded toward Elcon's prostrate figure. "It's a hard thing to see the Lof Shraen wounded and lying in a cave like an animal. How does he fare?"

Eathnor glanced at Arillia before answering. "Worse than before."

Dorann crossed the cave and knelt to examine Elcon. Arillia waited for what Dorann would say. As a tracker, Dorann knew something of medicine and had skill with herbs. Perhaps he could heal her husband. She folded her arms across her middle. If the tracker told the wrong story about her husband's prospects, she couldn't bear it. Elcon must recover. She needed him with her. Why had she wasted time on foolish bickering?

"His wound gathers poisons." Dorann announced at last. "A poultice of plaintain would draw them off. I saw a patch growing on the banks of Weild Aenor. I'll go and harvest some."

"No." Eathnor shook his head. "The Lof Shraen needs your care. I'll go after the herb." He reached for his pack, propped nearby.

"All right, then." Dorann looked up from Elcon with a sober face. "Make all speed, but mind yourself out there. You wouldn't want to bump into Pilaer's finest. I had trouble with them myself."

"Point well taken." Eathnor pulled on his pack, bowed to Arillia, and slipped out of the cave.

Without a word, Anders took up his station at the opening.

"Elcon will be all right, won't he?" Arillia couldn't help but ask.

"Lof Raelein..." Dorann gave her the cautious look she'd dreaded. "Only Lof Yuel knows what will happen, but the Lof Shraen lies closer to death than to life."

"No." Arillia shrank from him. "I'm sure you're mistaken." Heat rose into her face. She bent and dispatched the contents of her stomach.

⊗

Lyneth peered down the trail in both directions. Seeing no one, she climbed over the fallen log before her and onto the humus-covered path. Her skin felt prickly from the foliage that had brushed it while she'd struggled through thick underbrush. The tips of branches and thorns she'd encountered had raised welts on her arms. How many days had it been since she'd fled the high hold? She didn't know. The ordeal had merged into one long nightmare from which she would never wake. Having seen a group of servants from Torindan put to the sword while she'd hidden, trembling in terror, made her own suffering seem less important. She'd never understood the lust for war and hoped she never would. It had taken her friends, family, and home. She'd lost her cherished position as Lof Raelein Arillia's maid and the ease she had known at Torindan. It would not, however, rob her of life, not if she could prevent it.

Her stomach growled, gnawed by pangs. She hadn't eaten in days, beyond the berries she'd found along the trail and a few wild mushrooms she knew from childhood forays with her brothers into the kaba forest. The repasts she had shared with the other servants at the high hold of Faeraven had seemed humble then but a feast now. What she wouldn't give for a fat partridge roasted on a spit, a slice of coarse brown bread, and a cup of cider to wash it down.

She would welcome a warm drink, having come away from Torindan wearing only a chemise and kirtle. With the nights chill and the days cool, she'd had to learn to survive. After the warriors had murdered the servants near her, she'd taken a cloak from one of the slain. She'd known him as Jaret, a stable worker with a booming laugh. She could not take time to bury him but thought he would have understood. His cloak hung on her, dragged the ground, and kept catching on briers, but it shielded her from much of the cold.

Lyneth licked her cracked lips and traveled along the path searching for a place to go down to Weild Rivenn to drink. The river swelled its banks below her, roaring with the fury of awakening after a long winter's freeze. She rounded a bend and came upon a bridge slung across the water. Lyneth caught her breath at the sight of a partly-submerged net floating in the water. Someone had left a fish trap unattended.

Now hunger as well as thirst drove her forward. In her eagerness, she stumbled but picked herself up and went on. What would she discover in the trap? A fat percken would be nice, but she would take whatever it offered. A person in her situation could not pick and choose. The thought occurred to her that she might steal someone else's supper, but she pushed it away. Whoever had set the trap should not have left it unattended.

She went down the faint path to the bank. With a shaking hand, she grasped the rope anchoring the net. It would be too cruel to find the trap empty. She put gave the rope a heave.

A scuffling sound warned her. Before she could turn, a body slammed her to the ground. Someone pushed her face into the dirt and held her arms behind her back.

"What are you doing here?" A masculine voice snarled the words. "Stealing my fish, are you? Well, we'll see about that."

Lyneth's breath came in small gasps, more from fear than exertion. Whoever pinned her might have a blade ready. It could be a warrior or an outlaw who lurked in the deep woods.

She twisted free in a move her brothers had taught in her early days. He grunted and fell sideways, losing his grip. Lyneth took the advantage. Reversing the hold, she sat on his back with her dagger to his throat. He was a young man, and handsomer than most. "That's no way to court a maiden."

"A maiden, you say? With your tangled hair, dirty face, and man's cloak, I took you for a hag."

"You are quite a flatterer, aren't you?" He turned without warning. Lyneth's dagger went flying, and she fell. He pulled her into his strong arms in a restraining embrace. "I think you will not use that weapon on me."

"Let me go!" she protested in a breathy voice.

"Gladly." He stood her up, dragging her with him. Her captor held her at arm's length. "Raise your head and look at me. I want to talk to you."

She bit her lip, tempted to refuse but that would not win her a fish for supper. A change of tactics might. Pushing back her irritation, she raised her head. "Forgive me for trying to take your fish, but I haven't eaten in days."

He raked her with a glance. "Who are you and how come you into the wild lands?"

"It is not seemly to demand a lady's name without giving your own beforehand, and I'm certain good manners call for you to remove your mask."

He laughed, a pleasant sound that tugged an answering smile from her. "I'll do no such thing, but you may know that I am called Searcher."

"I've heard of you."

The corners of his mouth tilted. "I hope 'twas to my credit."

"I'm sure it wasn't." She gave into the urge to annoy him. In truth, servant's gossip made him into a misunderstood hero. His unusual title had claimed her attention, which was why she remembered hearing about him. "My name is Lyneth of Rivenn. I've come away from Torindan's burning." She didn't have to fake the tremor in her voice or the tears misting her eyes. "I've lost my mistress, and I fear for her life. I don't know what to do."

"You must not be afraid. I will protect you now that I know your peril. Who is your mistress?"

It didn't seem quite safe to have an outlaw as a protector. "Arillia, Lof Raelein of Faeraven. Have you seen her?"

He shook his head. "I'm sorry, but I haven't."

"She would be on her way to Cobbleford Castle."

"That is where I am headed, as it happens. You must allow me to escort you."

About to refuse, she hesitated. Her occupation as a lady's maid had not prepared her to survive in the forest. She could admit that, if left to herself in the wild lands, she would probably die. Going with this annoying and intriguing man, at the very least, would provide a fish supper.

4

THE PRISONER

Mara lifted yet another yellow tuber from a crockery bowl on the work-table made of boards supported by trestles and applied her knife to its peel.

Nadya, on the stool across from her, glanced up from peeling tubers. "Did you sleep well last night?"

"Thank you, yes." She'd fallen asleep almost as soon as she sank into the feather tick.

"I wondered if the wagon would seem strange to you."

Nadya might find sleeping in a building as unfamiliar as Mara did passing the night in a wagon. She couldn't imagine such a life as the wanderers led, although the thought of it had snared her imagination since childhood. She gazed across the clearing to Rand, sleeping in a sitting position while tethered to the tree. One of the outlaws kept watch beside him. She returned to her task with a sigh.

Nadya nodded toward Rand. "You are sad for that one?"

"Of course. He doesn't deserve to be tied up like a wild bruin." The heat of Mara's words must make her feelings on the matter plain. "Where is your leader this morning?"

"At the river checking the fish trap, but he should be back soon." Nadya dropped a peeled tuber into a pan of water beside the bowl and selected another. "I do not think you will talk him into freeing your bear."

Mara skinned the tuber she held with more force than necessary. A longing seized her with sudden force, the yearning to go home to Mam and Da. If only time would roll backward and she could go back to the life she'd known before. In the kitchen at the inn they would have chattered over a simple task like peeling tubers but never about a Kindren restrained against his will. Such things did not happen in their world. They would have discussed picking berries, the rising of bread, and how many eggs the hens had laid. Her lips curved into a rueful smile as she realized how small her worries had once been. The smile faded. She could not return to that life with Elderland in peril.

Nadya gave a toss of her head. "He comes now."

Mara looked in the direction she'd indicated. Hael strode toward them carrying a string of fish. The filthy urchin by his side seemed familiar. "Who is that with him?"

Nadya shrugged. "Another lost soul." She dropped a tuber back into the bowl and hurried to greet the newcomers.

Mara trailed her, not eager to welcome Hael after the way he'd treated Rand.

Hael introduced the urchin as Lyneth to Nadya. Lyneth, who was younger than she had at first seemed, stared at Nadya with a look of awe.

Mara remembered her own similar reaction upon first seeing the wanderer.

With pale blue eyes and a cloud of copper hair, Lyneth carried herself with a finer air than her stained and torn clothing called for. She wore shreds of what might once have been slippers on her feet, clinging by threads that must soon break.

"What is your story?" Nadya prodded.

"It's a sad one, I fear," Lyneth replied. "I am a refugee from Torindan and have been separated from my mistress, the Lof Raelein Arillia."

Mara started, recognizing Arillia's servant in the urchin before her.

Lyneth fastened her gaze on Mara, and her lips parted. "Lof Raena!" She bowed. "I am glad to find you well."

"Why do you call her that?" Hael stared at Mara but spoke to Lyneth.

Lyneth's eyes flared wider, and her forehead creased as she looked at Mara. "I'm sorry, Lof Raena. Should I not have given your title?"

"She is the high princess of the Kindren," Nadya answered Hael's question.

That a wanderer would know the term didn't surprise Mara. Nadya would have traveled far and wide. "Lof Shraen Elcon is my father." She gave up her secret. The place beneath the tree where Rand had sat was empty save for the rope that had bound him. The outlaws must be giving Rand a chance to walk about, perhaps to attend the needs of nature. Even knowing this, she couldn't help feeling concern at his absence. She drew in a breath, ready to ask about him.

Hael stared at her with a thunderstruck look on his face while the empty bucket he'd grasped tumbled to his feet "That explains why your Mam and Da let you fly off with Kai on his wingabeast. I thought they had taken leave of their senses. But why, if you are a Kindren, do you have black hair? And your eyes are more round like an Elder, not long like a Kindren's."

"My mother was an Elder. I am a half-caste." Her

words should drive away any desire he might have for her. That was just as well since she couldn't return it. Never mind that it made her sad that neither Elder nor Kindren would want her as a wife.

"How came you to the inn?" Hael asked.

"I am told that Kai brought me. My mother died there shortly after we arrived. Kai left me with my nurse and took my mother's body home to Cobbleford. He never returned and my nurse died in the boglands. Mam and Da kept my secret to safeguard me, or so they believed." She gave a slender account of events, careful not to say anything against Mam or Da, but her voice wobbled. She had forgiven them for lying to her, but the wound it had caused still hurt. She couldn't understand why they had deceived her father when he'd searched for her, saying she had died with her nurse. The truth might not have come out at all if she hadn't overheard Mam talking to Aunt Brynn that day.

"I had no idea," Hael murmured. "I'm sorry, Mara. If you'd told me, I'd have helped you."

"I think you are in want of washing," Nadya scolded Lyneth with a smile. "There's a place in the river where it's best for bathing. Come with me. I'll lend you clothes to change into and show you where it is." She led Lyneth toward her wagon.

Mara, suddenly alone with Hael, stepped aside while he went past her. He threw the string of fish on the table. "There'll be perckens for supper tonight." He drew his knife and went to work gutting the fish then stopped with a glance at Mara. "Lyneth tells me her mistress would go to Cobbleford. You have the same destination." He watched her face as he spoke, and she knew he was doing another kind of fishing. "Your mother came from there."

"Yes."

"That's where the king of Westerland dwells."

"It is to be hoped he will grant my step-mother asylum."

He pulled a fish from the stringer, sliced off its head with a deft stroke, gutted it, and dropped the offal in a bucket. He had done this many times before at the inn, but seeing him perform the familiar task in a different place seemed odd. "She is a queen without a country. From what I hear, Torindan is no more."

"And what of Rivenn?" She wasn't ready to accept the death of her kingdom. "It may rally."

"For your sake, I hope it does." He slapped another fish down. "Will Westerland's king shelter you, too?"

"He is my grandfather." Mara watched his hands at their task without really seeing them. She had never met King Euryon of Westerland, but she could hope he would take her in. Cowering in Westerland went against the grain, but no other choice remained to her. How could Rivenn rally with the stronghold fallen and her father wounded?

"I did not mean to make you sad." Hael's voice broke into her reflections.

She shook her head without speaking.

"When you flew off to Torindan, what did you find there?"

"The person I should have been." She pressed her lips together to stop their trembling. While doing the familiar chore, Hael made her think of the apple-cheeked stable boy she'd known at the inn. "Why do they call you Searcher?"

"Sounds rather grand, does it not?" He grinned. "I blame my grandfather, Taels. He was a great hunter who taught me not only wood craft but lore as well. From him I learned to gentle wildlife."

"What can that mean?"

"Do you not know? You saw it with horses."

Hael had been faultless as a stable hand. He'd seemed always to know what the horses had in mind, and they him. Thinking about life at the inn reminded her of a question to ask. "Have you word of Mam or Da?"

He raised a brow "It's taken you a while to wonder."

"I feared the answer."

"They're busy these days. You won't have heard yet, but Freaer's armies reached into Norwood."

Mara stared at him. "But the inn—"

"Taken." He bent his head to his task again.

Coldness swept over Mara, and she put down her knife to wrap her arms around herself. "I can't imagine such a thing."

He went on doggedly gutting fish. "It is nonetheless true."

"What has Elderland come to?" she wailed.

His jaw tensed. "I'm not certain."

"If that is true of you, why won't you let Rand go?"

Hael watched her from his dark eyes. "I haven't decided what to do with your friend." He carved into the last fish and tossed its entrails into the bucket. "Prepare for a journey, Mara. On the morrow we'll leave for Cobbleford."

Nadya returned from the river carrying a cloth bundle with Lyneth in tow. With her face clean, the maiden's delicate beauty shone forth. The colorful garments that dwarfed her slight frame must have come from Nadya. The maiden's thinness and haunted expression gave silent witness to the suffering she had endured.

"I see you found the soap." Hael wiped his hands on a rag and hefted a cauldron of water onto the tripod above the fire. "I'm off to feed the birds and bait the trap again, but I'll wash down the table when I return."

"We can see to it." Nadya waved him away. "I'm glad for the fish you brought for supper."

He picked up the pail of fish heads and entrails. "I'll make sure I'm back in time for that."

Nadya grinned. "Mind you do if you expect to find any."

Hael moved off along the path.

"Sit here," Nadya invited Lyneth with a gesture toward the stool she had occupied earlier. "You can help Mara peel the tubers while I hang your clothes to dry." She patted the bundle she carried.

Lyneth took her place at the work table. She picked up a knife while Nadya started for her wagon.

"I'm glad to find you alive." Mara took the chance to speak plainly now that they were alone. "The Lof Raelein feared that you died when her chambers caught fire."

"You spoke to my mistress afterward?" Lyneth's voice trembled. "I wondered the same about her."

"She lives," Mara hastened to assure her but frowned the next instant. "At least, she did when I saw her last."

Lyneth's knife slid beneath a tuber's peel. "I must comfort myself that she did not burn in dragonsfire."

Mara wondered if death at the hands of the welke riders who had chased them would have been preferable. "I hope to find my step-mother and father alive and well at Cobbleford."

"Searcher says he will escort me there as well." Lyneth's knife stopped moving, and she leaned toward Mara. "I assume he is the leader of this encampment. What do you make of him?"

"He is an outlaw." Rather than sort out the jumbled thoughts and feelings Hael inspired in her, Mara fell back on the simple truth. It served as a reminder and a warning, for an outlaw could not be trusted. With that in mind, she needed to stop trying to persuade Hael to free Rand and find a way to do it herself.

The thought of Rand had her searching him out. She found him awake and talking to his guard. On impulse, she reached to him with the soul touch, but he had cloaked himself, and she couldn't find him.

"That man you are looking at—I know him from Torindan." Lyneth exclaimed. "The Lof Raelein said he is Freaer's misbegotten son."

Mara turned back to her at once. "You must not tell that to anyone else."

Engrossed in reaching out to Rand, Mara hadn't heard anyone approaching from behind, but now Nadya stood staring at Lyneth with a shocked expression. "Searcher must know of this."

CR

Rand closed his eyes to shut out the sight of the merriment around the campfire, but the laughter intruded. That Mara joined in troubled him. Had she forgotten his plight? He had seen her talking with the outlaw leader as if they were old friends. She had reached for him with the soul touch earlier, but he had shut himself away lest she feel the jealousy raging through him. She didn't need to know his feelings when he couldn't claim her.

"Go on with you." Trader's voice intruded into his morose reflections. The wanderer gave a nod of his head to Rand's guard. "Nadya has a plate waiting for you. I'll mind the prisoner."

"And here was I thinking I'd missed out." The guard lifted his lips in a gap-toothed grin. "I'll return the favor sometime, see if I don't." He hurried off.

Hauling himself back from despair, Rand watched Trader set a plate on the boulder near him. "I've brought a bite of fish. Mark you, setting aside a morsel for you in that hungry pack was no mean feat." The wanderer bent to untie his hands. "Something has you bothered, or I wasn't born. What is it?"

Rand gave a bitter laugh. "You mean besides being trussed like a bruin ready for the spit?"

Trader glanced up at him. "It's the maiden, is it not?"

Rand clamped down on the emotions that hit him. Mara had him tied up in knots, of course. He'd been prepared to lose her, but not so soon, and not to an outlaw.

Trader finished untying Rand's hands. "Never mind answering, your face gives the tale away."

Rand took a bite of the buttery fish and wondered if Mara had guessed his feelings also. At the thought, his appetite deserted him.

"What's the trouble now?" The wanderer asked in a jovial voice. "Thinking of your lady love in the arms of another?"

"You have a strange way of offering comfort, if

that is what you intend."

Trader chuckled. "I doubt anything I could say would do that. No, Kindren, I came to feed your body not your soul. I can't stand by with a full belly and let another go hungry."

"He can, I'll warrant." Rand nodded toward the outlaw leader, talking with several of his men around the fire. He must have caught Rand's movement, for he lifted his head.

"He's not a bad sort, but you seem to have found the wrong side of him."

Acid churned Rand's stomach.

The outlaw leader detached from the group and strode toward him across the clearing. From the set of his shoulders and the way he carried himself, he would probably say something unpleasant.

Trader stepped aside as he neared.

His abandonment left Rand bereft. He refused to show any weakness, but met the outlaw leader's gaze squarely. "So nice of you to stop by."

"I know who you are." The outlaw leader ground out the words.

"Then you have the advantage." Rand deflected the remark, hoping the man knew less than he believed. A sinking feeling gripped him. How else would the outlaw leader know his identity unless Mara had told him? And if he knew Rand's identity, did he also know Mara's?

"I suppose you've forgotten me. I was the stable hand who saddled your horse when you came to the White Feather Inn." His jaw tightened. "That's how I knew you were lying about where you met Mara."

"I must have had a lapse of memory."

His nostrils flared. "Will you continue to lie? But

then you've learned to deceive from your wretched father."

Rand glared at the man before him. "My father never claimed me. He taught me nothing." He spoke the words lightly, although they summed up one of his deepest sorrows. "Nor do I serve him. I'm not his true-born son, a fact for which I am thankful."

"Since I have heard falsehoods from your lips, you will forgive my doubts."

He would never live down the misfortune of his birth. "What do you want with me?" Rand dragged out the words. "I've not harmed you. It lies within your power to release me."

"That I am not inclined to do."

Rand leaned his head against the tree behind him. "Is it my death you want?"

A faint smile tugged at the outlaw's lips. "Not your death, but your life."

"I don't understand."

"A man in my circumstances watches for opportunities." Speaking softly, as if talking to himself, he paced in front of Rand. "Even an illegitimate son might be worth something to Frear."

"Do you mean to sell me, then?"

The outlaw leader tilted his head. "I'm not sure yet."

"If you do, you'll send me to my death. Freaer would like nothing better than to kill me."

5

IN THE WILD LANDS

Arillia laid a damp cloth on her husband's forehead. He groaned and thrashed on the makeshift bed they had made from fallen logs and evergreen boughs, his movements as restless as the storm moaning outside the cave. Dorann leaned over Elcon with a restraining hand on his shoulder. "Why does Elcon seem so much worse?" she asked the tracker. "You said that the poultice would draw poisons from his wound."

"He's lain with a grave wound in a dank cave for too long." Dorann shook his head. 'The poultices and infusions I've given him may not be enough to counter that."

"Well, then, do something else!" Arillia immediately regretted snapping at Dorann.

"Milady..." Eathnor moved to her side. "My brother is doing everything within his power to help the Lof Shraen."

"Except remove him from this cave." Dorann's frustration came through despite the soft tone he used.

Anders's eyes gleamed as he glanced back from the cave entrance, where he stood guard. "Do we dare risk leaving?"

"It might save the Lof Shraen's life," Eathnor answered, "but at the risk of ending it. With Pilaer's warriors searching the forest for those fleeing Torindan, we could all be killed."

Dorann put a hand on the back of his neck. "I don't see how we can avoid taking the chance."

Arillia clasped her hands together. "I can't bear watching my husband fade away like this."

The wan light filtering from the cave entrance picked out the lines of strain in Eathnor's face. "When the storm ends, we could make a stretcher and bear him to a hunter's hut my brother and I know in the wild lands. It's remote and well-hidden."

"That's a good idea," Dorann approved. "We'd keep him warm and dry there."

"Provided we reach it," Eathnor pointed out. Thunder boomed, and he stopped speaking but continued when it stopped. "Exposing ourselves to danger might not end well."

Dorann straightened. "So could staying hidden. You know that, Eathnor. The longer we remain here, the greater the likelihood of being discovered."

Eathnor nodded. "True." He cut a glance toward Arillia. "The choice of course is yours, Lof Raelein."

Arillia closed her eyes. How could she possibly decide such a thing? She murmured a silent prayer. *Lof Yuel, help me know what to do.*

How had they come to this pass? She could remember in her early days how she and Elcon rode into this forest along paths now crawling with his enemies. They had made a game of racing one another and always ended with breathless laughter. The understanding that they would one day marry had grown up with them. When he had taken Aewen as wife instead, she had wept into her pillow and sworn never to marry. She might have kept that vow if Elcon hadn't asked her to break it. When he'd reached out to her from the midst of his sorrow, she'd agreed to marry him, never realizing that the shadow of his dead wife's memory still walked with him.

Lightning flared, and she opened her eyes to the sight of her husband's face streaming with sweat. The certainty that Elcon would soon follow Aewen to the grave fell upon her like a heavy hand. She hauled in a breath. "I'll do anything to save my husband."

CR

From the weeping in the bailey, Freaer guessed what he would see when he looked out his throne room window. He was not surprised when four guardians of Pilaer rode through the bailey escorting Draeg's riderless horse. The frothing equine bore his son's shield, sword, and helmet in the ceremonial manner denoting a death. If Draeg's body had been recovered, he would have been buried at the start of the journey from Torindan. Freaer gazed upon the crowd and found Amora weeping among them. He gazed at her smooth face with long eyes and plump lips, at her waving golden hair and curvaceous body, and hated her. He despised her for the son she had given him but who had died, for the lust she roused in him, and for the passion that even now held him in thrall.

He had wanted Shae, yearning to defile her. He would have howled over the slow corruption of her innocence, then cast her to his warriors when he'd tired of her. But she'd called upon Lof Yuel and put herself beyond his reach. Amora did not pretend to be pure, but flaunted herself knowingly. She was the opposite of Shae, and irresistible because of her lust for evil. Sampling her favors never tired him, but if he could bring himself to do without her, he would have her slain. He could not allow any living creature such a hold on him. The softer feelings weakened his soul, threatening his very survival. His mother, Meriwen of Old, had taught him that, and he'd never had reason to doubt her wisdom. She had taught him the dark magics that had brought him through the ages alive and powerful. He had even escaped the Viadrel, the flames of virtue that burned at the rotting heart of Maeg Waer, the forgotten mountain. And so he watched the horse bringing the last vestiges of his son home and did not weep.

He knew the knock at the door as Ladric's and called for a servant to answer it. The first guardian of Pilaer strode into his chambers and stopped before him. Garbed in the red surcoat emblazoned with the rampant golden dragon of Pilaer, he kept his pale hair clubbed back. "Lof Shraen, I am sorry to inform you —"

Freaer put up a hand. "I have seen."

"I am sorry, Lof Shraen." Ladric pushed out his lips in a gesture that always gave away his nervousness.

Freaer doubted that. His first guardian had always despised Draeg, although most of the time he'd been careful to hide it. Ladric seemed to fear a backlash, and Freaer was half-tempted to give him what he expected in order to amuse himself and remove the foul stench of sentiment from his nostrils. But no, that would take the edge off the torment he'd reserve for Amora. Still, he couldn't resist taunting the first guardian. "Have you intruded on me only to inform me of something I already know?"

Ladric looked gratifyingly terrified. "Forgive me, my Lord. I only thought to tell you —"

"If I wanted you to inform me of anything, I would have let you know." The heady fragrance of Ladric's fear infused the air, and Freaer hid a rush of glee. "But now you are here, make yourself useful. I am certain that Elcon's daughter lives. I found her with the shil shael." Syl Marinda had let down her guard while sleeping when he'd located her with the soul touch. Upon awakening, she had closed herself to him almost at once.

"Have you discovered her hiding place?"

Freaer would like to say that he had, for admitting that he had failed galled him. "I know where she is going," he hedged. "We must push into Westerland."

Ladric's eyes gleamed. "She must be stopped."

Freaer awarded him a look of approval. "I'm glad you understand what must be done."

Ladric nodded. "We can't allow her to persuade the Elder to strengthen Rivenn."

Freaer smiled. "Once Elcon and his daughter die, all of Faeraven will fall."

CR

"I don't need help." Mara jerked away from Hael more forcefully than she'd intended. He winced and drew back. She mounted the white horse he'd brought her with a sinking feeling in her stomach. Hurting Hael didn't sit right with her. She couldn't forget that he was the friend she had loved since childhood, no matter how much he upset her.

She glanced back to assure herself, yet again, that Rand would ride with them. Ropes secured him to the back of a roan horse with a graying muzzle and sagging belly. Trader held the horse's lead rein. Mara couldn't help wondering how a nag that had seen better days could keep up with the high-stepping black horse the wanderer rode.

Trader showed his strong teeth in a grin, winked at her, and gave an imperceptible nod of his head toward Rand.

Mara caught her breath. *Had he guessed her feelings?* She'd hidden her concern for Rand from the outlaws to protect his safety, and before that she'd kept them to herself for the sake of her pride.

Rand sat straighter in the saddle, gazing at her with his long eyes darkening to a shade more green than amber. The brush of his soul against hers caught her off guard, and she started at the yearning sorrow mingled with anger she sensed pulsing through him. She looked away and fought for composure. He waited for her to turn her head, to acknowledge him, but she pulled away and shielded herself. This was no time to reveal her emotions, and she would do nothing to aggravate Hael's jealousy of Rand.

Hael didn't seem to have noticed the exchange. He strode across the meadow with his back to her. When he reached the edge of the woods, he lifted a horn to his mouth. A hoarse note resounded. Hael stood still, his whole attention focused on something she could neither see nor feel.

"Are you cold, Lof Raena?" Lyneth, mounted on the horse beside Mara's, asked in a soft tone. "You shivered."

Mara shook her head. "'Twas only a passing

discomfort."

The outlaws on horseback who flanked Lyneth and Mara riveted their attention on Hael.

Mara tried to reconcile their reactions, which underscored his importance to the band, with the gentle stable boy she had known.

"Why does he stand there, waiting like that?" Lyneth asked.

"I wish I knew." Mara's horse shifted beneath her. "Whhst, now." She stroked the silken mane, aware that her voice sounded tense.

Movement flickered in the forest shadows.

"What's that?" Lyneth's cry gave away her uneasiness. "Do you see it? Look there!"

Mara nodded, not quite trusting her voice. A creature slipped from shadow to shadow with rapid grace, emerging into the light so briefly it plunged into darkness again before she could catch more than a glimpse. "I think it's—"

"A stag!" Lyneth exclaimed.

"I've never seen one so large," Mara marveled.

The stag stood tall as a horse, its magnificent antlers arching above its head. The magnificent animal knelt before Hael, who sat astride its broad back. The noble creature rose to its feet.

"Searcher rides in the forest," Trader bellowed. "Let our enemies take heed."

A cheer went up from the outlaws, and they fell in behind Hael with gusto.

"Come, Lof Raena." Lyneth called. "We need to keep up."

A guard leaned over behind Mara and a slap rang out. The white horse screamed and reared.

Mara gripped the pommel, fighting to keep her

seat. Her horse came down with a thud of hooves. Mara urged the frightened creature forward, and it plunged after the others. The forest closed about her. She'd lost track of Lyneth, but the guard remained at her side. Known as Jacko, he had dark hair and a swagger in keeping with his youth. He couldn't be older than twenty summers. She'd overheard him telling one of the other outlaws that he'd joined the band after being falsely accused of murder. What a tragedy, if he'd told the truth about his innocence. She hoped that he had. Having a murderer for an escort did not appeal to her.

She wouldn't have tried to run away. If that's what Hael had thought, by assigning Jacko to her, he was wrong. How could she leave and abandon Rand? Her decision to explore on her own had trapped them both. She could admit now that it had galled her to be so utterly dependent on Rand. She'd wanted to show him up, to assert her independence. That had been foolish. Rand knew more about finding his way in the wilderness than she did. If only she had trusted him to guide her, they wouldn't be in this predicament.

Hael's determination to deliver her to Cobbleford might reassure her more if she knew what he planned to do with Rand. Whatever it took, she would try her best to win his freedom. Hael's refusal to free Rand seemed absolute, which narrowed her choices to one.

If she escaped, it would be with Rand.

She caught up to Lyneth. Their escorts fell back and allowed them to ride together through the coolness beneath the trees.

Lyneth, her red-gold hair plaited down her back, glanced sideways at Mara. "Milady, I trust you were not harmed when your horse reared."

"Unless being scared out of my wits counts as an injury, I suffered none."

"Are you unused to horses?"

"No, but I've never ridden this sort."

"They are half-wild it's true, like the outlaws themselves."

"Let us hope they remember to be civil."

"Which do you mean? The outlaws or their horses?"

Mara laughed. "Both, of course."

The track descended a slope, and they fell silent while guiding their horses around a turn. With the wind in the trees, the river rushing, and the valley below glistening in the sun, they might be riding for pleasure.

"Have you known Searcher long?" Lyneth asked after the track straightened.

Mara hid her surprise. "Why do you ask?"

"Seeing you together made me wonder. You seem familiar with one another."

"Do we? I've known him since we were children. You're observant."

"I'm told that's a good trait in a lady's maid."

"I'm sure it came in handy with the Lof Raelein." Mara found Arillia's moods difficult to read. "Tell me about yourself, Lyneth. Where are you from?"

"Daeramor in the north. I grew up near the border of Whellein, home of the wild wingabeasts of Elderland."

"You must know all about Talan's ride."

Lyneth laughed, a musical sound. "I grew up with the tale. I can see why someone would want to tame a wingabeast, but I've never understood why a lof shraen's son would risk his life for the chance."

"Sometimes proving yourself is more important than life."

Lyneth's brow furrowed. "I can't imagine that."

Of course she couldn't. Lyneth seemed to do everything with grace. "You were born to a noble house, I expect."

Lyneth's eyes lost their shine. "I am one of the nine raenas of Daeramor."

The maid's sadness triggered a memory. Hadn't her father said something about Daeramor? "I seem to recall—" Mara couldn't hide the shock creeping over her. "Didn't Daeramor align with Freaer against my father?"

"It shames me to admit it. I disagreed with my father when he made that decision. I will always be grateful to Lof Raelein Arillia. Allowing me to remain at Torindan as her maid spared me from being cast upon my wits to survive." Tears glazed her blue eyes. "I can never go home."

"No wonder you tried so hard to find Arillia."

"I would have searched for her whether or not she stood between me and the open road. I've grown fond of her."

Mara nodded, having noticed Lyneth's devotion to Arillia. How strange to think of living at Torindan as part of the past. It still seemed she might return to find her father in his chambers. It hardly seemed possible that Faeraven had fallen with Torindan in ashes and her father at death's door. For all she knew, he had crossed the threshold into the world beyond. Arillia's whereabouts remained another mystery. When those who had escaped Torindan on wingabeasts had scattered while fleeing the welke riders, she'd lost track of anyone but Rand. What had become of Kai? If he had suffered harm, she would grieve. Hopefully she would find her father, Arillia, and Kai at Cobbleford, where they'd agreed to meet.

How would her grandfather react to her arrival? Would her resemblance to her mother endear her to him? Nothing she had heard about King Euryon suggested that possibility. He was more likely to turn her away. Her thoughts circled like a flitling denied a perch, as she tried to determine what she should do if he rejected her.

CR

Holding the wingabeasts' reins, Kai waited for Aerlic to return from the cliff for a final check. They'd traded watches since sundown and had seen no welke riders batting their wings in the sky.

How fitting that a night bird's lament should throb through the air, as if nature wept the tears of Lof Yuel. How many more Kindren would the warriors rout from their hiding places and murder on the morrow? Whatever happened tonight, Kai would not hear their death screams. One way or another, he would escape that torment.

Clouds raced across the moon's face, casting the land in uncertain light, sailing on a wind he could not feel so far below. Neither could he hear its wailing. The world about him lay in stillness, although he did not delude himself that all the warriors slept. Guards would stand duty in Pilaer's camp and might sound the alarm upon spotting two wingabeast riders in flight. That would awake all the fury of Pilaer's finest, but they had to take the risk. The mountain was too steep for the wingabeasts to descend on foot.

"Well?" Kai asked when Aerlic returned.

The archer took Argalent's rein. "Guards watch over Pilaer's encampment."

"We can hope they've fallen asleep."

Kai led Flecht to an open spot, and the archer followed. The wingabeast's hooves clattered on bare rock then came to a stop. Kai lifted into the saddle. Flecht quivered beneath him and stomped his feet. Kai laid a calming hand on Flecht's neck. Being grounded in a cave during daylight hours had been hardest on the wingabeasts, who craved the open air. Well, they would have their fill of flying tonight. Aerlic sat composed on Argalent, the Silver he'd long ridden, but Kai read eagerness in the archer's posture.

Kai slackened Flecht's reins and touched his heels to the wingabeast's side. Flecht spiraled upward with dizzying speed, and Kai leaned forward to compensate. A night bird whistled a sharp alarm from across the valley. Kai started. Had something attacked the bird or could that have been a signal from a guard? He pressed Flecht to hurry. The great wings rose and fell with speed, creating a draft that riffled the wingabeast's flight feathers and buffeted Kai's face. The wind snatched his breath away, and he turned his head sideways.

Flecht leveled off above the mountain, and Argalent came up beside him. They were most visible high in the sky. Kai wasted no time in sending Flecht downward, and Aerlic followed on Argalent.

The forest canopy slid by beneath him. Moonlight touched the highest branches, filtered through gaps into meadows below, and picked out bodies sprawled in the open, some half-eaten. Kai shuddered and averted his gaze. The dead were too far away to recognize, but he hoped he did not know any of them.

Weild Aenor threaded through grassland and forest, a dark mystery running between grassy banks on its way to the sea. A flight across the valley would take only a short while, but Kai brought Flecht down on a broad place in the path that would take them to the road north.

Aerlic landed, and they followed the path in the shifting moonlight. The way narrowed and the kaba trees closed in, hiding them in shadow. With branches meeting overhead to make dark tunnels, they could travel the road more safely than the air. This time of night brought little fear of discovery. Provided none of Pilaer's watchmen had noticed them flying down from the mountain, they could hope to escape. Kai did not relax his vigilance. They must rely upon the wingabeasts' eyesight to go forward, for beyond occasional glimmers that penetrated the forest, they journeyed in pitch blackness. Darkness could prove an enemy, failing to warn them of low branches or a wrong turn taken in error. He did not urge Flecht to caution, however, but leaned against his wingabeast's neck while straining his eyes and ears. Other denizens than those of Pilaer stalked the forest at night. Creatures of the night, not all of them mortal, might creep upon the unwary.

6

THE WILDERWEN

Arillia allowed Dorann to help her onto his wingabeast and peered about with a feeling of unease. Moonlight bathed the rock escarpment outside the mouth of the cave and swirled in light mists that caught in the trees beyond the cave. She couldn't help a shudder at the thought of venturing into the darkness that lurked beneath the trees. Since her early days she had heard the many and fabled tales of what happened to those unwise enough to venture into the wild lands that separated the Kindren ravens from the kingdoms of the Elder in the west.

Some fell prey to the wildcats that stalked by night. The smallfolk known as the Feiann led the unwary astray or cursed them with enchantments that tore away their reason. Other travelers lost their way or vanished into the Vale of Shadows, never to emerge. Few spoke of the wilderwen, a horned monster birthed of ancient evil. Lurking within forest shadows, a wilderwen thrived upon the blood of the unwary.

She could only hope that the two trackers knew their way well and had the wit to avoid such perils.

Dorann swung up to join her. "If you will allow me, Lof Raelein." He reached awkwardly around her to take the reins.

"Of course."

Eathnor's wingabeast snorted and pawed the ground, obviously more than ready for Eathnor to take the lead. Anders followed, carrying Elcon on his wingabeast. Dorann moved in behind. They traveled downhill through trees that stood like dark sentinels against the pewter sky. Clouds ran in great drifts across the face of the full moon and cast shifting shadows over the forest.

Arillia shivered in the night wind, despite the warmth of her cloak. She'd grown used to wearing the garment at all times, having fled Torindan clad only in her chemise. Even if there had been time for modesty that awful night, her chambers had become a raging inferno and every stitch of clothing she'd possessed had burned. She shook her head at the thought of her maidservant, lost in the blaze. Lyneth had not deserved her horrid fate.

How many of those she had known at Torindan were dead? She might never know the answer to that question. Those who survived the attack would have scattered and might never gather again. She had no doubt that if Elcon had the strength to speak, he would instruct her to turn over the Circlet of Elder to Syl Marinda along with the Scepter of Faeraven and Sword Rivenn. She'd noticed that Kai safeguarded the mighty sword, but the other two symbols of rulership were lost to her. If they had not been destroyed by the fires that ravaged Torindan, Freaer would make use of them to bolster his claim. What would become of Faeraven then?

A night bird's lament echoed across the valley and came to roost within her. She pulled her mind free. Letting her thoughts wander down such paths only made her melancholy. She needed to keep her spirits up. They would reach the hut, and Elcon could begin to recover. She had to believe that or lose the last shreds of her sanity.

The night dragged on, turning from an adventure to an ordeal. The journey narrowed to the muffled clopping of hooves, the creak of the saddle, and the rhythmic sway of the wingabeast. Clouds fled across the moon, and fitful light silvered the path, giving a false sensation of movement and making the trees jump at them.

A gap in the foliage revealed an encampment. Arillia squinted and made out the banner of Pilaer flying above the tents, although without seeing its rampant dragon she would have guessed that only the triumphant warriors of Elcon's enemy would dwell so openly. Most of the camp slumbered, but two guards sat around a fire. The flames lit their faces, and the murmur of their voices carried on the wind. Arillia sucked in a breath, thankful that darkness hid her. She prayed that any sounds made by their passage would not reach the wrong ears. Eathnor had refused to travel by air when Anders suggested it. She'd wondered about the wisdom of his decision but now understood why he'd made it. Although the wingabeasts could carry them to safety sooner when airborne, they couldn't count on the darkness to hide them. The guards might pick out wingabeasts in the sky and set welke riders upon them. At the thought, the hair on the back of her neck lifted. She wouldn't soon forget the precarious flight while escaping a welke rider that had delivered them to the cave. When Eathnor had brought the wingabeast down on the hillside behind the trees, she'd almost screamed at him to keep going. Had she given into her panic and commanded Eathnor to obey her whim, they might not now draw air.

The path unfolded beneath the wingabeasts, carrying them closer to the encampment, and Arillia reminded herself once again to trust those who had charge of her safety. Every hoofbeat seemed loud in her ears, the rasping of her own breaths a betrayal. A rhythmic growling claimed her attention. Her heart thudded. What manner of beast made such a fearsome noise? Her fevered imagination supplied the answer, much to her discomfort, but then she remembered a similar sound she'd heard beyond her father's closed chamber door. Her maidservant had smiled from beside her. "You'll have to come another time. Shraen Ferran arrived home late last night and still snores in his bed." Elcon did not snore while he slept, and she'd forgotten the sound until now. Tension ebbed from her body in a silent flood.

The path curved away from camp, and they slipped like wraiths through the night.

❧

Orange light flickered along the trees from the fire in Pilaer's encampment, and Kai guided Flecht off the path to hide in a meadow. He rode toward the stand of weilo trees lining the banks of Weild Aenor. A breeze lifted from the surface, which gleamed like black silk, and here at last he felt night's breath in his face.

Flecht stumbled, and his hooves thudded as he regained his footing.

"What's that?" one of the guards near the fire cried out. He jumped to his feet and peered across the meadow toward them.

Kai halted his wingabeast. Aerlic also drew rein.

"What'd you hear?" A second guard joined the first.

"I'm not sure. Maybe a horse."

"We'd better take a look."

Kai rested his hand on Sword Rivenn's hilt. He'd picked up the weapon from beside the Lof Shraen, who had fallen after his fight with Draegmor of Pilaer. Kai had forgotten to give the sword to Elcon before they'd parted. Hopefully he would soon return the mighty weapon to its rightful owner. But first, he might need to use it against the two guards who stalked into the meadow with swords in hand. They advanced slowly, squinting into the shadows that concealed him. The guards halted nearby, the stench of their perspiration mingling with the over-sweet odor of mead. Kai strained to hear but couldn't make out their whispers.

One of the guards started forward.

Kai tightened his grasp on Sword Rivenn. His pulse pounded his temples. Blood hummed in his veins. He rasped in a breath.

The second guard to move caught up to the first and took him by the arm. "Careful. The wilderwen lurk in dark forests, ready to make off with the careless."

"Don't talk your northern nonsense." The first guard's protest might have been more believable if fear hadn't edged his voice.

"You southern Kindren think you know everything. I'm telling you, the wilderwen haunt places where the old magics linger, such as these woods. Can't you sense one watching us?"

In other circumstances, Kai might have smiled.

He'd never been called a wilderwen before. In his early days at Whellein, he'd learned of the ancient evil that took shape as gangly creatures with long noses, large ears, pointed teeth, and sharp talons. The wilderwen satisfied their taste for blood by attacking those who lost their way in the forest.

"All I feel right now is you holding onto me." The southern guard took a step nearer to Kai. "I could swear I heard something…"

"Whatever it was will be gone by now. Let's go back to the fire."

"All right, but I'm not afraid of shadows." The southern guard turned around with a promptness that belied his claim.

His companion threw an arm around his shoulder. "A bit of prudence stands a body in good stead." The guards moved off toward camp.

The light shifted with the clouds, sending the shadows into retreat and making the wingabeasts' silver coats glow in the moonlight. The hair at Kai's nape bristled. The guards had only to look behind to see them. When he could stand the suspense no longer, Kai urged Flecht forward but reined in when darkness again concealed them. Aerlic had hidden also.

The southern guard looked over his shoulder. "Did you hear anything?"

"Nothing but the wind in the treetops."

"I'm not convinced of that."

The northern guard removed his arm from around the other's shoulder. "I'll watch you investigate from here."

A small pause followed, during which Kai caught the night bird's lament.

"Never mind, then."

The guards returned to the fire. After the two stopped sending anxious glances toward where he hid, Kai led the way along the edge of the meadow. With Aerlic beside him, Kai held steady, despite the tremors crawling down his spine.

Kai let out a breath of relief when they reached the road to Norwood. Traveling off the path had been slow and treacherous, but they'd made it. It had cost them time, however. He'd expected to end the night's journey farther from the enemy encampment. With the sky lightening, he revised his plans. Once long ago while searching for shelter during a rain storm, he'd discovered a cave on a forested hillside, well back from the road. It would make a secret refuge to hide in, provided he could find it again.

Daybreak was bursting over the horizon when he finally found the mouth of the cave. Aerlic dismounted and went in first, his bow drawn. He reappeared a short while later and waved Kai inside.

The wingabeasts balked at entering yet another cave, and Kai needed Aerlic's assistance to bring them inside. Kai didn't blame the winged horses the small rebellion after their taste of freedom, but it made him uneasy. What had spooked them? He stepped inside, and the smell of damp stone rose to him. The cave extended well back into a dark place where water dripped. All the better for watering the horses. "What's this?" He asked when his vision cleared.

"It's a tracker's bed, made of deadfall and evergreen boughs." Aerlic pointed to a bloody bandage between the bed and wall. "A wounded person lay here, and not that long ago."

"Anders rode this way with Elcon. I wonder if

Eathnor and Dorann knew of this cave."

"It seems likely."

"We can't know for certain, but it's comforting to think they might have escaped to shelter here."

"I'm surprised *we* did. Those guards almost came upon us. If they'd roused the camp, I doubt we'd have survived."

"I am thankful for the High One's protection."

"Let us hope it continues. We've a long and perilous journey before us."

ॐ

Arillia glanced back at her half-conscious husband, who was swaying in Anders' arms. She drew her brows together. In the sunlight, Elcon's face looked waxen. "How long can you hold onto him?" She called to the servant in the loudest voice she dared, aware that any sound could draw the wrong sort of attention from the creatures that inhabited the thickening forest. Shaycats and jaggercats were more fearsome than bruins, Elcon had told her. The wildcats would stalk a victim without mercy, leaping from branch to branch until they pounced without warning.

Although the spring day was not warm, Anders' face glistened with moisture. "As long as I must."

Dorann reined in his wingabeast. "I don't doubt your intention, Anders, but after keeping the Lof Shraen upright for so long, your strength flags. Let me carry him."

Eathnor turned his wingabeast in a wide space in the path. "Dorann is right. You must dedicate yourself to safeguarding the Lof Raelein instead."

"I will watch over the Lof Raelein gladly," Anders declared, "as my master would wish."

Dorann dismounted. "Milady?"

Arillia nodded. "Don't bother with me, Dorann. Go and see to the Lof Shraen."

"If you're certain..." At her nod, the tracker went to lift Elcon down.

Eathnor dismounted also and hurried to help.

The wingabeast pranced beneath Arillia. Rather than calling attention away from her husband, she reached for the reins, ready to restrain the restless creature. She froze, and her mouth went dry.

The leaves of the kaba trees surrounding them shivered in a steady rhythm, driven by a stiff wind. Whatever storm made this disturbance left the sky unravaged. A gap in the trees showed her that the clouds had blown away, and the sun now shone in a blue sky. The trees' shaking increased.

Eathnor released Elcon to his brother's arms and scanned the forest. "That's an ill wind." He drew his sword and faced the shaking trees.

Dorann laid Elcon on the ground, and standing over him, pulled the slingshot from his belt. He bent and loaded a stone into the weapon.

Movement caught the corner of Arillia's eye. She turned her head, her heart thudding, and glimpsed a creature ducking behind the kabas nearest her. Her throat clogged, choking off her cry. The wingabeast she rode did not suffer the same handicap but screamed and batted its wings. The other wingabeasts echoed the alarm. "Help!" Arillia tightened her hold on the reins. If the terrified creature flew off with her, she'd have no idea how to land.

Neither Eathnor nor Dorann responded. Eathnor

had gone strangely still, and Dorann was winding up to make a throw from his slingshot.

Anders hurried to Arillia and took hold of her wingabeast's bridle. "Lof Raelein, come down from that beast, if you will." He added his last words with a flourish, as if suddenly mindful of protocol.

She slipped from the saddle, dizzy with relief.

Anders' dagger gleamed in his hand. "Stand behind me, Milady, and I'll defend you."

Arillia wanted to trust Anders, but how could a single servant with only a dagger, no matter how brave-hearted and loyal, defend her from the horned monster? Thoughts gibbered in her head, and the urge to escape gripped her. She backed and turned to run, ignoring Anders' shout.

Arillia reached the end of the sunlight and fetched against a tree, breathing in small gasps. Even in the midst of panic, she knew to avoid forest shadows with a wilderwen near. Long shudders wracked her, and she darted glances about, alert to any movement. She hadn't gone far, and Anders would soon reach her. She could hear his running footfalls now.

Aewen appeared beneath the trees before Arillia, her rounded eyes blue, a sapphire band at her brow, and her dark hair bound in a braid that fell to her waist. A smile lit her face, as if something amused her. "Come, Arillia. I'll tell you a secret."

Aewen seemed very real, and yet this wraith could only be a specter of her own mind. "Go away. I don't care what you have to say." Arillia spat out the words, but then realized her lips hadn't moved. She struggled against what could only be an enchantment. How long could she resist so strong an urge to obey? She could no longer hear Anders' footsteps. Had the wilderwen captivated him as well?

Aewen's forehead puckered in a frown. "Don't you want to know why Elcon still grieves for me?"

"Why should I listen to a figment of my imagination?" She issued the challenge with a sense of irony, aware she argued with herself.

Aewen laughed, a musical sound. "Is that all you think I am?"

"What else can you be?"

Aewen's smile twisted. "Elcon abandoned you for me."

"He apologized for that."

"All he desired, he found in me. I am everything you are not."

"Stop this."

"Afraid of the truth?" Aewen shook her head. "I gave him his firstborn child."

"I hate you."

"Do you think I care?" Aewen's eyes glittered. "You will never be good enough, not while I live in his thoughts."

Arillia put her hands over her ears. "I don't want to hear any more."

"You were wrong, you know." Aewen continued speaking. "I come from Elcon's mind, not yours."

Arillia gasped, but then recovered her wits. "Why should I believe you?"

Aewen shrugged. "To drive me from Elcon's thoughts forever, you have only to kill me now."

Arillia stared at the apparition. She longed to free Elcon from Aewen's memory. What if the enchantment could give her what she desired most? Still, she held back. "I'm no murderess."

"If I am, as you say, a figment, it wouldn't be

murder. Draw your dagger and you'll be doing Elcon a favor. It will be as if I never lived."

Arillia fingered her weapon. How easy it would be to give in. Why not, if it meant she could have her husband to herself? She pulled her dagger, its hilt more solid in her hands than the wraith in front of her. She started forward.

"Arillia, no!" Eathnor's voice penetrated the fog surrounding her.

She halted and stared at the dagger in her hand. What had she been about to do?

"No." Elcon's voice reverberated like a knell.

Arillia backed away from Aewen, who seemed to be shifting into another form. Horns sprouted from her head while her face transformed into a hideous mask with distorted features.

"You'll regret displaying a conscience," the specter that was no longer Aewen snarled.

"Move aside from it!" Dorann called.

"Gladly." Arillia backed away.

A thud followed a hissing sound. A rock struck the wilderwen in the forehead. The monster stared blankly then toppled. The enchantment fading, Arillia turned toward her companions. Eathnor stabbed the vile creature that had fallen, then rushed at a darker shape beneath the leafy shadows. Dorann bent over Anders, who lay on the ground with his eyes closed. Elcon lay on the ground without stirring.

"Is my husband all right?" Arillia asked in sharp alarm.

"His condition hasn't changed," Dorann answered in soothing tones.

"And you, Lof Raena," Eathnor sheathed his sword and strode toward her — "are you unharmed?"

She nodded, but her shaking told a different story. "I'd never want to repeat the experience."

"Understood."

"What's happened to Anders?"

Dorann glanced up from checking the servant's pulse. "A rock from my slingshot knocked him cold."

She glanced at him in surprise.

Dorann shrugged. "It's true, I'm afraid."

"But, why—"

"The wilderwen holding him in thrall wouldn't give me a clear shot. I had either to render Anders senseless or see him drained of blood before my eyes."

Arillia grimaced at the idea.

"Begging your pardon, Lof Raelein," Dorann bowed to her.

"He has a hard head," Eathnor said approvingly. "I expect he'll live."

The servant's chest rose and fell, confirming this. Leaving the servant to Dorann, Arillia went to her husband. "Elcon, can you hear me?" She bent close and caught his mutterings. She laid a hand on his brow. "The Lof Shraen is feverish. How much farther must we travel before we reach the hut?"

"I know it's hard to wait, Lof Raelein," Eathnor comforted her in a soft voice. "We should arrive tomorrow, depending on how far we can travel."

She cradled her husband's head on her lap. "Tell me what happened with the wilderwen."

"Wilderwens," Eathnor corrected her. "More than one of the foul beasts set upon us. I would have come to your aid sooner, Milady, had I not been a bit preoccupied."

"I'm glad you won free."

"That was entirely Dorann's fault. I'm afraid I was

taken in, as you were, by an enchantment."

"Anders also fell prey to the creatures." Dorann chimed in. "I escaped only because a wilderwen can't enchant more than one person at once."

"Do you mean to say that three of those monsters attacked us?" She peered into the shadows, her skin crawling. "Do any more of the fiends hide in this forest?"

"That is something I hope and pray we will never discover."

7

THE GIFT

Mara opened her eyes to the dim light filtering into the wagon around the closed window hangings. Lyneth stirred and stretched beside her on the bed Nadya had made for them in the wagon after banishing her husband. Trader slept beneath the wagon at night, a fact that gave Mara a feeling of safety in the midst of the wilderness. Trader showed his gentle side to the females under his care, but she had no doubt he could prove a tough opponent in any fight that came his way. No sound came from behind the closed doors that hid Nadya's bed from view.

"You're awake early." Lyneth gave her a sleepy smile, rolled over, and said nothing more. Soon her breathing came in small rasps.

Mara lay awake, unable to sleep again, for this day Hael would deliver her to Cobbleford Castle. Her thoughts carried her forward in time to the moment she would meet her grandparents. Her stomach turned over and her mouth went dry. She'd thought about this occasion many times. Now that it was upon her she couldn't remember anything she'd planned to say. If only she knew how they would receive her, she might better endure the waiting. Not knowing led to fretting. Time and again she convinced herself that worrying made her feel sick, only to ignore her own advice.

Perhaps if so much did not rest upon her grandfather's help, she would not suffer these pangs. She'd never known King Euryon of Westerland, after all. She wouldn't deceive herself that they could form any real connection. With this logic, she could almost convince herself that she didn't care how her grandparents reacted to her. When she was honest with herself, as now, she could admit that their reaction mattered. For her mother's sake as well as her own, she wanted them to accept her. Her father had told Mara how he had compromised her mother by meeting her secretly. They'd been caught in the garden alone, which had ended her betrothal and shamed her household. Her parents had accepted his offer to marry her because he'd left them little choice. Her father had regretted his actions, as he'd told her, and wished he had acted with more honor. Her mother never returned to her family except in death, but now Mara could give them something of the daughter they had lost. She could hope that they would return the favor and help her discover more about the mother she'd never known.

Trader's deep voice rumbled outside the wagon, to be answered by Hael's resonant tones. Trader had risen early to care for the prisoner before they broke camp. How he'd acquired the responsibility, she didn't know, but he'd taken it to heart. She worried less about Rand knowing that Trader looked after him. If only she could say that of Hael, but he saw Rand only through his anger. Abandoning Rand after he'd saved her life on so many occasions was unthinkable. Nor could she fathom not knowing where he might be or how he fared. She had to ask Hael to release Rand, and the sooner the better. Mara stood up on the thought and dressed quickly.

"Where are you going in such a hurry?" Lyneth called.

"Good morn," Mara greeted her with a smile. "I've an errand that can't wait."

A knowing look came over Lyneth's face, and she glanced toward the sleeping-cupboard doors. Painted with red, blue, and gold crests showing a crowned stag above crossed laurel branches, they remained closed. "You must hurry."

Mara took her point. Nadya would soon burst upon the world and sweep everyone in her path along to do her will. Because she commanded out of kindness, her gentle bullying brought her devotion rather than rebellion. Mara usually didn't mind putting herself to whatever tasks Nadya assigned her, but this was no ordinary day. The camp would remain at a safe distance, as Hael had explained, while he and a small band of the outlaws escorted her and Lyneth to the gates of Cobbleford Castle.

She slipped out the wagon door, too late to catch Hael.

Trader strode toward the tree where they'd tethered Rand.

She hated to see the collar, fit only for a dog, around his neck and the rope by which they led him around camp. Restraining the urge to follow Trader and assure herself of Rand's well-being, she turned her steps the opposite direction. Hael had gone to tend the horses, just as he'd done every morn at the Whitefeather Inn. Picking up the striped skirt in shades of blue and gold that Nadya had bestowed upon her, she followed him. The wingabeast she'd ridden with Rand what seemed a long time ago lifted its head and whickered. Hael spun. The startled expression he wore brought her sadness. At the inn, he'd never had to fear the approach of a friend.

His shoulders relaxed, and he nodded to her. "You're on a mission, I see."

"What makes you say that?" He was right, of course, but how had she betrayed herself?

He shrugged. "I know you, remember? You might as well tell me what you're about."

She'd once wheedled him with smiles and flattery, but the time for that lay in the past. "All right." She looked him square in the eye. "I want you to release Rand."

He gave a slight shake of his head. "You know where I stand on that."

She pulled her gaze away, blinked to stop the tears from gathering, and waited until she could speak. "I hoped you'd change your mind." She turned back to him. "*Why* won't you?" It was the closest she would come to begging.

"What would you do if I did? Euryon might take a dim view of your marching into Cobbleford Castle in the company of Freaer's son."

She hadn't thought about that. It wouldn't be fair to betray her grandfather's trust by not telling him Rand's identity, but doing so might bring dire consequences. "What will you do with him?" she asked in a defeated voice.

"I've an idea that someone might want him enough to barter for him."

"Have you become so mercenary?" She snapped out the words. "You would never do such a thing before."

He grinned. "Have I shocked you? Life has a way

of changing a person."

"You fault life itself for your avarice. If anything has twisted you, it is the path you've taken."

His laugh rang out. "You speak as if I had a choice. Another man made a fugitive of me with false accusations. Would you like to know his name?"

"Why do you ask me that?" Fear crept into her voice, despite her attempt to quell it.

"You would recognize it, I think."

She bit her lip. "I shouldn't let you draw me."

"You're curious, I'll warrant."

"Of course."

He smiled at her maddeningly and said nothing.

"Tell me this instant."

"Rohan."

"I was well rid of him as a suitor, it's clear. But I don't understand. Why would he do such a thing? He seemed interested only in working his farm and boasting of his gold."

Hael looked into the distance. "To get back at me. He—well, he came out the worst when I fought him after you left. In my mind, he'd driven you to it."

"I see." Hael had become an outlaw because of her. By running away she had hurt the people she cared about most. She'd never realized before how closely twined were all their lives. She hung her head. "I'm sorry, Hael."

He lifted her chin and stroked her cheek. "I'd do it again."

"I'd better go." She pulled away from his touch.

Lyneth watched them from beside the wagon but turned away quickly and ducked inside.

Mara hurried toward Nadya's camp, but before reaching it she followed her heart to Rand.

CR

Rand opened his eyes and pulled his mind back from the dark places it had wandered. Seeing Mara follow the outlaw leader, whom Trader had called Searcher, had pained Rand more than he cared to admit. What Mara saw in Searcher he didn't know. The man struck him as cocky. Why Searcher gathered so many loyal followers remained elusive, although they might prefer a leader who displayed strength of mind. For all his faults, Searcher certainly did.

Trader stood apart from him, watching something in the trees across the meadow.

"What do you see?" Rand shifted for a better view but could make out no movement.

"With my eyes? Nothing much." Trader cast a glance over his shoulder. "My mind, on the other hand, shows me many things."

"What do you mean?" It wasn't the first time the wanderer had said something similar. "Do you see into the other worlds?"

"Only those of my invention." Trader grinned. "Do you never daydream?"

Rand considered the question. "Not since my early days."

"That's where you've gone wrong." Trader nodded agreement with himself. "Daydreaming is a particular habit of wanderers."

Rand tried and failed to picture what it would be like to carry this mark of innocence. "I'm glad."

At the soft thump of a footfall, he turned his head, unprepared to find Mara walking toward him through the meadow grass.

Trader chuckled and moved a small distance away, obviously intent on granting them privacy.

Mara's smile fell flat as she met Rand's gaze, and her puckered brow revealed that some problem disturbed her thoughts.

"Why the frown, Lof Raena? Had a falling out with Searcher?" The mockery in Rand's voice gave away his glee at the idea.

Her chin tilted in that irritating way that made him want to kiss her. "My friendship with him has nothing to do with you."

"That's plain enough." He slanted his glance downward to avoid looking at her, which only made him ache. An ant carrying a crumb too heavy for such a tiny creature struggled past the toe of his boot. "I'd rather keep it that way, if you don't mind."

She stirred as if irritated. "I didn't seek you out to talk about Searcher, if that's what you mean."

He glanced up, surprising an expression of sorrow on her face. "What do you want with me?" He went on in a softer tone.

Her chest rose and fell on a sigh. "Only to say goodbye. We'll ride for Cobbleford soon."

He swept his gaze over her face, taking in every plane and curve, although he already knew it by heart. Why did her eyes shadow and her lower lip tremble? He could almost believe that she cared for him as he did for her. What did that matter? Her destiny did not include him, and his held no room for her. A rose's thorns wounded even while they protected its beauty, he reminded himself. Mara was not for him, and he was thankful he hadn't taken more from her than a stolen kiss. He'd expected them to part ways, but not like this. Words lay between them that would never be spoken. Once she took her rightful place as granddaughter of King Euryon, she'd be lost to him. Life in a castle as grand as Cobbleford would drive everything that had brought her to it from her mind. She would think of him no more, except perhaps when caught by a stray memory. Would she smile or frown when that happened? He would never know. "Safe journeys."

She leaned nearer, taking him off-guard, and whispered near his ear. "I have a gift for you." Her face lowered and her lips brushed his cheek.

"What are you doing, Lof Raena?" he asked, but then the hilt of a blade slid into his palm.

She pulled away, breathing faster than before. "May God keep you safe."

He gave a quick nod. "Thank you."

Her smile faltered as she stepped backward. Her skirts swayed as she walked away. She looked back from the wagon before going inside.

Trader seemed to have returned to his daydreams, which was just as well. Rand leaned against the tree and fancied he felt the sap running behind its bark. He angled the knife to cut his bonds, but then hesitated. He had no desire to confront Trader, who had been kind to him. Besides, he had an inkling that in a fight the wanderer would prove a formidable opponent. Escaping by night would be better.

☙

Rand had trouble keeping the knife hidden when the outlaws took him to relieve himself in the woods, and Trader proved too perceptive. "Something on your mind?" he'd asked more than once. Fortunately, Mara's departure gave an excuse for his distraction. In truth, that was a large part of it. The guard who normally watched him at night nodded off, as was his wont. Finally, the familiar, gasping snores wafted from the outlaw slouched against a tree. Rand pulled the small dagger from behind his belt and applied the sharp side of the blade to the bonds restraining his hands. They came free, and he bent to cut the rope around his ankles.

His guard snorted and jerked into a sitting position.

Rand straightened and placed his hands behind his back barely in time to avoid discovery. His heart thudded, but he closed his eyes and pretended to sleep. Silence followed. At last the gasping snores carried to him again.

Rand made quick work of his remaining bonds. Cramped from sitting, he eased into a standing position and looked out over the slumbering encampment. The full moon shone from a clear sky, sending its light to bathe the forest. A jaggercat yowled in the distance, reminding him of the perils a trek through the woods could pit against him. He'd be better off flying. He crept toward the livestock. The outlaws had hobbled his wingabeast and strapped down the poor creature's wings.

The wingabeast nickered at his approach, an unplanned complication. Even a small sound might bring one of the outlaws down upon him. Feeling the need to hurry, he sliced through the straps constraining his wingabeast's wings and sawed off the hobbling rope.

A twig snapped close behind him. He spun about. A body hurtled into his. Rand slammed to the ground with his assailant on top of him. Hands gripped his throat.

Rand threw off his attacker, who fell to the ground. The moonlight revealed the face of his night guard. The man gasped for breath and didn't try to rise. That circumstance wouldn't last long, Rand suspected. He flung himself onto his wingabeast's back and gathered the reins.

"The prisoner is escaping. Stop him!" His guard had regained his powers of speech.

Rand didn't wait to find out what would happen next but sent his wingabeast skyward. He gripped the creature's mane, fighting dizziness, then leveled out above the camp. His head cleared, and he looked down at his guard shaking his fist while other outlaws ran from their tents. "Be sure to thank your leader for his hospitality." He couldn't resist the taunt. "Tell him I decided not to wait to express my appreciation in person."

Rand sent the wingabeast upward, grateful that his riding had improved since he'd first taken the reins at Torindan. He adjusted more readily to sudden shifts and experienced less often the alarming sensation of being accidentally airborne without a mount. He'd taken the wingabeast too high, though. The thin air made breathing harder, and they were both shivering in the chill. He guided the wingabeast lower.

Something large and dark flapped in the sky, just catching the edge of his vision. He turned his head and drew a sharp breath.

Two welkes bearing riders on their backs sailed toward him.

Rand urged his wingabeast to fly faster. Keeping his seat at a high rate of speed wasn't so easy. He held on, aware that the dagger Mara had given him was no match for the swords the welke riders brandished. They arrowed in his direction and would soon flank the wingabeast. What could he do? He lacked the skill to outmaneuver the warriors and their trained raptor birds.

In a desperate move, he gave the wingabeast its head. The frightened creature pulled ahead, twisting to avoid the welkes' sharp talons. Rand slipped sideways in the saddle but hung on with the tenacity of terror.

The welke's shriek echoed from the hills below. The welkes pulled forward for another pass, so close the huffing of their breathing reached Rand. The wingabeast screamed. Blood spattered. The wingabeast angled toward the ground, almost catapulting Rand out of the saddle. He held on. His ears clogged, and the world tilted.

The wingabeast flew beneath the kaba tree canopy with the welkes in pursuit. Leaves and twigs lashed Rand, and he ducked to avoid being decapitated by a branch. Ahead loomed a fern-covered canyon with water seeping down its side. The wingabeast flew lower and dove into a grove of keirkens.

A shriek was followed by a thud. The welke landed beside it's rider, who flailed on the ground.

The remaining rider bared his teeth and shook his sword, With the wingabeast darting through the canyon at a terrifying speed, Rand couldn't pay much attention to the rider's posturing. The canyon stopped at a sheer face of rock cut by a waterfall. The welkes followed, and the solitary rider leveled his sword at Rand.

The wingabeast slanted upward at a precarious angle. Rand tried to hold on, but his grip broke and he tumbled.

The tops of the kierkens lining the river lay to one side, out of Rand's path. Otherwise, he might have broken his landing by clutching at branches. Nothing could save him now. The fall seemed to take a long time, giving him time for regrets. He'd failed to save his mother and failed to protect Mara. Trying his best had not been enough to save anyone, not even himself. After everything he'd gone through that should have killed him and hadn't, dying like this hardly felt fair.

8

COBBLEFORD CASTLE

The canyon wall passed in a blur, picking up speed. Rand crashed into something that yielded downward, slowing his descent. His fingers tangled in a silken mane. Wings rose like a curtain around him and batted downward. The wingabeast leveled in flight. Rand gripped the saddle and hauled himself forward to take a seat on its back.

Wings flapped above them, and long shudders wracked the wingabeast. Rand looked upward, his heart thudding.

Beaks snapping and talons gleaming, the welkes closed in for the kill.

From somewhere below bows rasped, followed by the whoosh and thud of arrows. The welkes' shrieks told him that the arrows had found their marks. The rider's sword spun by while the raptor birds plunged past, creating a current that rocked the wingabeast's flight. The rider screamed as he fell.

The wingabeast pulled upward, but Rand took over the reins and signaled to land. Three archers, clad in the green and gold of Rivenn, stood at the edge of the keirken grove. He'd not approach them on his own account, but for Mara's sake, he would. The wingabeast spiraled downward but lifted away to hover above the broken bodies of their pursuers.

The archers did not lower their bows. "Name yourself," called the one who stood in the lead.

"I know him." Recognizing the speaker's voice, Rand stiffened. Craelin strode out from the trees. It seemed strange to find him here, as if he should not exist apart from Torindan. The sunlight picked out a scar on his throat and made shadows in the lines at the corners of his blue eyes, sketched no doubt by a lifetime of squinting into the distance. "Come down from that wingabeast."

With three arrows aimed his direction at close quarters, Rand had little choice but to dismount.

"Water the wingabeast." Craelin commanded.

A guardian emerged from the small group at the edge of the grove. He took the reins from Rand and led the wingabeast to the river bank.

"That wingabeast belongs to the guardians of Rivenn," Craelin thundered.

Rand nodded. "He does."

"How came you to ride him?"

"Honorably." Rand refused to flinch beneath Craelin's glare. "I carried the Lof Raena away from Torindan on this wingabeast."

Craelin's eyebrows shot upward. "The Lof Raena escaped Torindan?"

"She did."

"What have you done with her since?"

"I lost her to the outlaws who kidnapped her."

Craelin peered at him as if trying to see into his mind. "Where did this happen?"

"On the road to Cobbleford. I descended to inform you of it."

"Oh, did you? Just as you warned me at Torindan, I suppose — after the damage was done? For all I know, you let Freaer's warriors in through the sallyport."

"That's not fair—"

"Why should I believe anything you say, son of Freaer?" He waved a hand, and several guardians started forward.

Rand bit back his frustration and adopted a reasonable tone. "I've committed myself to Faeraven."

"Under which ruler?" Craelin pinned Rand with a piercing glance. "Elcon or your father?"

"You saw me bend my knee to Lof Shraen Elcon."

"That would make you a traitor, then."

"*If* I did wrong."

"Whether you did is a question I intend to answer." Craelin flicked a glance to the guardians watching from the grove. "Take him prisoner."

ଔ

Mara reined in her horse and stared at the gates of Cobbleford Castle, looming on the other side of an arching bridge. The awe and wariness on Lyneth's face, who had halted her horse beside Mara's, matched her own. She could never grow used to the grandeur bound to reside behind the pleated stone columns and ornamented arches of the gatehouse. She reminded herself that if her grandparents refused to accept her, she would never have the opportunity.

"I won't come inside, if it's all the same to you." Hael, on a black horse beside her pulled down his brimmed cap to shade his eyes and gave Mara a rakish grin. "I'm not in the mood to dance in the wind quite yet."

She frowned. "I'll see if I can help you avoid it altogether."

His eyes glinted, and he caught her hand for a kiss. "I'd appreciate that." He looked across her to Lyneth, gazing at him with an intent expression. "I hope you find your mistress here."

"As do I." Lyneth's smile seemed a little forced. The relentless journey to reach Cobbleford before afternoon must have wearied her. Or perhaps she felt the same strain Mara did at casting herself upon the mercy of people she didn't know.

Hael turned his horse but looked over his shoulder. "I'll watch to make sure you're allowed inside."

"Thank you." Relief washed over Mara, a measure of her anxiety.

His smile slipped. "Mara—" He looked away but then back again with his smile firmly in place. "Humor me, will you? Tie a scrap of linen in your window when you know you're safe."

"All right," Mara agreed.

"Goodbye, then." Hael pulled the brim of his cap lower and rode a little way along the river bank.

Lyneth's face took on a look of distaste, as if she'd eaten something unpleasant. "I'm not quite sure why I'm sorry to see him go."

Mara laughed. "Searcher has a way of growing on a person."

"You seem to know him well."

"I do." Lyneth's statement was really a question, one too complicated for Mara to answer. She squared her shoulders and pushed her horse forward. The familiar clop of hooves on the bridge comforted her.

Lyneth kept pace beside her. "Are you frightened,

Milady?"

"Yes." Mara immediately regretted the sharpness of her reply. "Are you?" she added in a softer tone.

Lyneth nodded. "What if the guards throw us out?"

"Then Searcher will come for us."

Lyneth sent her a sideways glance. "You seem sure of that."

"He would." Mara spoke with more confidence than warranted perhaps, but the Hael she'd known couldn't have vanished completely. The waters of the Cobbleford River rushed beneath the bridge and emerged on the westward side, hurrying along on its voyage to Maer Ibris, the western sea she'd noticed glimmering on the horizon. Maybe someday she'd dip her foot into it. How did salt waters feel against the skin? The fierceness of her desire to know gave her pause. Had Nadya's wanderlust rubbed off on her or was she desperate to put distance between herself and Cobbleford? She'd wanted to meet her grandparents and to be accepted by them, but the closer they came to the castle, the more her stomach churned. Mara set her jaw and forced herself to continue. Running away from the inn had taught her that the only way to deal with trials was to travel the path through them.

The wooden gates yawned open but would probably close at nightfall. The metal teeth of the portcullis behind them bit into the cobblestones, allowing no admittance.

"State your business."

Mara squinted upward but with the sun behind the ramparts, she could barely make out the guard who had called to them. He stood as a dark figure against a bright light that hurt her eyes. She summoned a smile anyway. "Please tell King Euryon that his relative has arrived."

"What names do you give?" His tone warmed a little but held an edge of wariness.

"Syl Marinda."

"And I'm the servant, Lyneth."

The guard grunted. "How comes an Elder maiden into the company of a Kindren, and why do you have such a strange name?"

Mara squinted up at him. "That is a tale for the king's ears."

"Is he expecting you?"

"No." Lyneth's voice joined hers.

"My visit is meant as a surprise." Mara spoke into the silence that followed.

"And where do you come from?"

Mara hesitated. If she told him Norwood, he would wonder how she'd escaped Freaer's forces to reach Cobbleford. If she explained that she'd come from Torindan, she could lose any help he might offer her. She drew herself taller and did her best imitation of Arillia in a commanding mood. "That is no concern of a mere guard. I will explain myself to King Euryon."

"Move on with you. I've no patience for a waif who will not state her business or where she's from."

Mara exchanged a glance with Lyneth. The servant's face reflected Mara's own dismay. Strange how she'd dreaded entering Cobbleford while on the bridge but now yearned to do so. Going away might ease her nerves but would bring her no closer to her goals. She decided to try a different tack. "I will tell you what you want to know, but in private." She glanced about for emphasis. "I would not want the wrong ears to hear."

The guard folded his arms. "Who would those belong to?" he scoffed.

Mara tamped down on her irritation. Ranting at this obstinate man would not help, and might possibly harm her chances of gaining an audience with her grandfather. "I will tell you privately."

"Wait!" a woman's voice shouted from behind the portcullis. "You must let her in at once."

The guard looked downward. "Go away, Merwith, or I'll report you for interfering with official business."

"Don't be daft, Arctar. Can you not see that she's the very image of Aewen?"

"I'm too young to remember Aewen."

"Trust me when I say that this woman must be Euryon's kin."

"I'm not convinced of that."

"Because you won't listen to reason. Look at the poor waifs. Let me feed them at least before you send them away."

"They can have a share of the alms in your basket."

"A bit of bread won't help them much. They need a proper meal and a cot by the fire."

"Cobbleford is not a sanctuary for the poor."

"Where's your sense of decency, man? They're thin as starved cats and likely as weak. What threat can they be to anyone?"

The guard paced on the wall. "All right. You can take them into the kitchen for the night. Set them on the road early tomorrow or I'll know about it."

With the screech of metal and clank of chains the portcullis began its upward journey. Mara, with Lyneth beside her, urged her horse forward into the corridor where a woman in the dark dress, mob cap, and white apron of a kitchen maid stood, a large basket filled with bread over one arm. Mara stopped before the servant, who had looked youthful but on closer inspection bore the marks of age in her wrinkled throat and thickening waist. "Thank you for your help."

The woman hoisted the basket and tilted her chin in the direction of the guard. "Meddling, he'd call it. I'm Merwith, as you might have heard."

"I did indeed." Mara dismounted. "I'm Mara, and this is Lyneth."

"Welcome to you both."

Lyneth slid from her horse's back. "How kind of you to speak for us."

"That guard…" She shook her head. "Never mind. You're in now. Bring your horses and come with me."

Fading light fell through arrow slits in the walls of the corridor, forming bars of pale gray for them to walk through. Their feet left the cobblestone at times and thudded hollowly on wooden trap doors. Kai had told Mara that in time of war, the castle defenders could trap an invading enemy between the portcullis at the entrance and the one raised before them. They passed out of the corridor, and the clanking behind them announced the lowering of the second portcullis. An arched doorway led into the outer bailey where horses whinnied in a long, low building and smoke curled from kitchen chimneys across a green sward. Men garbed in short tunics and leather leggings or wearing the dark blue of the castle garrison traveled the cobbled paths.

"You there!" The woman called.

A lanky youth with shaggy hair the color of buckskin looked over his shoulder, then came to greet them with a wide smile for Lyneth. "Shall I take your horse, Milady?"

"Yes, you shall," the kitchen maid informed him, "and without gawking at the ladies."

The youth's face reddened. He ducked his head. "I meant no disrespect, Milady."

"Of course you didn't," Lyneth assured him with a quick smile. "Thank you for your service."

The red staining the youth's face spread to his ear tips. "I'm happy to do it." He gathered the horse's reins and led them toward the stables.

Merwith transferred her basket to a young maid in the kitchen doorway. "Take these alms, Aela, and give them to the poor."

Aela turned round green eyes on Merwith. "The poor will ask after you."

"You must tell them I am occupied but will come tomorrow."

Mara turned to her. "I'm sorry we're keeping you from your duty."

Merwith's lips curved in a gentle smile. "Why would you think that? You are God's creatures in need, given into my care. Come and eat, then I will listen to your stories."

ભ

Shae woke with the certainty that Kai was in danger. She sat up in the leafy bower and swung her legs down from the bench where she'd lain. Birds sang from the trees surrounding the garden. Their joy at the beauty of Creation would have spread to her if worry did not cloud her mind. When it came to Kai, she couldn't relax. She'd seen him suffer but lacked the ability to do more than comfort him. Going to him in his world, at least in part, had made it easier to accept their separation. Traveling through the weak places where the worlds didn't quite mesh had cost her a price that had risen each time.

Trapped between worlds, she felt the pressure of their shifting. The weak places had grown more numerous, but she could no longer travel them. The effort she'd made to show Kai the location of the sallyport had almost killed her. She had no doubt she would not survive another attempt to reach him. Her death would cause the ancient prophecy to fail, with horrifying consequences. Freaer would rule over Elderland with an iron fist and destroy every scrap of virtue it possessed.

Her feet made little sound on the marble path as she rushed to the gazing pool at the garden's heart. If Lof Yuel smiled upon her, she would be able to see Kai, to understand his peril.

Dense foliage nodded at the edge of the pool. The waters churned and frothed. Shae held back, suddenly afraid. What would the reflection show her when the waters smoothed? Did she dare to find out? She pressed forward, certain that not knowing would take more of a toll than facing the truth.

The waters stilled in an instant and shone clear as glass. Glimpsing the scene that unfolded within the pool, Shae fell to her knees. She couldn't go to Kai again, but Lof Yuel could. "Keep him safe," she prayed. "I release him to You."

ॐ

The drumming of hooves drove Kai off the road and into the green shade beneath a spreading keirken. He signaled to Flecht to remain still and waited with Aerlic in tense silence. The dark branches twisting above dripped lobed leaves to screen them, the best hiding place he could find on sudden notice. In the uncertain light in the aftermath of a storm, it might serve well enough to hide them. He couldn't guess for certain the number of horses approaching, but he counted many. He'd ridden the rough wagon road that connected Norwood with Westerland many times but could not remember ever coming upon so many wayfarers. Only one explanation presented itself, although he wished it wrong. The hoofbeats grew louder, and he picked out the creak of leather.

A contingent of Pilaer's soldiers hove into sight, confirming his suspicion. He'd heard that Freaer's forces had invaded Norwood, but had they also taken more of the Elder lands? If so, he might have sent Mara to seek her grandfather's help in a castle that no longer remained in his power. The thought strengthened his resolve to reach her at all costs. Kai had given his word to Elcon to protect his daughter. He could do that much for Elcon after failing him when he'd fallen on Draegmor's sword. When Elcon had sent him away from his chambers for privacy while spending the night with the Lof Raelein, Kai should have slept on a pallet in the corridor outside Elcon's door. Instead, he'd sought the comfort of the bed in his gatehouse chamber. He'd chased after Shae when she appeared to him in the night, never thinking he should be elsewhere. She'd led him to the hidden sallyport Pilaer's warriors breached, but barely in time to warn of the danger. Had he remained near Elcon, he'd have been present to defend the Lof Shraen when Pilaer's warriors broke into the keep. If the Lof Shraen died, Kai would hold himself responsible.

He must not fail in his duty to protect Elcon's daughter and heir or the Alliance of Faeraven might end. If Elcon died, Mara would be the only hope remaining to the scattered Kindren. They would look to her for leadership and sustenance. Kai must support her in that. At all costs, Freaer's forces must be stopped.

Warriors garbed in the red surcoat emblazoned with the gold dragon of Pilaer rode across his vision. Resisting the urge to press into the shadows, he held still. Any movement could invite discovery, and he would rather keep his life to spend it for Faeraven. That had been his desire since his early days, when he'd bent his knee in service to Faeraven and the ruling House of Rivenn. He'd exchanged the raiment of a second son of Whellein for the simple garb of a squire. In that humble capacity, he'd rescued Elcon's sister Shae as an infant when Kindren loyal to Freaer had tried to take her life. After delivering Shae to his parents in Whellein for safekeeping, he'd returned to Torindan to a hero's welcome. After being promoted into the ranks of the guardians of Rivenn, he'd applied himself to his training and had risen to the status of personal guard to Maeven, Elcon's beautiful mother. Kai's throat swelled as memory swamped him. He could still see Maeven's lifeless body lying on her funeral bier. He'd told himself he couldn't have known her maidservant would poison her, but he couldn't help the uneasy suspicion that somehow he had failed her too.

The contingent of Pilaer's warriors filed by, some familiar to him. Even with a faceplate hiding his features, that large warrior with flaming red hair showing at the edges of his helm could only be Draggon of Merboth. Kai had bested him once in hand battle, a defeat Enric would acknowledge with a grin whenever they met thereafter. And there must ride Darvin of Tallyrand, whose crouching posture vied with the prowess shown by the locks of defeated opponents tied to his horse's bridle. Kai swallowed against a lump in his throat.

These Kindren followed Freaer for various reasons, but deception lay at the root of each one. No Shraen ruled perfectly, as Kai had learned. Elcon's mistakes weren't the only that divided the Kindren. His father Timraen had made his share. Trusting too quickly left room for betrayal, but Timraen had scorned the advice that might have saved him from the murder that took his life. With Elcon so young, Timraen had chosen on his death bed to pass Sword Rivenn and the Sceptor of Faeraven to his wife. This lapse in protocol had offended those of the Kindren unwilling to submit to a female ruler. They'd questioned Maeven's fitness to lead and also her loyalty as a Lof Raelein from a vanished raven. A garn invasion had ended the House of Braeth in her youth, leaving the stronghold and outlands in ruins and the bewildered raena orphaned and alone. She had risen above that crisis and become Lof Raelein of Faeraven upon marrying her rescuer. And later, when tragedy took Timraen from her, she'd continued with unshakable grace to give herself to her people. Having long admired her example, Kai would not do less.

The warrior's horses must have been schooled to

silence, for they passed without drawing attention to the wingabeasts they must sense in the shadows.

Kai let out his breath as the last of them started by. He and Aerlic would burrow deeper into the forest and wait for the warriors to put distance between them before setting off again. Traveling off the road would make for a slower journey, but they'd be more likely to win through alive.

One of the horses let out a long whinny, halted, and pointed its head at their hiding place beneath the keirken tree. Flecht trembled, and without thinking Kai put a calming hand on his wingabeast's neck.

The warrior riding the horse that had whinnied whipped his head around to stare in Kai's direction. "What was that?"

The few who came up behind the warrior on the errant horse went around him, but a lanky archer glanced back. "Come now, Harrick. Can't you control that beast?"

"Something moved in the shadows, Naetar. I swear it."

Naetar snorted. "Are you seeing wilderwens again?"

"I saw what I saw." Harrick insisted in a wounded voice.

"All the more reason to keep up with the others, I'd say." Naetar scanned the forest, but his gaze stopped at the keirken tree, and his eyes narrowed.

Kai's heart thudded, but he held himself in check. No good would come of striking when the pair might ride on.

"To your target!" Naetar shouted. He palmed his short bow in an instant and slotted an arrow with deft skill.

9

ABANDONED HOMEFARM

Reacting in the brief space between Naetar's shout and the twang of his bow, Kai urged Flecht sideways. His wingabeast moved out from under the tree, missing the arrow aimed for its heart. Shouts rang out from the warriors racing to challenge them, and he caught Aerlic's voice calling commands to Argalent. Kai had no time to spare a glance for his companion while guiding Flecht into the air by the quickest and safest route possible. That meant a direct launch. A gentle spiral made adjusting into flight easier on the rider, but they had no time for such niceties. Flecht lifted at once, a greater target stretched out for flight, but Kai had no choice but to take the risk. He drew his sword, sent up a prayer, and held onas arrows flashed by.

Altitude came quickly. Pain thrummed in Kai's ears, the world spun, and his gut clenched. He would not hold back for his own sake, but the need to locate Aerlic stayed his impulse to flee. The archer came up beside him with his bow drawn. A shaft shot downward would carry farther than one sent up after them, a fact he used to advantage. Cries carried up to them, and Kai hardened his heart to the thought of Enric, Darvin, and the others he'd once called friend in harm's way.

A horn blasted the air below them, its hoarse blare an ancient call that stirred the blood. Kai knew it for the signal it was — a call to any welke riders in the area. Aerlic must have read it too, for he shouldered his bow and turned Argalent to follow Flecht. Kai set out due west, drinking in gulps of air to settle his nausea. The battle cries and screams of Pilaer's warriors sloughed away like the mold off a wheel of cheese. The kaba forest canopy unfolded all the way to the coasts of Darksea, a soothing sight. He didn't let himself relax however. Welke riders might even now scour the countryside for them. Searching for a clear place to land and shelter, he pressed onward.

The homefarm sprawled at the end of an overgrown track. One of its doors hung open negligently, as if whoever had abandoned it had left in a hurry. The tumbledown barn behind the house tilted on its foundation like a drunkard. Its blasted-out windows made entrances for clouds of flitlings that drifted from the barn, hovered in the air, then dove in again. Whatever usefulness this ruined remnant of a forgotten past had once boasted ingratiated it no longer. No foot fell here save the soft padding of forest creatures as nature reclaimed the land.

Kai sent Flecht downward into what had once been a pasture beside the barn. Sections of barbed wire still guarded their domain, although an equal number lay flattened on the ground at odd angles wherever wind or snow had carried them. The pasture held an apple tree with twisted branches and gnarled bark. Its fruit must once have delighted the creatures confined to graze this enclosure. Perhaps some now-forgotten kindness had prompted its planting for that reason.

Kai dismounted and led Flecht beside Aerlic and

Argalent toward the barn. The front doors sagged on their hinges, too derelict to function. A side door creaked open, the sound startling a flurry of wings into motion. The tiny birds flew at Kai's face, and he batted his arms to deter them. "*Fiends.* Be gone with you."

Aerlic laughed. "Don't hold a grudge against them. Even gentle birds will defend their nests."

Kai rubbed away a spot of blood on his hand. "Maybe stopping here wasn't such a good idea."

"We make ourselves the intruders, my friend. We will do better if we respect the homes already established here."

Kai nodded his agreement with the archer's wisdom. They checked the barn for other hazards and found none. "I think it's safe to hide the wingabeasts here for a short while. Let's check the house."

Aerlic rubbed Argalent's neck. "We may find it a more convenient environment."

The sky seemed more open than ever, leaving Kai grateful when they could duck inside the homefarm. Even with grass growing in the floor cracks and moldy walls, the house had a welcoming feel. Kai dismissed this impression as mere fancy but it persisted, following him from room to room like a faithful cur he couldn't shake. By unspoken agreement, he and Aerlic didn't speak until they'd swept through every nook.

Kai turned to Aerlic. "I think the house will work for our needs, and the barn will do for the wingabeasts."

A smile touched Aerlic's lips. "The birds aren't nearly as put out by the horses."

"For that I'm thankful. We'll have to trade watches, but this night should give us sleep."

"I hope you are right about that. Something has

me on edge."

Kai went to the grime-spotted parlor window. No welke riders stood out against the afternoon sky. He and Aerlic shouldn't move from this place tonight, but he'd be happy when they could. "I share your feeling."

CR

Kai peered out the dining room window in the abandoned homefarm. Dawn lightened the sky and unfurled on the horizon in hues of pink and gold.

A welke rider stood out against the pearl grey sky.

Kai pulled back from the window. The rhythmic sound of Aerlic's snores drifted from the other room. Neither he nor the archer had spent a comfortable might, but their training had taught them to disregard distractions and sleep when necessary. The night passed in relative safety, regardless of the uneasiness that continued to haunt Kai. Perhaps the long journey had taken a toll on his nerves. By all appearances, it seemed they would escape this place unharmed. The only life they had seen besides the birds had been a nest of mice in the barn.

He worked a kink out of his neck. Sleeping on the improvised bed made of branches had not helped the aches he'd gathered on the road. Somewhere outside a kaeroc whistled and fell silent. The last time he'd seen one of the reclusive birds had been long ago in the ruins of Braith. Thinking of the spidery waevens that had held him enchanted on that journey did nothing to restore his peace of mind. This lonely place seemed a likely home for such hideous creatures. His skin crawled, and he peered behind him into the shadows.

Nothing stirred.

Only a little longer, and he'd wake Aerlic. He wouldn't wait for full daylight to leave. He couldn't stomach this place much longer. Being out and about while most Elders hadn't risen yet would be wise anyway. They would need to travel by land, a prospect not entirely welcome. If two Kindren journeying through Elder lands didn't attract attention, the wingabeasts would. Standing out usually led to trouble, especially in Lancert, which had a reputation for drawing a high-spirited crowd. The buying and selling of horseflesh, the trade that gave the town its primary sustenance, apparently called for a great deal of drinking and gaming. If he could avoid the place he would, but all roads led there. They joined and ran parallel or intersected at crossroads, of which there were many. He and Aerlic would take the junction that led south and east to Cobbleford.

He could hope to find Mara and Elcon there. Splitting up when the welke riders pursued them had been the right choice to make, but sometimes he had to remind himself of that fact. By doing so, he'd sent both of the people he'd promised to protect out of his reach. Rand had proven himself by alerting Craelin of the danger at Torindan, but sending Mara off with him wouldn't have been his choice. He'd had no time to arrange anything else. Thinking of Elcon in the care of Eathnor, Dorann, and Anders would give him more comfort if they hadn't taken Arillia with them. Watching over Elcon would be difficult enough without also protecting the Lof Raelein. Elcon had been in no condition to gainsay her wishes, but Kai had no doubt he'd have objected to keeping her with him for her sake.

The flitlings began their morning chatter and flew from the barn into nearby trees to peck for bugs. Good. Kai and Aerlic could retrieve the wingabeasts without upsetting the entire flock. With that in mind, he started toward the parlor door, which Aerlic had left ajar. A scuffling from within the room alerted him. He slowed his steps and drew his sword. He'd not been particularly quiet. Whoever or whatever lurked behind that door might have heard his approach. He couldn't change that, but he might gain the upper hand regardless. He'd know more once he discovered what had happened to Aerlic. That something was amiss seemed obvious, since Aerlic hadn't cried out and no sounds of battle emerged from the room. If anything had happened to him…

Letting his emotions rule wouldn't help. He applied his boot to the door, and it shuddered open. Inside the room, waevens did not hum to weave magics. No wraiths ran at him wearing the faces of those he loved. The feiann did not cast nets of trickery. Only Aerlic, starting up from sleep, met him. "Is something wrong?"

Kai did not relax his guard but scoured the room for signs of intrusion. "I thought I heard someone in here with you."

"I'd have known it. I sleep light." Despite his disclaimer, Aerlic darted glances about.

"Now that you're awake, why don't we continue our journey?"

"Gladly."

"I'll be happy to leave this place behind." Kai turned to go but stopped short.

An Elder man with his sword leveled stood outside the parlor doorway. "State your business."

Kai reached for his sword hilt.

"I wouldn't." The man spoke in a bored voice. "I should tell you that I'm quite good at swordplay."

"Who are you?" Kai threw out the question while watching the Elder's every movement.

The man wore disheveled clothing and shoes with holes in them. Morning shadow on his face and rumpled hair beneath a tattered cap completed the picture of a vagabond. "Trespassers have no call to ask questions."

"Neither should vagabonds defend what they do not own," Kai shot back.

"Have you never heard of squatter's rights?" The man brandished his sword. "I'll ask you a final time. What do you Kindren want in these parts?"

"Nothing but a way through them." Kai changed tactics.

"That so? Then I'll give you my blessing to be on your way."

"We'll take it then."

"Stay out of the barn when you leave. Those winged horses belong to me."

Kai drew his sword. "We differ on that point."

Aerlic came up beside Kai, his bow drawn.

The curtains at the window billowed, and a wild-haired man appeared. "You heard what Tam said." He flicked his head, making his riotous curls bounce. "Go on with you."

A man with a broken nose that had healed in a flattened shape stepped out from the shadows while the first was speaking. "Topper and me don't take it well when someone draws a weapon on Tam. Understand?"

Garbed in ragged clothes, they seemed little more

than tattered scarecrows, but the knives the two wielded meant business.

"Put away your weapons." Tam called from the doorway. "You don't want to learn how well Topper and Jost can throw a knife."

Topper displayed a gap-toothed smile. "That's a fine sword he has. I'm sure it belongs to you, Tam."

Kai remained in a fighting stance, ready to defend Sword Rivenn. "You'll not take my weapon."

"Squatter's rights," Jost crowed.

"Is that what they call theft in Westerland these days?" Aerlic drawled.

"Westerland law does not apply to Kindren property." Kai remained alert for movement.

Tam tilted his head, clearly considering a novel idea. "It does on this home farm."

"So now you declare these lands your realm? I wonder what King Euryon would make of that."

"Why do you quibble over rules when I'm giving you the chance to escape with your lives? Go peacefully and I'll let you keep your weapons."

Kai bit back a sarcastic retort. With both sides evenly matched, no good would come of a fight, which Tam must have guessed. "Move aside, and we'll see our own way out."

"You've made a wise decision." Still leveling his sword, Tam stepped back out of the doorway.

Kai started forward. Aerlic positioned himself as rear guard. Topper and Jost closed in behind them, and Tam followed.

"You've seen us off the property," Kai said when they reached the road. "How much farther did you plan to travel with us?"

"Stay well away from here." Tam spoke in tones

that brooked no refusal. "There'll be no second chances."

Kai frowned. "You've made your point."

"Mind you remember it." Tam nodded to Topper and Jost and turned back.

The other two vagabonds followed them as far as the next town before turning back.

Kai watched them out of earshot. "We'll wait a couple of days, then take back the wingabeasts."

Aerlic shouldered his bow, which he'd kept in his hands with the vagabonds near. "My thought exactly."

 Ω

With the pots scoured and the flames burning lower in the cavernous fireplace, Mara sipped the warm cider in the tankard Merwith had thumped onto the scarred table before her. Thankful for a hot meal, she'd eaten with gratitude the coarse bread they'd never have been offered at the Lof Shraen's table. Across from her, Lyneth mopped up the last of her stew and sighed. The shadows under her eyes testified to her exhaustion. The servants who had sat on benches at the trestle tables had gone elsewhere. Later some would return to spread pallets on the floor.

Merwith sat beside Lyneth. "You're weary, child. Have you traveled far?"

Lyneth nodded. "All the way through the wild lands."

The light from the lantern suspended by a rope above the table picked out Merwith's frown. "What reason had you for such a treacherous journey?"

Lyneth sent Mara a questioning look, obviously

wondering how much to tell.

"A desperate one," Mara answered. "We've come from Torindan."

Merwith's eyes flared in a look of surprise. "I've heard rumors..."

"Only rumors?" That must mean that none of the others had arrived yet. Her father would need to travel slowly, but Kai should have been here by now.

"People say that Pilaer has taken more of the Kindren lands."

"It's true, sadly. Torindan has fallen." The words fell from her lips, each dropping by its own weight. Speaking them made the tragedy more real in her mind.

"Not the High Hold of Faeraven!"

"You know of it then."

"As does everyone at Cobbleford with a memory. It's where the Kindren high king took Princess Aewen to become his bride."

"Did you know her?" Mara asked, diverted.

"Of course I did. She spent as much time mingling with the kitchen staff as she did with her father's guests. She came each night and gave alms to the poor. They looked for her far more than they do for me." Merwith's gaze wandered over Mara's face. "You've the look of her."

"She was my mother."

"That explains it, then." Merwith nodded. "We must tell the king."

"That's what I came to do."

"I'll try my best to help you, but we don't have much time."

Remembering the guard's threat, Mara nodded. She could guess that if they didn't leave willingly, they'd be thrust out the gate. "Is there any way of sending word to King Euryon?"

"Let me think about that. Meanwhile, your servant is falling asleep. I should lay down a pallet for her."

A door opened. "Merwith, I've brought the decoction for your lungs," a feminine voice called from behind Mara.

Merwith half-stood. "Your Serenity—"

Mara turned to see the newcomer.

A white-faced woman stared back at her with dark eyes. She wore a dark dress and a winged cap with a veil falling down her back. "Aewen!" A small vial slipped from her grasp. Shards flew, and a dark liquid spread across the stone floor. The woman's chest heaved, and she swayed on her feet.

Merwith rushed to her and put an arm across her shoulders. "You must sit down, Your Serenity. You've had a shock."

The woman pulled away from Merwith. A frown puckered her brow. "What wraith has come to haunt Cobbleford? My sister is dead."

Strong emotions distorted the woman's features, but Mara could detect a slight resemblance to herself in the high brow and the curve of her cheeks. She cast back in memory. What had Father called her mother's sister? "Aunt Caerla?"

The woman stared at her. "*What* did you call me?"

"She says she's Aewen's daughter," Merwith supplied. "You have only to look at her to know it's true. Who else can she be?"

"I believe it. Has my father seen her?"

"The guard wouldn't tell him she's here."

Tears sparkled in Caerla's eyes. "God in his kindness has given me a second chance to help my sister."

Part 2
Castle Intrigue

10

Audience with the King

Mara stood before the double doors to the king's chambers with a sinking feeling in her stomach. She had traveled a long way and endured many hardships to reach her grandfather. Why hesitate on the brink of meeting him? She should be more glad than fearful. What if she discovered him cruel? Could that have been the reason for her father's reluctance to ask King Euryon for help? Euryon had sent his own daughter away to live in a foreign land among relative strangers. Her mother had brought shame to her family, but even so what kind of father would retaliate so harshly? She balled her hands into fists but couldn't quite gather the courage to move.

Arctar, the guard who had refused to allow her into the castle last night, now stood ready with another member of the garrison to admit her to the king's chambers. Either coincidence or God had placed him there. She would not inquire as to which but resisted the urge to gloat at the sheepish expression on Arctar's face.

Caerla, who had walked beside her from the kitchen, pressed her back with the lightest of touches. "You mustn't keep the king waiting, little bird."

Mara forced herself to walk forward, and the guards swung open the doors. She slowed her steps at the realization that her aunt had remained behind. She glanced back, and Caerla waved her onward. Mara squared her shoulders and entered the king's chambers alone. Arctar and the other guard positioned themselves just inside the doorway. Other members of the garrison stood at intervals down the sides of the long chamber. The others present faded into the background as Mara gave her attention to the man at the end of the long stretch of dark stone paving who did not look anything like the curmudgeon she had imagined.

King Euryon sat on his carved and gilded throne with a noble bearing, although the wrinkled hands splayed around the armrests revealed the toll time had taken on him. Beneath the armrests roared the same lions sewn into Westerland's flag and carved into the entrance doors. The twin lions of Westerland adorned the king's chest, embroidered in gold thread on cloth of twined purple and green.

He studied her with narrowed eyes and an air of deep concentration. "Caerla said you would look like Aewen, but she didn't prepare me to see this vision of my daughter. You closely resemble her."

"This I have heard many times." She made her bow. "King Euryan." She would not call him grandfather without invitation.

"How I wish she had not died." His voice

quavered and brightness filled his eyes.

She looked away from his grief, which made her ache for the mother she had never known. "I share your wish."

He blinked away tears and sat taller. "Come closer, child."

The light from the overhead chandelier cast shadows that shifted as she moved toward him. He watched her with sad eyes and a wary expression. It comforted her somewhat to recognize that her grandfather might have similar feelings about this meeting. She could see Caerla's rough features arranged more happily in his face. More suited to a man, they gave him a becoming ruggedness.

A frown puckered his brow. "You have Elcon's eyes."

"He *is* my father."

He lifted his head like a bird, and his eyes lit with quick interest. "And how does the high king fare these days?"

She searched his face and found only concern written there. "Not well, I'm afraid. A battle at Torindan left him with a grave wound."

"Will he recover?"

"I hope that he will." She folded her arms against the draft that blew against her. "No one could say when I left him."

His eyes widened. "What would take a daughter away from her father's side at such a time?"

He must not realize that she had responsibilities other than those of a daughter. "A kingdom."

Euryon leaned forward. "Explain yourself."

She returned her attention to him. "Have you not heard? Torindan lies in ruins."

"I am sorry that the high hold of Faeraven has come to such a pass."

Mara pulled in a breath. "My father wanted to ask your help." The statement came as near the truth as she dared go. "I have come in his stead."

Euryon's wrinkled hands gripped the rests above the lions caught perpetually in voiceless roars. "What can Westerland do with Torindan already fallen?"

Mara held onto her patience. "Faeraven doesn't have to fall with it. I am heir of Faeraven and can gather the Kindren."

"You are like your mother in more ways than appearance."

"Won't you help us? We can't stand against Freaer alone. His forces are great and Faeraven is divided."

"If that is the case, perhaps the alliance of Faeraven should end."

She stared at him, then found her voice. "You don't understand your danger. Freaer won't stop at bringing down Faeraven."

"The garrison will repel any who trouble our borders."

"I must warn you. Resisting Freaer will not be so simple." How could she make her grandfather understand the horror of the enemy he would face? Freaer taught his warriors to value death above all else. He used old magics to control minds and corrupt souls. He set himself to destroy a kingdom from within.

Euryon shook his head. "You received more from your father than his eyes, apparently. Long ago Elcon asked me to stand with Faeraven against Freaer, and I gave him the same answer you will receive. When and if Freaer attacks Westerland, I'll face him, not before. It is the way among the Elder. We do not seek out war but address it swiftly when it arrives on our doorstep."

Mara blinked at the speed with which he'd dashed her hopes. Would it make any difference if she told him that Emmerich had told her father to ask him for help? Not at present, judging by his scowl. If she argued with him, he might have her escorted out of the castle. It would be better to bide her time and hope she could win him over. "I wanted to see you for another reason."

"What is it?"

She couldn't help but smile at the hunted expression that crossed his face. "I only want your permission to remain at Cobbleford."

The humor that lit his eyes gave him a youthful look. "I'd like more of your conversation, but on pleasanter topics."

She smiled. "Then you shall have it. May I meet the queen?"

The frown returned to his face. "I'll send for her. Guards! Summon Queen Inydde from her chambers."

ભ

Queen Inydde leaned against one of the pillars supporting the small alcove at the rear of the king's chamber and behind the throne. The light from the chandelier could not reach her here, but she remained behind the statue of Euryon anyway. Her own likeness graced a similar alcove on the other side of the throne, but she'd never liked the weak way it portrayed her. The statue had been Euryon's vision, which explained why the soft marble showed her poised like a handmaiden, ready to do her king's bidding. That she would never do, although she made sure he did not know it. She should have been rendered in ironstone, holding herself erect like a woman who knew her own mind and what she wanted.

She couldn't see her husband's face but could just make out the features of her wayward daughter on the new arrival's face. Emotions flooded her, too many to name, turning her stomach into a churning cauldron of acid. Aewen had been an errant daughter, lowly in thought, and brazen in action. After disgracing their royal household, she'd richly deserved the banishment she'd received. Her death had brought relief to her family, although Innyde still could not reconcile herself fully to that fact.

Inydde directed her attention back to the conversation she'd hidden in the throne room to spy upon. Caerla shouldn't have interfered to foist Aewen's brat upon the king. Now that she had, it was up to Inydde to guard her family against more shame. Euryon was too soft to be counted upon in that regard. She could hear him now, inviting the brat to stay. That wouldn't work. Aewen's child, by her very presence, could only stir memories long forgotten.

So she wanted to meet the queen, did she? Inydde slipped into the secret passageway that had brought her to the throne room. She would give the brat what she wanted, but with an outcome different than she might anticipate. Inydde hurried along the passageway to her inner chamber, a plan forming in her mind.

☙

Mara followed Inydde up the stairs with mixed emotions. The queen had greeted her in the throne room with politeness and promised to see her to a private bedchamber, but something in her behavior didn't ring true. The king had seemed ill at ease, and Mara had caught the queen giving her a glittering glance that chilled her spine.

One of the chamber doors on the flight above stood ajar, shedding light from a window partway down the stairs. The queen continued up the tower stairs to the next level, and then led the way along the corridor to the corner tower.

Mara walked behind her up the circular stairwell with daylight from arrow loops in the walls falling across her at intervals. Their steps stirred dust motes, and the air smelled musty, as if these stairs did not often see a broom and mop. It became obvious that the queen intended to hide her like a poor relation in the attic or another obscure corner of the castle.

Queen Inydde reached the landing and looked down at her with an expression that might have been contempt.

Mara hesitated, no longer certain she should follow this woman.

"Come now, we're almost there." Queen Inydde gave her a charming smile. "I know it's a long way up, but the view is beautiful."

"Really?" Mara's interest piqued.

The queen nodded. "You can see all the way to the waves of Maer Ibris." She warmed to her subject. "When I first arrived in Cobbleford, I spent many long days embroidering in this tower and gazing at the sea. With the breeze at the window, it was like being in an aerie."

After requesting to become a guest at the castle, it would be strange for her to object to being shown to a chamber. Mara tamped down her reluctance and followed the queen past the studded door at the top of the stairwell.

The bar that closed off the tower chamber lifted in the queen's hands. She turned and smiled at Mara. "Come in."

Mara held back. The inflexion of the queen's voice, the barred tower room, and the forcefulness with which she gestured her forward triggered a warning in Mara's mind. "I'd rather sleep in the kitchen, if you don't mind."

Quick as a snake striking, the queen caught her by the upper arm. "I do mind."

"What are you doing?" Mara tried to pull away.

The queen reached back her free hand and slapped her palm across Mara's cheek. The force of the blow snapped her head backward. Mara jerked her arm but the queen's grasp tightened.

"I'm afraid there's not much hope of escape. I don't want you wandering Cobbleford."

"Release me, and I promise to go away."

"If only I believed you." The queen unleashed a bitter laugh. "But I doubt that. You will talk to someone, whether inside Cobbleford or without its gates. Either way, I intend to silence you before that can happen."

"I don't know what you mean."

"Don't play the fool with me. We both know that I can't take the risk of allowing you to stir trouble. Most of the kingdoms have forgotten about Aewen's disgrace, and I mean to keep it that way." The Queen flung Mara into the tower chamber. She fetched hard against the wall and slid to the floor.

"If you won't free me, what are your plans?" Mara asked, although she dreaded the answer she might receive.

The queen's mask of civility slipped sideways, and the bitterness ingrained in her soul revealed itself in every line of her face. "I haven't made up my mind. You will remain in this chamber until I do. It is where I imprisoned your mother long ago."

"How can you do this? Don't you think the king will question my absence?"

A smile lit the queen's face. "I have no doubt that he will, but Euryon is weak-minded. He will accept what I say when I tell him you changed your mind about remaining with us."

"After our conversation, he will guess that's not true. Let me go and I won't tell anyone about what happened here."

The queen's laugh rang through the sparsely-furnished chamber. "The King does not question me." The finality of her words told Mara who held the real power at Cobbleford.

Her grandmother turned and vanished into the stairwell, closing the studded door behind her.

Mara breathed a prayer, but God seemed far away. Using the support of the wall, she stood and peered around the chamber. She'd had no time to gain more than an impression of the room. Its furnishings consisted of a bedstead with a worn coverlet, a meager washstand with a cracked mirror above it, and a bucket that must stand in for a chamber pot. Dust balls scattered across the floor, and a pile of ancient droppings might have belonged to mice. She went to the barred window to breathe in the cool air.

The queen might have lied about other things, but the view really did stretch to Maer Ibris. It was the room's one redemption. She stood for a long time looking out. What would she do? From the way the queen had talked, she wouldn't allow her to leave Cobbleford. Would she keep her imprisoned or do away with her? Mara suspected the latter.

CR

Beside her mother at the high king's table, Caerla sat with her gaze fixed on the trencher of bread before her. She would put only a few of the delicacies brought to her on this slab of bread. Since taking her place at the abbey, she'd learned from Brother Robb's example to live a disciplined life in contrast to the luxuries her parents and their guests enjoyed. She glanced at her father, already in his cups before the repast began. Her mother ignored him. She would bear his behavior, although she'd told Caerla privately she despised his drinking.

The servants brought the first course, which consisted of small pastries stuffed with cod liver, meat tidbits in cinnamon sauce, beef marrow fritters, spiced eel, percken fish in a green sauce, and roasted elk. Steadfast in her resolve to avoid gorging herself with too much food, Caerla took small portions, even of the eel, which she favored. She frowned and glanced about, then touched her mother's arm. "Where is Mara?"

Mother gave her a blank look. "Do I know someone by that name?"

"Aewen's daughter, Syl Marinda, goes by Mara.

Where is she? I understood she would stay with us."

"Yes, yes! I granted her permission." Father bent his head toward her mother. "What have you done with her, Inydde?"

Caerla knew he did not ask the question in jest. Mother dealt with people who displeased her in harsh ways. She'd learned in childhood not to ask questions, but she couldn't ignore her dead sister's child.

Her mother laughed lightly, never a good sign. "Didn't I tell you? She decided not to stay with us after all."

Father frowned at the wine in his drinking horn. "She wouldn't have gone without taking her leave of us."

"Do you know her so well after one meeting? She said something about giving up trying to persuade you to help her." She sipped her cider. "What did she mean?"

"Pity. I liked her." Father tossed back his wine and drew his sleeve across his mouth. "Where did she go, did she say?"

Mother gave a small shake of her head and took a delicate bite from the food on her trencher.

Caerla swallowed a bite of eel and washed it down with cider. She had no illusions left when it came to Mother. From the expression on her mother's face, she was lying. She'd had everything to do with Mara's departure, that much was easy to read. Caerla's jaw set. She couldn't overlook her mother's actions this time. She had removed Caerla's one chance to make amends for parting in anger from Aewen. Her sister had deserved better from her, just as Mara should have received kindness at Cobbleford. She considered the possibility that Mother had placed Mara under lock and key. She'd done such a thing before.

Caerla resolved to sleep this night in her old chamber, as she did upon occasion. Brother Robb did not like the indulgence, but Mother had insisted. The chamber beside Caerla's had belonged to Aewen. No one ever resided there now, by her father's command. She'd gone into it once and found it as Aewen had left it with the bedclothes thrown back and the tick still bearing the impression her sister had made upon it. The floor looked newly swept and no dust marred the furniture. Father would have seen to that.

Mother, as eager to forget Aewen as father was to remember her, had disparaged his shrine. Normally accommodating to his queen's wishes, Father had stood his ground. He'd kept the key to the chamber hidden after that. Caerla knew where to find it, but she no longer wished to enter the chamber where her past foolishness reproached her. She'd seen Father coming from the room brushing away tears. If Mother ever found the key, Caerla had no doubt she would erase every trace that Aewen had ever lived.

11

IN THE KEIRKEN GROVE

Arillia sat up with a start. She searched the darkness, which was heavy with breathing. Her pulse raced and fear tightened her throat. The breathing continued, sounding all at once familiar. She frowned. Where had the wilderwen chasing her gone? The forest had vanished, too. She seemed to be—yes, in a bed.

It had only been a dream.

Relief washed through her. Any monsters that stalked the night did so outside the hut.

"Lof Raelein?" Dorann's voice came from the other side of the flimsy door that separated the sleeping chamber from the main room. "Is all well?"

She couldn't make out Elcon on his bed next to hers, but his breathing sounded strong. "I think so. I had a nightmare."

"I wouldn't wonder, after everything that's happened. Do you want a draught to help you sleep?"

Elcon shifted and breathed lighter.

Arillia got up and to avoid waking him only cracked the door open. She couldn't see Dorann in the blackness. "No, but thank you."

"I should check the Lof Shraen."

"All right."

"I'll light the lanthorn."

Arillia groped for her cloak. Her fingers closed

over the woolen garment, and she pulled it from the wall peg where it hung. The warm folds settled about her, and she fastened the garment to conceal her chemise.

Dorann returned and went to Elcon. The light from the lanthorn the tracker placed on a table beside the bed showed her husband sleeping with a quiet look on his face. "Is he better?" she asked.

"He's quieter." Dorann kept his voice low. "I'll tend his wound in the morning. Restful slumber is what he most needs now."

"I'm grateful he will find it here." She saw him to the door.

"Arillia?" Elcon called from behind her. "Why is that tracker in my bed chamber?"

Dorann turned with a look of joy on his face. "So, you've decided to wake."

"Why do you make that sound remarkable?" Elcon asked in a fainter voice. "I do that every day. Why are you crying, Arillia?" He closed his eyes.

"Elcon?" She rushed to him.

"He's gone back to sleep." Dorann spoke from the other side of Elcon's bed. "We should let him rest."

She reined in her emotions. "Yes, of course."

"He'll wake again soon enough, I'm sure."

"Do you think—"

"It's a good sign, anyway." Dorann withdrew, taking the lanthorn with him. In the newly-darkened room, Arillia felt her way back to bed, only to lie awake. Sleep no longer mattered. She pressed a hand to her stomach, where a tiny flutter of hope stirred. Her husband had called her name.

Dawn painted the edges of the shutters that guarded the room's tiny window, while outside the little hut birds broke into song.

Arillia swung her legs out of bed and sat up to watch over her husband.

Voices carried from the main room, where the others had spent the night.

She didn't join them. When Elcon woke again, she wanted to be by his side.

A tap summoned her to the door. Anders stood on the other side holding a wafer of waybread and a hunk of cheese. "Forgive me if I woke you, Lof Raelein, but I wondered if you wanted food."

"I'm famished." Arillia smiled her thanks. She ate too quickly, and the repast turned into an uncomfortable lump in her stomach. She sat on her bed and clasped her hands around her knees, waiting for the sensation to pass.

"Why do you look so aggrieved, wife?" Elcon asked. "Have I done something wrong?"

She went to him. "No, indeed, my husband. You have done just the right thing by opening your eyes."

He cast glances about him. "Where am I?"

"Somewhere safe. We're in a tracker's hut in the wild lands."

His brows drew together. "Why?"

"What do you remember happening last?"

"I watched Syl Marinda run through the smoke and flame. No wait. There's something more." He closed his eyes for so long it seemed he might have fallen asleep, but then he opened them again. "I fought Draegmor."

She held his hand. "That's right. You took a wound."

"That must be why my side pains me so wretchedly. Syl Marinda—is she well?"

"To my knowledge, yes. We had to separate. She should be waiting in Cobbleford."

"So, she's managed to seek Euryon's help after all." His eyes wore a distant expression, as if gazing backward in time. "What's happened to Torindan?"

If she told him of the high hold's fall, would the shock be too much for him? A knock at the door spared her from answering. Arillia kissed her husband's hand and released it. Elcon smiled, looking so like the youth he had once been that an ache throbbed inside her. She blinked away stray tears.

Dorann, with Eathnor beside him, stood waiting on the other side of the door. "Forgive us for intruding, Lof Raelein." We heard the Lof Shraen's voice."

Eathnor smiled. "'Twas a welcome sound."

"You must come in and tell him so." She stood back to allow them entry.

Eathnor bowed to Elcon. "I'm glad to find you better."

"Thank you."

"What has the Lof Shraen said?" Dorann whispered to Arillia.

"He went over what happened to him."

"That's only natural. How much does he recall?"

"He didn't mention anything after his fight with Draegmor. His shoulder pains him."

"I should change that bandage soon." Dorann left her and made his bow to Elcon. "Lof Shraen."

Elcon tried to sit up but gave up with a groan.

Dorann bent over Elcon and prodded his injury. "If you can bring yourself to lie still, Lof Shraen, you'll avoid straining your wound."

"Thanks for the suggestion, Dorann. I think I've"—Elcon grimaced—"figured that out."

Another knock rattled the door, and Arillia admitted Anders.

"There's a face I'm happy to see," Elcon proclaimed.

Anders made his bow, beaming all the while. "It's a delight to find you restored to us, Lof Shraen."

"Tell me, why are we not at Torindan?"

"My husband's wound needs to be dressed, I am told," Arillia spoke before Anders could.

Elcon studied her face. "Is the news so bad that you would keep it from me? Don't spare me."

Arillia would rather have waited to break the news to him, but she would not deny him the truth. "Torindan lies in ruins."

Elcon's face paled.

"I thought as much." His words hung in the air as if reluctant to leave. He took in air and let it out again. "May Lof Yuel protect the alliance of Faeraven."

Dorann stepped forward. "You tire yourself, Lof Shraen."

Elcon nodded. "I'm weary to the depths of my being. I'm not sure how to rise from this blow, but somehow I must."

"You will, Elcon." Arillia's voice caught

Her husband's gaze swung to her. "You should be at Cobbleford with Syl Marinda."

She'd expected him to gainsay her, but not quite so soon. "We'll all go there once you regain your strength."

"I'll not have you waiting on my recovery. The wild lands hold too much danger. Eathnor, I command you to escort Lof Raelein Arillia to Cobbleford at once. Dorann, you will accompany them."

"You can't be serious, Elcon!" Arillia burst out.

"I'll not leave you with only a servant to protect you."

"I must agree with the Lof Raelein," Eathnor chimed in.

"Then take Anders and leave Dorann."

"With all respect, Lof Shraen, I am the only trained fighter among us. I should watch over the Lof Shraen of Faeraven. My brother is well able to stay out of harm's way in the wild lands, and Anders would lay down his own life before he'd let injury come to the Lof Raelein."

Elcon sighed. "Very well."

Arillia fumed inwardly. Once again Elcon had overruled her before she could voice an objection, but it wouldn't be fair to vent her anger with Elcon so ill. "Pray allow me to remain with you until tomorrow morning."

He gave her a look that warned her he meant to refuse. "I'd rather have you safe. Promise me you'll leave today."

"If I do, Dorann must remain to dress your wounds."

"I can do that," Eathnor assured her. "Our grandmother taught us both healing arts." She nodded and looked away to hide the tears in her eyes. "I will go."

"Don't take it so badly, Arillia." Elcon's voice softened. "I need you to persuade Euryon to join Faeraven's forces against Freaer."

She stared at him. "But Pilaer has put Torindan to flight. Who knows what he has done at Whellein, Graelinn, and the other loyal ravens? The alliance of Faeraven may already have fallen."

He closed his eyes. "If only I had the strength, I would rally the Kindren."

She took his hand. "I know, Elcon."

His eyes flew open. "Syl Marinda must go in my place."

CR

Kai squinted to see better in the early light. Moving with caution, he and Aerlic kept to the shadows alongside the road. Attempting to reclaim the wingabeasts at dawn made the most sense. The flitlings that roosted in the barn would take issue with a nocturnal disturbance and raise a racket. The vagabonds might expect the wingabeast's owners to return by night but were less likely to look for them with the dawn. If Lof Yuel smiled upon Kai and Aerlic, the vagabonds would sleep through their visit.

Living in the kaba forest the past two days had presented its share of challenges, but he'd found the delay in reaching Cobbleford more of an irritation. He chafed to find out if Mara had reached her grandfather and whether Elcon had survived. He had doubts on the second count but Aerlic's presence beside him was a reminder that Lof Yuel could perform miracles. Hadn't the archer returned to life when the DawnSinger's song rolled through Elderland?

Reaching Cobbleford by foot would take longer than he wanted. Mara, Elcon, or Arillia were likely to need him before he arrived. He had no intention of lagging due to the whims of a vagabond. Tam had bragged of his prowess with a sword, but in Kai's experience, those who boasted usually fought the worst. Kai felt sure he could prevail against Tam. The knife throwers troubled him more. As first archer of

Torindan, Aerlic could hold his own with a bow and arrow, even deflect airborne weapons, but the knife throwers outnumbered him. If they took aim at Aerlic, his leather armor might not ward off their knives.

They'd broken camp a little later than intended. He'd hoped to reach the homefarm earlier, but the colors of dawn were already fading from the sky. They left the road when the barn, which stood on a rise, came into view. The woods thickened before reaching the homefarm, which made this tactic uncomfortable, but Kai deemed it necessary. Antlers branching above the undergrowth in a clearing alerted him to the stag watching them. They left the magnificent creature unchallenged and followed the stream that ran past the barn.

A cloud of flitlings lifted into the sky at their approach and settled into the trees for their morning feast. No movement came from the homefarm. The silent building couldn't have seemed more abandoned. Kai crept alongside the barn. The door complained when pushed inward. They slipped inside.

Kai blinked to adjust his vision, but he could already tell that the wingabeasts were gone.

"Where are they?" Aerlic asked.

"I wish I knew. At a guess, the house is unoccupied too."

The glimmer of an idea stirred within Kai. "If you were a vagabond, where would you take a pair of winged horses?"

"I'd want to sell them." Aerlic nodded. "I see where you think they're headed."

"It's obvious, wouldn't you say?" He glanced at a steaming pile of horse droppings. "They'd want to leave early to reach Lancert. Looks as if we just missed their departure."

"We can track them."

"That depends on whether they fly or not."

Aerlic winced, a reaction Kai understood well. Those who attempted to ride one of the wingabeasts, a feat that required training and sensitivity, often regretted it. To make matters worse, the wingabeasts would draw the attention of any welke riders still hunting them. In that event, the vagabonds had better be as good at fighting as their leader claimed.

ᘒ

It took two days to reach Lancert on a road that carried them through rich farmlands. After reaching the outskirts of the sprawling town, they stopped at the merchant camp, located beside the field where tents were going up for the horse fair.

Kai put a warning finger to his lips and gestured with his head. Aerlic's eyes opened wider. At Kai's nod, the archer glanced over his shoulder. He faced forward at once, and they walked away from the camp. Kai turned off the road into the shade of a weilo tree with drooping branches that concealed them. He peered out through the leafy veil, from which they could spy on the camp.

Kai had glimpsed the wingabeasts before turning away. Flecht and Argalent didn't appear mistreated. The opposite seemed true. The vagabonds had spared no effort to present the wingabeasts in the best light, probably with an eye to fetching the best price they could. With silver coats brushed to a shine, hooves polished, and many-colored ribbons braiding their manes and tails, the beautiful creatures were making a stir among the horse traders. The vagabonds had cleaned themselves up also, but the improvements they'd made were by no means vast. An excited crowd now gathered around them amid laughter and the playful calling of bids. Several tried and failed to make serious offers in amounts that represented fortunes. Tam smiled and refused them all. He obviously understood the value of the wingabeasts and aimed to take no less than the highest possible cost.

"I might be interested in your winged horses," a tall man in jean cloth declared. "What name can I call their owner?"

"I'm Tammerlee of Norwood, although I've settled in Westerland of late." He smiled. "Now you know more about me than I do you."

"True enough." The tall man laughed. "I'm Abermerle of Darksea."

"You're a long way from home."

"That I am, which is why I only come once a year to trade."

"Well then, I hope we can make your journey worthwhile."

If they didn't act soon, Kai had no doubt that Tam would find a buyer. That would complicate matters. Taking back his rightful property from thieves was one thing. Stealing the wingabeasts from an innocent party who had paid a sum to own them was quite another. Kai left the road and entered the forest. Aerlic kept pace. They came to a small clearing where grasses waved and wildflowers nodded. Kai sat with his back to a fallen log and the sun warming his face. "I have no idea how to proceed," he complained to Aerlic. "The wingabeasts are sure to draw a crowd wherever they go, making any attempt to reclaim them difficult by day and near impossible at night. The vagabonds will guard them well in that crowd."

Aerlic perched on the log Kai leaned against. "I wish I had an idea to offer, but I lack your skill at strategy."

"I don't think we can make a plan. We'll have to wait for an opportunity, although watching for one without showing ourselves won't be easy. If we walk about among the Elder, the vagabonds will learn of our presence." He shook his head. "This is more difficult than I imagined."

"Weariness guides your words. If you'll rest a while, our situation will look brighter and a solution clearer."

Kai nodded. "You've been a good companion during the trials we've suffered since leaving Torindan."

Aerlic smiled. "I'm happy to travel with you also."

"I'd rather we'd joined forces under better circumstances." He ran a hand over his face. "That couldn't be helped."

"We'll sort ourselves out." Aerlic stood and stretched, his hair lighting to gold in a ray of sunlight. "Meanwhile, I've our supper to hunt. Did you know? A full belly can be counted upon to change the blackest mood."

Kai smiled despite himself. "I'll start a fire to roast the venison you bring us."

Aerlic laughed. "I'll do my best." He picked up his bow and strode off.

Kai leaned his head against the log behind him.

The archer was probably right about exhaustion coloring his thoughts. How long it seemed since he'd shared a table with the other guardians of Rivenn at Torindan. That many of his friends had died seemed too hard. He had only to think of the last battle of Torindan and time folded back like a curtain. He heard again the screams of the dying, felt his gut churning, and tasted the ashes of defeat. He had to reach Cobbleford.

Lof Yuel, tell me what to do.

He waited for an answer, but none came, not even the breath of wind that sometimes stirred the air in the allerstaed when he prayed.

CR

Arillia held onto Anders while he guided the wingabeast carrying them along the forest path. She'd chosen to ride with the servant in order to free Dorann to lead them. They'd made good progress after leaving the cabin and had reached a place where the road narrowed and grew wilder. Gazing into the distance did not reassure her. They had so far avoided encounters with the horrors that stalked this forest. Going down this neglected road, which they must, could well change that.

Anders had ridden behind Dorann for most of the journey, leaving her riding behind him with shivers traveling up her spine. She couldn't help being nervous, although perhaps her thoughts prompted the feeling. When Dorann dropped into the rear, she did not ask if he'd heard something following them.

The sun warmed the day, it's heat uncomfortable

in her wool cloak, but she would not remove the garment for modesty's sake. How she longed to bathe and put on clean clothing afterward. The life she'd led at Torindan seemed a golden time. If she'd known then how events would turn out, she'd have appreciated it more. She could only go into the future, however, and shouldn't dwell on the past.

They must travel the difficult road before them to reach Cobbleford. After abandoning her husband in the hut, she refused to do less. She intended to keep her promise to Elcon. Once she reached Cobbleford Castle, she would add her voice to Syl Marinda's in trying to persuade King Euryon to unite with the remnant of Faeraven against Freaer. Sometimes war was the only way to peace. She had to believe that Syl Marinda had reached Cobbleford. With Elcon incapacitated, the responsibility of gathering the Kindren fell to the heir of Faeraven, but if Syl Marinda did not shoulder it, Arillia would. She had married Elcon with the knowledge that her life might take second place to the needs of Faeraven. Such were the responsibilities of rulership. They belonged to her until she released them to Syl Marinda at Elcon's decree. She refused to think about the other way Elcon's daughter might ascend to the throne of Faeraven—his death. Her husband would survive, she assured herself fiercely. Surely Lof Yuel could not be so cruel as to take him from her.

They left the sunshine for the shade of a grove of kierken trees that lined the path. Welcome coolness settled over her, but as the wingabeast moved through the enclosing branches of the trees, the hair at her nape bristled. A jaggercat stalked them, jumping with stealth from tree to tree. A wilderwen lurked within the green shadows. The Feiann waited to trick them into the bog.

Arillia tamped down her wild imaginings. She would behave like a high queen, even when the soughing of the trees sounded like voices whispering. If she didn't take herself in hand, she would arrive at Cobbleford gibbering with fear.

Dorann slowed and dropped back to ride in the rear. Arillia couldn't decide if that made her feel better or not. She'd rather have his protective presence behind her if it didn't signal that they were in peril. Anders continued along the path at a faster clip. She didn't blame him for wanting to win clear of this grove. A strange hush hung over the twisted trees where no bird sang, the stench of decay emanated from the bog behind them, and an army could hide in the tangled undergrowth.

Something stirred in the leafy screen near the road, and she swerved her head in time to glimpse a pale woman vanishing into the trees. Before she could alert her companions, the woman walked onto the road in front of them. Arillia had never seen such a lovely vision. Her pale hair floated around her as if on an unseen wind, and the robe she wore glittered like the stars.

The wingabeast let out a shrill cry and lifted onto its hind legs, batting its wings and pawing the air.

Arillia held onto Anders but couldn't stop her slide. She slammed to the ground.

"Lof Raelein!" Anders divided his attention between her and the frightened wingabeast he fought to control.

Arillia sat up, desperate to pull in air, but could not.

Dorann supported her with an arm around her shoulders while she struggled to breathe.

Anders brought the wingabeast under control. "Is she all right?"

With a strangling sound, Arillia pulled air past the constriction in her chest.

"She's winded from the fall." Dorann glanced at Anders. "What made your wingabeast rear like that?"

"I don't know."

Arillia stared at them both. "Did you not see her?"

They exchanged glances.

"Who?" Dorann prompted her.

"The pale-haired woman in shining robes. She walked out from beneath the trees."

Dorann looked past her down the road.

"She's gone now." Arillia clutched his sleeve. "Who could she have been?"

"One of the Feiann."

Arillia gasped. "The woman looked so innocent. You'd never know that she could lure you to your death." She glanced about, frightened by her own words.

"As an ancient race, the Feiann count the rest of Elderland's occupants as intruders. They delight in playing tricks on us, and yes, they sometimes lure travelers to their deaths. Are you ready to stand, Lof Raelein? We should leave this place at once."

She accepted his help and regained her feet, but hesitated before climbing back onto the wingabeast she'd fallen from. She didn't blame the poor creature for reacting with fear to the mysterious woman. In truth, that emotion still crawled like a spider along her own skin. While they passed beneath through the leafy tunnel made by the trees, she peered into the forest shadows. The woman seemed to have vanished, but Arillia thought she glimpsed faces peering out at her.

The keirken grove fell away behind them, but Arillia couldn't escape the sensation of being followed.

12

At the Horse Fair

The wolf howls reached Eathnor's ears from far away, but they raised the hair on his arms just the same. He'd faced the beasts often while hunting for the Lof Shraen's table. They favored the scent of blood. Darkness pressed the tiny window, making him glad for the lanthorn's light. He'd left it here long ago for his own use and to benefit the other trackers who relied on the safety of this hut. The jar of lanthorn oil never ran empty, for they all kept it replenished. A variety of food usually graced the kitchen shelves, for which he'd been grateful on more than one occasion. This was one, for it meant he could care for Elcon without leaving him alone in order to hunt or gather food. Plenty of earlyberries grew nearby, but he'd leave them to the deer that wandered the clearing where the hut and stable stood. Elcon's condition improved daily. He stayed awake through most of the day and had regained his appetite. He should be ready to depart for Cobbleford soon. Chafing to leave the hut behind, Eathnor couldn't be more delighted about that. Each day that he and Elcon remained here put them in greater peril. From what he had learned during his captivity at Pilaer, its warriors would venture far afield to satisfy their lust for blood. If any of the remnant fleeing Torindan ran this way, he and Elcon might be found out. He hadn't seen welke riders flying overhead, but if any did, they would spot the hut.

"Why are you staring at that window?" Elcon's voice was more alert than it had been in a while. "Did you hear something?"

"Wolves." Eathnor glanced at Elcon, sitting up in his bed. "They're not near."

"That's happy news. I encountered wolves from the wild lands once while hunting. Wretched fiends."

"All creatures in the wild lands grow larger and fiercer than elsewhere in Elderland. Why that should be, I have no idea."

"Some say an ancient evil binds the land."

Eathnor thought over the idea. "The presence of wilderwen seems to confirm that."

"You have knowledge of wilderwen in the wild lands?"

Eathnor stared at Elcon in surprise before remembering that he had been too ill to pay attention. "Have you no memory of the wilderwen attacking us?"

"I recall very little of the journey and thankfully nothing about that."

"We escaped, obviously."

"Are the monsters as hideous as the bards say?"

"More so. No tale can describe the terror they breed."

Elcon shook his head. "This forest is not a fit place to travel."

"I agree. All manner of perils lie in wait, and many blunder into the Vale of Shadows. I am one of the few who returned from the place, and only by Emmerich's grace."

"I hope the Lof Raelein will not stumble into it."

"Dorann knows the pathways that avoid it. My brother and Anders should be well on the way to Cobbleford with the Lof Raelein." Eathnor would rather not have had to safeguard Elcon, injured and alone in a forest where anything could happen, but he couldn't have refused the Lof Shraen's direct command. Elcon's determination to send his wife to safety made sense to him. With no skills to survive in the woods, she'd endured the ordeal well, but watching out for her had proven a distraction. Anders had acquitted himself little better. Eathnor would rather have kept his brother with him, but neither the Lof Raelein nor Anders would have been equal to the journey without Dorann.

Elcon frowned. "We should follow them at daybreak."

Eathnor considered this idea. "Are you well enough?"

"I'll make certain that I am. Remaining here would be precarious, at best."

A snapping sound came from outside, as if to confirm his words.

Eathnor swiveled to look out. "That was no wolf."

Elcon nodded and reached for the knife on the scarred table beside his bed. Eathnor had used it earlier to slice a cake of raisins.

Eathnor doused the lanthorn and crept to the window. The moon stood above the clearing, a silent sentinel in an army of stars. He caught a flicker of movement that might have been an animal but nothing more. Still he lingered, held to his post by what felt like a certainty.

Someone was out there.

CR

Boots thumped on the stoop outside, and a heavy hand pounded the door. "Open to the guardians of Rivenn."

Eathnor pressed against the wall beside the door. "Name yourself," he called, although the voice had sounded familiar.

"Eathnor? This is Craelin. For the love of mercy, let us in."

Eathnor held back. "What if it's a trick?"

"Do as he says." Elcon ordered, taking the decision out of his hands.

Eathnor cracked open the door. On the stoop stood Craelin and others he recognized. Rand stood with them, but with his hands bound. Had this small company of guardians escaped from Torindan or were these wraith images formed from his own mind? He'd heard of such deceits in the wild lands.

"I recognized you through the window," Craelin told him. "Your lanthorn went out, but before it did I thought I saw—"

"Craelin, I'm glad to find you alive," Elcon called.

"Lof Shraen!" The joy in Craelin's voice sounded genuine. Eathnor edged closer to accepting him as flesh and blood.

"Come in! Eathnor, light the lanthorn."

Eathnor backed away from the door. He felt for his flint and, finding it, added tinder to the stone bowl from the small pile beside it on the table. Laying down his sword with reluctance, he scraped the flint with his knife, setting sparks smoking in the tinder bowl. He blew until a flame burst forth, then carried a burning brand to the wick. It flared, and light climbed the walls to spread across the ceiling. The faces around the hut stood out in relief, revealing their thinness. The haunted look in their eyes did not reassure him of their mortality. "How came you here?" He couldn't help that his voice quavered.

Craelin's gaze grew distant. "Through much hardship. After the keep went up in flames, we escaped Torindan by way of the sallyport. We'd lost you, Lof Shraen, or so we'd thought. The guardhouse and stables were burning. The hall still stood and the allerstaed, but most of the other buildings had been destroyed." He shook his head. "I gave the order to escape too late for most of the guardians, a fact I'll regret to my dying day. Only a few remained to flee with me."

Elcon's nostrils flared, and his jaw tensed. "Freaer will pay for what he has done. I will make sure of it."

Craelin nodded. "We are ready to stand with you, Lof Shraen, and to die for the alliance of Faeraven."

"Thank you for your loyalty, but hopefully that won't be necessary." Elcon turned his attention to Rand. "Why have you taken Randolph of Pilaer prisoner?"

Craelin's jaw tightened. "He's Freaer's son. Given what's happened since he arrived at Torindan, that's reason enough."

Elcon continued to study Rand. "Has he done anything that warrants captivity?"

"By his own admission, he violated your command to avoid the Lof Raena."

Elcon lifted his eyebrows. "What have you to say for yourself?"

Craelin jerked. "Why do you give him the chance to speak?"

"Pray content yourself to listen, Craelin." Elcon's voice held an edge.

Rand lifted his chin. "Craelin is right, but only because I valued Mara's life above that promise. Do you remember nothing of my carrying her away from Torindan?"

Elcon shook his head. "It's all a blank. Tell me, where is my daughter now?"

"At Cobbleford Castle, assuming an outlaw can be trusted."

Craelin frowned. "It's a long story, Lof Shraen. Whether it's true remains to be proven." He ended with a glare at Rand.

"I have the time to listen to the tale, but I suppose we'd better feed you all first. It looks as if a strong wind could knock you down. Eathnor, what stores do we have?"

Eathnor brought waybread and divided the last of the cheese from the kitchen shelf. The guardians fell upon the food, ending his reservations about their mortality. A wraith, no matter how real it appeared, could never consume a portion of cheese.

Craelin finished eating and drew up one of the benches at the table to sit on one side of Elcon's bed. Eathnor stood on the other.

Elcon leaned against his pillows. "Tell me all you've seen since leaving Torindan."

"Death, and plenty of it." Craelin paced. "Pilaer's warriors crawl through the wild lands, eager to strike down male or female, old or young. It matters not to them." He shook his head. "I have seen cooking pots filled with the flesh of the slain. The warriors have lost any shred of humanity, if they ever possessed it. They have become creatures of darkness who answer only to their evil overlord."

"I am sorry but not surprised to learn this. If the Contender's invasion is not checked, those who survive will become like these sad souls."

Craelin frowned. "We must strive for a better future."

"Have you heard or seen warriors searching near this place?" Elcon pressed him.

"No, but I have no doubt they will come. Freaer won't stop at taking Torindan, and his warriors will devour the Elder with equal glee."

ᏣᏍ

Kai listened to the early activity within the merchant's camp from the shelter of the weilo tree and exchanged a glance with Aerlic. The vagabonds were already up and about, which wouldn't work at all. He and Aerlic might have to go back to camp and try tomorrow. The trouble with that idea was that Tam might find a buyer for the wingabeasts before then.

He looked past the cascading weilo leaves to discover Topper and Jost taking the wingabeasts to the small stream that wended through the camp. Kai held his breath as the vagabonds turned their steps toward the weilo tree.

Topper, holding Flecht's reins, turned his gaze toward Jost who led Argalent. "I'll buy myself all the food and drink I want. That's what I'll do."

"You can throw your share down your gullet," Jost retorted. "I want a bath and some tailored clothes. Maybe I'll find a maiden willing to marry the likes of me. Wouldn't that be sweet?"

Topper laughed. "You've always been soft for the ladies."

Jost chuckled. "A wife would keep you a lot cozier at night than a mug of ale."

"Provided you find a woman who won't leave you cold unless you do her bidding. No, thank you." Topper shook his head, sending his curls bouncing. "Think I'll stick to ale."

The vagabonds passed the weilo tree and continued down an incline to the stream. They would be hidden from the camp while watering the horses. Reading the excitement in Aerlic's face, Kai gave a nod and stepped out from the weilo tree.

"Do you see them?" A masculine voice called from within the merchant camp. "What are Kindren doing in Westerland?"

Several others joined in. Kai caught Tam's deep tones intermingled with the voice of the buyer who had called himself Abermerle.

"We'd better hurry," Aerlic nocked an arrow to his bowstring.

"My thought exactly." Kai drew his sword and picked up his pace, hurrying as quickly as possible without making noise that would give away their approach. He could hope that the stream's burbling would mask the ruckus in camp, but either way the time to strike had come.

Topper and Jost stood with their backs turned. Holding the wingabeasts by long reins, the vagabonds watched them drink from the stream. The wingabeasts stood where the stream spread wide and flowed over a rocky bed. Flecht reached for a mouthful of the bright water, then lifted his head in a graceful motion. He tossed his mane and whickered. At the same time,

Argalent neighed.

Kai sprinted the rest of the way.

Topper looked over his shoulder, his eyes widening. "Behind you," he warned his companion.

Jost had already turned, a knife in his hand.

Topper went for his knife, but too late. Kai rammed him, and they went down together. Kai dropped his sword and fought with both hands to keep the vagabond from pulling his throwing knife. Kai drew the weapon and struggled to his feet. He hauled back his arm and hurtled the blade into the stream.

Topper threw himself toward Sword Rivenn.

Kai pulled him back by the waist.

Topper responded with a fist to the jaw.

Kai returned the favor.

The vagabond went down, out cold. Kai picked up Sword Rivenn and stood over the vagabond. Topper might be good at throwing a knife, but he couldn't hold his own in hand combat.

Aerlic's arrow had found its mark, pinning Jost to the ground by his tunic. The knife the vagabond had unsheathed was nowhere in sight. Kai suspected it had suffered a fate similar to Topper's blade. The vagabond freed himself and ran toward camp with Aerlic's arrows dogging his heels.

"He's already fleeing." Kai pointed out. "And he has no idea he's in the hands of a master archer."

"All right, I'll stop." Aerlic shouldered his bow.

Jost had met Tam and Abermerle. He stood before them, gesturing wildly,

"We'd better go." Kai unclipped the long rein from Flecht.

Argalent had come up out of the water. The Silver nuzzled Aerlic's neck, getting in the way while Aerlic tried to remove the long rein.

Tam and Abermerle were running toward them, and Jost had turned back.

"Do hurry," Kai urged.

Aerlic dropped the long rein and leaped onto Argalent's back. "Can I help it that my wingabeast loves me?" His gaze shifted. "Look out!"

Kai needed no warning but braced himself for Topper's lunge, which carried him sideways. Before he could regain his balance, the vagabond trapped his arms at his side, preventing him from drawing his weapon.

Aerlic, who had no such restriction, drew his bow.

Topper thrust Kai between himself and the archer. He clamped a hand across Kai's throat, then squeezed. Kai gasped for air. "Drop that bow or I'll throttle your friend." Aerlic laid down his bow.

Topper's hold on Kai eased.

Taking the advantage, Kai forced his arms up and twisted away from the vagabond.

Aerlic retrieved his bow and came up shooting.

Warm droplets spattered Kai's face. The vagabond screamed and backed away, cradling his bloodied arm. The shaft of Aerlic's arrow protruded from his forearm.

Aerlic nocked another lethal missile to his bowstring. "You have one chance to save yourself. I suggest you do it now."

Topper turned and ran, passing Tam and Abermerle as they reached the weilo.

Aerlic lifted an eyebrow. "If you're ready?"

Biting back his retort, Kai vaulted onto Flecht and

sent him skyward.

©ℛ

Arillia bent and dipped her hands into the stream, letting its silken flow pull through her fingers. The longing seized her to lower herself into the water and let its coolness soothe the aches gathered during a long day of riding. A fallen log quieted the water and formed the pool at her feet. She hardly recognized herself in the solemn face that gazed back from her reflection. Recent events had taken a toll on her. Would she ever be carefree again?

She plucked a handful of earlyberries that grew along the bank and crammed them into her mouth. Chewing them slowly, she savored their moisture and sweetness. Waybread and jerked elk grew wearisome after a while. Remembering the lavish feasts that had been her portion at Torindan didn't help. She should be grateful that at least they had food. The ravages of hunger would be too much to endure on top of her other sufferings.

She'd left Anders and Dorann setting up camp for the night. The snap of deadfall being broken into firewood came sharply. Cupping her hands, she scooped water from the pool to bathe her face. A rivulet ran down her neck and dampened the chemise under her cloak, but she didn't care. She would sit by the fire and dry out before the night could chill her. She would persuade Dorann to relieve the dreariness with one of his tales. Once she reached Cobbleford, it would be a long time before she'd want to travel again.

Something moved at the edge of sight. She turned

her head but couldn't catch it. What had she seen? The feeling of being watched that had plagued her since leaving the hut returned. She peered about, suddenly aware of the distance between herself and her companions. She stepped backward out of the water. The snap of a twig breaking carried from the other bank. Arillia flicked a glance across the stream. Fern fronds waved in the breeze lifting off the surface. Otherwise, nothing stirred.

A flicker of movement drew her attention to the pool. She gasped. On a branch behind and above her, a jaggercat crouched with its hindquarters raised as if ready to spring. The wildcat's hypnotic eyes gazed into Arillia's reflection. Fighting for air, she eased sideways. She couldn't draw breath enough to scream.

The wildcat's nose quivered, and it adjusted its position, tracking her.

Arillia's heart thudded in her ears. Every tale she'd heard about these predatory beasts arose in her mind. What could she do? If she screamed, the jaggercat would pounce. She could not outrun the fearsome creature, and it would never allow her to leave. Why, oh why had she wandered off on her own? Arillia at last hauled in air and released it in a scream, but only a whisper came out. A chill ran through her. She would die here, in this spot, within a short walk of her companions.

13

FOREST PREDATORS

The jaggercat shifted lower on the branch, which swayed beneath its weight. The beast waggled its hindquarters and extended razor-tipped claws.

Arillia whimpered.

The jaggercat sprang.

Pffft. An arrow sang in flight and thudded on impact.

The jaggercat slammed into her, taking her down. A shriek tore from Arillia's throat. She twisted out from beneath the big cat, which had an arrow protruding from one eye. The other stared flatly. Her gorge rising, Arillia kicked away from the creature's twitching body..

The jaggercat spasmed and went still.

Arillia leaned over and vomited.

Dorann reached her first. He slid to a stop. "Are you unharmed?"

Gasping and with tears wetting her cheeks, she nodded.

Dorann drew his dagger and stared into the forest across the stream. "The arrow came from over there. Did you see anyone?"

Arillia shook her head.

Anders arrived, panting, and knelt beside her. "Milady!"

She stood on unsteady feet while Anders hovered beside her.

Dorann bent over the jaggercat and whistled. "A master of the bow shot this arrow."

"Thank you." A masculine voice spoke from behind them. "Now drop that knife and turn around slowly."

A masked man stood with feet apart, his bow aimed at Dorann. Behind him stood more archers with arrows ready. They seemed a rough lot, garbed in ill-fitting clothes with their hair and beards shaggy. Their leader nodded to Dorann. "Why have you traveled into my domain?"

Arillia straightened to her tallest height, refusing to be cowed by a pack of outlaws. "Stop aiming your weapons at us. I'm on my way to Cobbleford Castle to dine with the king. You must not impede us."

The masked man grinned. "You weren't so high and mighty when that jaggercat went for you."

"You will show respect to the lady," Dorann demanded.

The outlaw leader's jaw tightened.

Arillia spoke quickly to avoid a fight. "Thank you to whoever slew that beast."

The masked man pulled his gaze from Dorann. "You'd have died but for me. Have you no reward to give?"

She glared at him, stricken speechless by his rudeness. A true gallant would not have pointed out her weakness or his own heroism, nor would he have asked for recompense. "You have been properly thanked."

"How thoughtful of you to make it official."

It galled her to think that she owed her life to this

outlaw, but she did not enlighten him to that fact. From the mocking way he watched her, he guessed her thoughts.

His lips curled. "What is your name and kingdom?"

"I am Arillia of Rivenn."

"Rivenn, did you say?" He glanced from her to Dorann and Anders, then back again. "Is that not where Torindan lies?"

"It is." She volunteered nothing further.

"And you are *Arillia*?" The surprised note in his voice hinted that he'd figured out her identity.

"Why should Milady's name mean anything to you?" Anders asked with suspicion.

The outlaw leader lowered his bow, and his men did the same. "I will see you safely to your destination. You will find your servant, Lyneth, awaiting you."

She stared at him, befuddled by his abrupt change in manner. "That's impossible. Lyneth died."

"She did not, I assure you. I found her in the wild lands and delivered her to Cobbleford. She spoke of you."

"Why would she mention me?"

"She feared that you had died."

It could have happened as he said, but Arillia needed more proof. "What is your name and where are you from?"

"My followers call me Searcher, and this forest is my home."

An outlaw would not identify himself. She should have been cautious in that regard herself. Tramping through the kaba forest like a gypsy should have convinced her that she no longer resided in the high hold of Faeraven under the protection of the guardians of Rivenn. She could not cast the die again and must take the consequences for revealing herself, if they came. Meanwhile, she could try to divert his attention away from her. "Well, Searcher, why do you haunt the kaba forest when others avoid it?"

That annoying grin spread over his face again. "I'll tell you my reason for being in the kaba forest after you give yours."

She'd already revealed more than she should have to an outlaw and mercenary. Glaring at him, she remained silent.

He laughed. "Give my regards to Lyneth."

CR

Arillia gazed across the river, where Cobbleford Castle stood on a rocky buttress. Clouds blushed pink and purple swept across the darkening sky behind the fortress. Would she find a welcome or rejection there?

Dorann came up beside her. "We'll reach our destination on the morrow."

He meant it by way of comfort, but she did not care to cast herself upon the parents of her husband's first wife. She had not often visited the Elder lands, but once when Elcon had accepted an invitation to the coronation of Gaerlic of Daeramor, he'd taken her with him. Meeting King Euryon and Queen Inydde had proven a strain. With too much unspoken between them for casual conversation, they had lapsed into silence. Elcon had asked this of her, and she would not deny her husband's wishes while he hovered on the border of the world beyond. She crossed her arms over herself to ward off the chill of encroaching night.

"Thank you for guiding me through that forest."

"That was my privilege, Lof Raelein."

She shuddered. "I'd prefer never to take that journey again."

Dorann nodded. "The paths through the wild lands are not easily traveled."

"No wonder so many forsake them." She turned to him. "I must ask you to go back to help Eathnor with Elcon."

He slanted a glance at her. "I had that in mind as well."

"Then we are agreed. Only deliver me to the castle and you can depart."

Dorann gave a slight shake of his head. "I cannot leave you so soon. By the Lof Shraen's command, I am to see you settled before starting back."

The tracker did not sound any happier at the prospect than she felt. "Then I will apply myself to becoming oriented to Cobbleford." Arillia tamped down on her irritation at her vexing husband even as warmth curled through her at the awareness that he placed her safety above his own. She had married Elcon knowing he would not allow her to rule over him. His domineering ways were ingrained in him and not subject to change. The truth, if she could admit it, was that she needed her husband's strong-mindedness to counter her own.

Anders came down to the water carrying a bundle of branches and set to work building a fish trap, a skill she'd watched Dorann teach him. The servant pushed branches into the river bed to form a small enclosure, leaving an opening fish could enter. It amazed her how the finned creatures could find their way into the trap but not out again. His task completed, Anders started back.

"Milady?" Dorann stood at the edge of the trees.

She glanced up from watching the clear water slide above rocks. Remembering the jaggercat, as Dorann also must, she followed him without complaint into the forest and along an animal trail to camp. Anders had laid a fire which Dorann now lit. With a diet consisting of waybread and jerked game, they had nothing to cook, but the fire kept nocturnal beasts at bay. She would never forget the eyes that glowed from the blackened forest. She shut out the watching eyes by bringing the hood of her cloak down to cover her own. Nothing could drive away the predatory creatures, but the fire provided a barrier they would not cross. She stretched out to sleep within the golden circle of firelight in the comfort of that knowledge.

Something woke her while it was yet dark. She sat up, letting her hood fall back. The eyes had crept nearer. Anders sat sleeping, propped against a boulder near the fire. He must have dozed off during his watch. The flames guttered within the ring of rocks, and the night breeze sparked tiny embers to fly upward. She drew breath to call a warning to Anders.

The glittering woman from the keirken grove stood outside the waning firelight. She needed no illumination as she glowed from within. Her face radiated light, and her robe sparkled as if impregnated with myriad stars. She held out a hand. *Come and I will show you the future.*

A shiver ran over Arillia, and a warning whispered within her. She held back.

Don't fear me, sweet dove. I can give you everything you wish.

What had Dorann said about this woman? Why

couldn't she remember?

Follow me. The woman walked a few steps into the forest, but then turned back.

Curiosity tugged at Arillia. Where did the woman want to take her? She wouldn't find out unless she went along.

Why do you hesitate?

Arillia's resistance broke, and she stumbled toward the woman.

Anders snorted awake. "Who's there?"

Hurry!

The warning grew more urgent. Arillia halted in confusion.

"Milady!" Anders's voice penetrated her thoughts.

The woman's face transformed into a hideous mask. The light shining from her faded and extinguished.

Eyes glared at Arillia from the forest. She shrank back, her heart thudding. Jaws snapped in the place she had stood, and a snarl ripped the air.

Arms hauled her backward. She screamed and turned to fight.

"Lof Raelein, it's me, Dorann. I'm sorry to startle you, but I had to pull you into the light. You nearly walked into a pack of wolves."

Tremors ran over her. She steadied herself and pulled away. "Did you see the lady?"

His eyes narrowed. "Who do you mean? Have the Feiann troubled you again?"

She stared at him in shock. "What did I almost do?"

"You wouldn't be the first they've tricked into danger."

She shuddered. "I'll be glad to leave this forest."

"We'll do that soon enough." Anders stirred up the fire.

He was right, of course. Arillia welcomed the sight of dawn gilding the sky above the trees. Today they would arrive at Cobbleford.

"We might as well make an early start." Dorann spoke briskly.

They arrived at Cobbleford Castle while roosters crowed and morning mist drifted above the river. The wingabeasts clattered across the bridge toward the castle gatehouse. Approaching the home where Aewen had lived with her parents brought her vividly to life. A long time had passed since she'd met Elcon's first wife, but an image of the dark-haired beauty stood out in Arillia's mind. How strange to feel connected to the woman whom Elcon had once called wife. Arillia sighed. She had wanted to hate Aewen for taking her betrothed from her, but that had been impossible in the face of Aewen's gentleness. If circumstances had been different, they might have become friends.

The wingabeasts left the bridge and clacked across cobblestones to stand before the gatehouse.

"Name yourself." A guard looked down upon them from the parapet.

"I am Dorann of Rivenn. Pray open the gate to Arillia, Lof Raelein of Faeraven."

"Does she have an invitation from King Euryon?"

"She does not, but she calls upon the king's mercy in time of war."

"The king may be merciful, but he is not foolish. State your business."

"I have already told you." A trace of impatience crept into Dorann's voice. "The Lof Raelein requires refuge."

"Can she prove she is who you say?"

Dorann's jaw tightened. "The King will recognize her."

"She could be an imposter."

Arillia peered up at the guard, a portly fellow with a ruddy complexion. "What are you called?"

"I am Arctar of Westerland, guardian of the realm."

She summoned her most imperious voice. "I would speak to your captain." He smirked. "Is that right? Who do you suppose will summon him?"

"Speak to the Lof Raelein with respect." Dorann's voice made his irritation clear.

The guard laughed. "Until she can prove her identity, she's no high queen to me."

"I can testify for her." Anders spoke up.

"And who might you be?"

"I am Anders of Rivenn, Lof Shraen Elcon's manservant."

The guard barked with laughter. "And how do I know that's true?"

Anders tensed. "I stand upon my word."

"Let them in, Arctar," Aewen's voice called from behind them. "I've met Lof Raelein Arillia."

Arillia looked toward the woman and drew in a shaky breath. "Caerla."

Aewen's sister smiled. "You remember me too. I'm pleased. I've never forgotten your golden hair. You haven't aged a bit."

"The Kindren do, but more slowly than the Elder."

"You are fortunate indeed." Caerla hoisted the basket of herbs she carried. "I heard something about seeking refuge. Is all well with you?"

Arillia shook her head. "Freaer's forces defeated

Torindan."

Caerla's brows drew together. "Why would you come to us? I would think you'd go to another of your kingdoms for help."

"That's a matter I shouldn't discuss before the castle gates."

"Yes, of course. Follow me inside." Caerla walked toward the gates, which Arctar cranked open without comment. Caerla would have renounced her princess title when she joined the abbey, but she'd always be the king's daughter. She led them to the stables in the outer bailey and summoned stable hands to tend the wingabeasts. Afterwards, they followed her past the chapel to the abbey. Silence reigned inside the stone building. Caerla turned into the kitchen. "I assume you're hungry. I'll bring cheese and bread, also some of my earlyberry jam. Will you take tea?"

Arillia tried to hold back her tears, but they burst out anyway. She put her hands over her face while sobs racked her body.

ભ

Rand opened his eyes to darkness. He sat up, the task made difficult by the cords that bound his hands and feet. Keening howls pierced the night, and the hair at the back of his neck bristled. The wolves had followed them from the hut, growing bolder with each passing night.

Rand rolled onto his side. Glowing eyes from the darkness beyond the watchfire stared into his. He closed his eyes with determination. He had learned in his early days to sleep despite the intrusions of the wraiths of Pilaer. He could not afford to allow the presence of marauding wer-beasts, wolves, wildcats, and whatever other foul creatures inhabited the wild lands to rob his rest while guards kept watch.

Snarls carried to him, then thuds, followed by silence.

He settled to sleep again.

A cold touch dragged him from slumber, swarmed over him, and pinned him to the ground.

Rand opened his eyes, gasping. His worst fear had come to pass.

Freaer had found him.

Rand withdrew to the small still place inside himself where Lof Yuel waited. He sheltered there until the stifling attacker slithered into darkness.

Mara's soul touch flooded him then, soothing and sweet. He clung to her until the horror passed and released her with reluctance. Connecting through the shil shael only made him yearn to hold her. He should shield himself from Mara so she wouldn't look to him. Their futures could not lie further apart. For her sake, he must not let it continue.

Freaer had more power than a wraith or monster to inspire terror in him, which made falling back asleep harder than before. He stumbled into a waking dream where he searched through mists for a murky destination.

Rand startled awake, his heart thumping, and stared into the sky, which lightened toward morning. What had disturbed him?

The howling began again, although this sounded like a different pack.

Resolved to sleep while he could, he closed his eyes.

The wolves' cries intruded.

He rolled over and tried to shut out the sounds.

The wolf howls stopped. A soft cry carried to him. Something thudded to the ground.

He sat up.

Dark shapes ran toward the camp.

"To your weapons!" Rand shouted.

The guardians sprang to their feet with trained efficiency. Swords scraped and shields gleamed.

Pilaer's battle cry pulsed the air, raising Rand's hackles. With cords restraining his hands and feet, he had no way to protect himself.

Pilaer's warriors burst into camp with swords leveled.

The guardians of Rivenn exploded into action. Swords clanged against metal as fighters engaged in a feverish frenzy.

A figure ran toward Rand, who threw himself sideways.

"Stop thrashing about." Eathnor took hold of Rand's hands. His blade flashed, and the cords around Rand's wrist fell away. Eathnor bent to perform the same service on Rand's feet.

"Why trouble with me?" Rand shook his head. "You should be defending the Lof Shraen."

"Craelin's guarding him with several others. Elcon sent me to free you." Eathnor pushed the hilt of his dagger into Rand's hand. "To your weapon." A warrior lunged toward him from behind.

"Watch out!"

Eathnor spun about in time to deflect his assailant's sword. Sparks flew as the swords met in a fierce fray.

Rand stumbled to his feet, painfully aware of the

inadequacy of his weapon. He scanned the camp, searching for a fallen sword.

One of Pilaer's warriors charged with a roar, his sword thrusting toward Rand's throat.

Rand held his position. At the last instant, he dropped and rolled into his opponent's legs. The warrior went down and lay still. Rand caught up the sword by his side and jumped to his feet.

Rand ran in the direction Eathnor had taken but stopped short before reaching his friend. He wanted only to help protect Elcon, but he doubted Craelin would let him near the Lof Shraen. A scuffling sound turned him around.

Merrick, one of Draeg's friends, clanged his blade against the helm of the guardian behind Rand. Merrick crowed while the guardian slid to the ground. He lifted his blade, ready to strike the fallen Kindren.

Rand lunged, thrusting his sword to avert the blow. Metal clanged. Sparks flew.

Merrick roared. He cut his sword sideways.

Rand countered the blow. They stood together, held by their clashing blades.

"You're a traitor in need of killing." Merrick snarled. "I'm pleased to do the honors."

Rand gagged on the stench of his former guard's breath. He broke away and backed to avoid being sliced by Merrick's downward cut.

Merrick followed, wearing him down with a constant barrage of blows.

Rand hurled himself sideways and away in a move he'd used many times to escape his brother Draeg.

Merrick glared at him but gasped in air rather than advancing.

Pushing himself to the point of dizziness, Rand hurtled toward his opponent.

Merrick fended him off, but with a slower swing. He rained blows on Rand in a renewed attack, driving him backward. Rand fought to hold his ground, but he could barely raise his sword. Calling upon his own agility against his opponent's strength, he spun and crouched to miss the blow that followed. Rand dove to the side, rolling out of reach. The maneuver bought him an instant to catch his breath.

"You can only play your tricks so long, Misbegotten," Merrick walked forward while Rand yielded. "After that, you'll dance at the end of my sword."

Rand stumbled against something behind him. He flailed and went down. The warrior he'd tripped over stared at him with glazed eyes, his mouth opened in a scream he would never again voice. Rand pushed away from the dead warrior.

Merrick roared with laughter. "You're not the only one with something up your sleeve. Stand and fight."

Rand snatched up his sword, which had fallen by his side. He scrambled to his feet and met Merrick's blow as the contest began again. How long it lasted, Rand couldn't have said. They were evenly matched, with neither gaining an advantage.

The sounds of battle faded, replaced by the cries of the wounded.

Merrick cast frightened glances about, then broke for the forest. Rand made his way through the bodies and detritus of battle toward Eathnor.

Craelin peered into the distance after the retreating warriors. "They'll return and bring others."

"We'll be ready for them." Elcon stood behind his

guard but with sword ready.

"Lof Shraen, the danger is over now." Eathnor spoke over his shoulder to Elcon. "Perhaps you should rest until we leave."

"I'll not be coddled." Elcon frowned. "Bring me my wingabeast."

"Certainly, Lof Shraen." Craelin turned to Elcon. "But Eathnor's suggestion holds merit. Why not save your strength? You'll wish today's journey at an end before it's over."

Rand smiled in sympathy with Elcon, who scowled and pulled in a breath as if about to unleash a tirade.

Craelin's gaze shifted onto Rand. "What are you doing with that sword? Seize the prisoner!"

The swords of the three guardians nearest Rand scraped.

"Stand down!" Elcon thundered.

The guardians lowered their swords but kept them unsheathed. They watched Rand with suspicion written on their faces.

"I don't understand, Lof Shraen." Craelin gazed at Elcon with a stricken expression. "Why have you countered my order? The prisoner is loose and carrying a weapon."

"Did you not hear Rand's voice warning the camp before the fighting began? Without his help, more guardians would have died. I wasn't willing to leave him tied up and helpless during an ambush, so I sent Eathnor to free him."

Rand gave Elcon a grateful smile. "Thank you, Lof Shraen. I'll do my best to remain worthy of your trust."

"Mind you keep your word," Craelin sniped, but with the faintest of smiles.

14

TOWER PRISON

Mara breathed the fresh air pouring into the tower chamber through the barred window, The panes had broken at some point in the past and had never been replaced. The breech brought welcome relief during the warmth of day, but she shivered in the chill of night, even with her cloak pulled about her. The bed clothes on the ancient tick were not adequate. Neither was the food the queen's frightened-looking servant brought her. Her appetite had largely fled, but she choked down the thin gruel anyway. She would need strength for whatever the future held.

The storm-tossed scene outside perfectly matched her mood. With nothing to occupy her, she had done her share of pacing. Her body did not pine for food, but her mind yearned for nourishment. She had counted and recounted the stones in the floor. She knew the cracks in the wall and the place where a former inhabitant had marked scratches in the stone. It wasn't hard to understand how a prisoner would resort to such measures. Darkness followed day in a pattern that never varied, and she had lost track of time. An eagle flew past the window, a stray that had not yet found a roost. Its wings cupped the air then fanned upward in frantic flight. Even a strong bird of prey could not withstand the storm blowing up. She cheered the solitary creature until it moved out of sight. Forlorn at losing sight of the bird, she left the window and laid down on the tick, which smelled of dust and mold. The storm might have entertained her with booming thunder and flashes of lightning, but she no longer wished to look upon it. Turning her face to the wall, she let her tears flow. She was like that eagle, struggling through a storm and in search of a safe perch.

A dark soul reached across time and space to seek hers. She curled into a ball. The presence twined about her like a snake, squeezing until she gasped in air. She fought the pull to surrender, resisting with the knowledge that Freaer could not claim her unless she gave in.

The assault ended, leaving her spent. Rain blew in through the window and dampened the straw tick. She sat up and put her arms around her knees, no longer ecstatic about the storm. The gentlest of touches brushed her soul, making her want to weep. He had seemed distant when they'd parted, but his touch came to comfort her. She turned into his embrace as darkness fell, flooded by peace.

The door scraped open, and a light fell over her. She sat up with a cry of alarm. The queen's servant had already brought food. Who could this be? Mara tried to make out the figure holding the lanthorn but couldn't see past its light. She shrank against the wall. "Who's there?"

"There's nothing to fear." Caerla's voice braced her. "I've come to free you."

Equal measures of curiosity and suspicion tugged at Mara. "Why would you counter your mother's wish to hold me captive?"

"I follow God's will above that of mortal creatures."

"Would God have you free me?"

"You and any other soul imprisoned by anger."

Mara swung her legs onto the floor. "How did you find me?"

"The longer we talk, the greater the chances we'll be found out." Caerla strode to the door but turned back, holding the lanthorn aloft. "Follow me."

Mara balanced on her feet, a harder task than when she'd first arrived at Cobbleford. Her aunt led her past the studded doors that shut off the tower and down the circular staircase she'd climbed with Queen Inydde. The lanthorn light thinned as Caerla descended. Mara needed no instruction on why her aunt feared discovery. Catching Caerla's urgency, she hurried after her.

Caerla stopped with a finger pressed to her lips at the base of the tower stairs. Mara nodded and tiptoed with her down the torchlit corridor that branched off the landing. Beyond the carved strongwood doors that stood tall on either side, Caerla rounded the corner into a passage strung with cobwebs. Their footsteps stirred clouds of dust that hung in the air. Once-ornamental stonework that bracketed the sagging doors had crumbled into piles of rubble here and there, the work of dampness that seeped from a neglected roof. The scent of stale water arose from the stone walls and floors to blend with the stench of rodent urine.

Mara continued behind her aunt with reluctance. For all she knew, Caerla shared her mother's derangement. Where was she taking her?

They reached the end of the corridor, and Caerla hauled open a massive door guarded by the carved lions of Westerland. She gave Mara a bolstering smile. "Only a little farther." Caerla slipped behind the door.

Mara took a deep breath and did the same. Her footsteps echoed hollowly in the tall chamber where light struggled through high windows coated with grime. A stone balcony spanned the rear of the chamber and a dais stood on one end. Every decoration had been removed from the chamber, except for those etched in wood or stone. Even so, it retained an air of grandeur.

Caerla pulled the door shut and joined her in the center of the room.

"What is this place?" Mara asked in an awed voice.

"It's been forgotten since my great-grandfather built the chapel, but the abbey priests used to lead the royal family and castle guests in worship here."

"It's breathtaking," Mara breathed. Even neglect could not shroud the chamber's beauty or diminish the mantle of peace that covered it.

Caerla smiled. "Yes, but we shouldn't linger to admire it. The dust will show our footprints to any who follow." Her boots tapped while climbing the steps to the dais. Two alcoves graced the wall behind them, and she went into the one nearest the window. Mara expected her to open the door in the center of the alcove, but instead she felt along the edge of its wooden paneling. Something behind the paneling snicked, and a previously hidden door gaped open. Caerla stood poised. "Hurry. You won't be safe until we reach the abbey."

Needing no more warning, Mara entered the arched tunnel. The stone floor gave way to beaten dirt, and the damp coldness had her pulling her cloak close.

Caerla shut the door to the tunnel, her movement swaying the lanthorn, which swung in dizzying arcs. Mara put a hand to the wall and closed her eyes to steady herself. Her aunt brushed past her, and she hurried in her wake through the long tunnel. Caerla stopped before a rough door and threw it open.

Mara followed her into a small chamber without windows, furniture, or adornment. "Where are we?"

"We're in the abbey's private prayer chamber."

"It seems so stark."

"Embellishments would distract from reaching the inner place of beauty through prayer. It's hard to describe."

Mara nodded, understanding better than Caerla might think. She'd learned when attacked by Freaer's soul touch to hide within an inner place of prayer. She couldn't have explained that either.

Caerla looked her over. "You're thinner than when we first met. I imagine some food and drink wouldn't go amiss."

"Thank you."

"Let's see what we can find."

In the kitchen, Caerla brewed tea and settled Mara at the scrubbed table with a joint of smoked elk, a slab of cheese, and a thick slice of dried-apple pie. Mara picked the meat bone clean.

Caerla's lips curved. "Your mother could eat as heartily when she came in from the field."

Mara broke off a bite of cheese. "My father told me that she gathered herbs in the wild. How did she dare go alone into the kaba forest?"

"Through faith in God, I suppose, and belief in her purpose. Did you know that the poor came to her with their stricken? She'd heal them by natural arts, if she could."

"I don't share that passion, although I love gathering food in the wild."

"You can do that here all you like. The abbey always needs extra food to give to the disadvantaged." A frown marred her brow. "You'll have to keep to the abbey until Mother comes around and accepts your presence at the abbey."

Mara cradled the steaming mug of tea Caerla had poured for her. "Do you really think she will?"

"She's bound to."

Mara would have believed her aunt's words better if she hadn't looked away while speaking them. "The queen seemed determined to be rid of me."

"She can't touch you here."

"Are you certain of that?"

Caerla nodded. "This abbey has the power to shelter political refuges independent of the throne. If the queen forgets that, I'll remind her."

Mara chewed a bite of apple pie and kept her reservations to herself.

"Come with me." Caerla stood and picked up the lanthorn. "I have a surprise for you."

Mara rocked on her feet. After the food and warm drink, she longed to sleep. "I'm not sure I can manage a surprise right now."

Caerla smiled. "You'll change your mind, I think."

Possessed by a curious sensation of floating, Mara moved beside her aunt down the echoing corridors of Cobbleford Abbey.

Caerla knocked on a door much like many others they'd passed.

"Who's there?" Lyneth called from behind the wooden panel.

"It's me, Caerla."

The door opened and Lyneth looked out. "I'm sorry, Prioress. The Lof Raelein is on her way to bed." She glanced at Mara and started. "Lof Raena! I'm glad to find you well."

"Syl Marinda?" Arillia came to the door with her hair unbound and her vest laces loosened. "I'd heard you'd left the castle." She glanced at Caerla questioningly, then stepped back. "Come inside."

Compared to Arillia's lavish chambers at Torindan, the rooms she occupied at the abbey seemed even more spartan than they otherwise might. No adornments hung on the outer chamber wall save a faded tapestry of a deer in the forest above the fireplace mantel. Sparse furniture sat on the stone floor, only a strongwood desk and a couple of serviceable benches by the hearth.

Lyneth closed the outer door and went through into what would be her own chamber.

Arillia turned to Mara. "Why did you go away?"

"She didn't," Caerla explained, "That's what I was told also, but I had my doubts."

"I don't understand." Arillia's brow puckered. "Are you saying that Syl Marinda has been in the castle all this time?"

"Explanations can wait until tomorrow, I think." Mara found her tongue. "How is my father?" Arillia's face softened. "He's recovering."

Mara brightened. "Is he in the abbey also?"

Arilla shook her head. "I left him in the wild lands under Eathnor's protection. Elcon needed more time to recover. Eathnor remains to protect him. Elcon will come to us when he can withstand the journey."

"I hope that may be soon. Has anyone else in our

party arrived?"

"Dorann and Anders brought me here. I thought Rand had traveled with you."

"We became separated."

Arillia swept her gaze over Mara's face. "That must have been upsetting."

"It was. What of Kai and the archer?"

"They haven't arrived. I hope we may not assume the worst for them."

⊂⊃

With the afternoon softening toward nightfall, Kai dismounted and led Flecht onto the cobblestone bar that extended into the river. The old ford had fallen out of use when the bridge had gone in to make reaching Cobbleford Castle easier, but in its early days wagon and rider alike had splashed across in this place. Travel into the Elder lands had been more common before Freaer, the Contender of Prophecy, had launched wingabeast attacks to divide the Kindren and Elder nations.

"That perverse cousin to a donkey doesn't deserve a position in the castle garrison." The stone Aerlic flung into the Cobbleford River plunked below the surface and spread a widening circle across the surface.

"Have a care how you speak," Kai warned. "You wouldn't want to insult a donkey."

Aerlic smiled, as Kai had intended, and gave him a sheepish look. "I'm a little testy."

"After that maddening interview, it's no wonder." The archer rarely lost his composure, but the rounds of increasingly ridiculous questions hurled down upon them from the gatehouse would have tried the mildest of tempers.

Kai had stopped to water the wingabeasts, and also to give himself time to think. The possibility of being turned away from the castle had occurred to him, but by Euryon. The guard's steadfast refusal to make his presence known to the king had not. He felt as cast adrift as the half-submerged log floating past, pulled along by deep currents. "I have no idea what to do next."

"That's easy." Aerlic left the edge of the river and came to stand beside him. "Make camp."

Kai smiled, tension easing from him. Aerlic's practical mindset always exerted itself. "Any suggestions as to where?"

"Assuming we'll try the gatehouse again tomorrow, somewhere around here would work best."

This location had long served as a camping ground, but during a gentler time. In these troubled times, they'd have to trade watches through the night.

Aerlic pointed to a level bank with a clearing that extended well back from the Cobbleford River. "That's a good spot."

Kai squinted across the water. "It's more open than I'd like."

"What about there?" Aerlic pointed again, to a place where the bank lifted high to avoid being washed away in a flash flood not too high to make drawing water a chore. The trees hung their branches low enough to hide it.

"All right."

They allowed the wingabeasts to drink their fill then turned them out on the grassy bank to graze until nightfall. Kai joined the archer in foraging berries and mushrooms to supplement their steady diet of waybread and elk jerky. They traveled along a scant trail winding around the gnarled feet of a stand of ancient kabas. The aromatic scent of tree resin mingled with the sweetness of wild roses. A sense of quiet stole over Kai, and he released his burdens to Lof Yuel.

Bright feathers erupted from a clump of sheaf grass at Kai's elbow. He cried out, his heart pounding.

Aerlic drew his bow and shot. His arrow's impact was followed by a second thud that cut off the pheasant's scream. The bird fell from the sky. Aerlic did not rush to retrieve it, but stood waiting.

"Nice shot, archer." A man with tousled brown hair stood up from behind a bush dotted with pink roses. Garbed in a leather jerkin, he held a bow in his hand. "Although you have cheated me out of supper."

Aerlic shouldered his bow. "Sorry, I didn't know you were there."

"I gathered that." The man shrugged. "You shot first. The pheasant belongs to you."

Aerlic retrieved the fallen bird.

"What business do you Kindren have in Westerland?"

The man's casual tone didn't ring true to Kai. From Aerlic's guarded expression, he'd also caught the hint of a stronger interest in the stranger's voice. The man looked familiar. Kai scanned his face, trying to place him. "We've come to pay our respects to the king."

"You've come a long way for such a purpose."

"That we have." Kai glanced about, searching for signs of an ambush. He found no one hidden nearby in the forest.

"What brings you into these woods?" Aerlic asked

somewhat inanely since the man had been hunting. His question turned the conversation, however, which might have been its true purpose.

The stranger nodded to the fat pheasant dangling from Aerlic's hand. "A quest for game. Stuffed with mushrooms and greens, that bird will make a fine meal."

"Would you like to join us?" Kai asked, giving in to his curiosity about this stranger.

"You'd be welcome," Aerlic added his own invitation despite the puzzled look he gave Kai.

The stranger smiled. "I'd like that. Thank you."

"I'm Kai of Whellein, and this is Aerlic of Glindenn raven."

"Whellein! Isn't that to the north beside Norwood?"

"It is." Kai waited for the stranger to reveal his own name.

"And Glindenn lies to the south, does it not?"

"Yes, along the coast." Aerlic answered with a touch of wistfulness, as if taken by a bout of homesickness.

"And your name?" Kai asked pointedly.

The stranger glanced from Aerlic to Kai. "I'm called Searcher."

Kai frowned. The man hid his identity behind an alias, a thing that didn't recommend him. "Where do you hail from?"

"Me?" Searcher glanced about him. "I belong to this forest."

"You will have tales of it then." Kai started toward camp.

Searcher kept pace beside him. "More than I care to tell."

"I can well believe that." Aerlic spoke from behind them. "It's a fearsome place."

"Surely you have a few to give us," Kai urged.

"I do, if I must tell tales for my supper," Searcher laughed.

While the pheasant cooked, Searcher regaled them with lively sagas of heroes and cowards, monsters and maidens.

Kai cut a joint from the pheasant and passed it to the man. "Your stories take a bardic turn, if ever I heard one."

"A bard?" Searcher's mouth ticked upward in a wry smile. "I'd never have claimed that title for myself."

"He's right," Aerlic chimed in. "You bring your tales to life."

Searcher shook his head. "I've wondered sometimes what I might have been had life turned out differently."

"Why are you called Searcher?" Kai watched the stranger's face. "What do you seek?"

"I hardly know these days. Once I'd have said the love of a maiden, but I lost her."

"What happened?"

"She ran away from the inn where I worked." He gave a bitter laugh. "I've talked to her since, but she's given her heart to another."

Kai hid his surprise. "Where did this happen?"

"In Norwood, at the Whitefeather Inn, a place you know well."

Kai stared at him. "How do you know that?"

"You don't remember me at all, do you? But then, you only saw me briefly when you brought Mara back to the inn."

"You look familiar..." Kai shook his head. "My apologies, but I've forgotten you."

The man leaned forward. "Think back, Kai, to the young stable hand who greeted you."

Kai sprang to his feet. "Hael? Is it you?" Could this stranger be the exuberant boy he'd known? He had the same rumpled hair, which must have been the clue Kai had recognized. The plains of his face had firmed, along with his jaw. He'd changed in less favorable ways, though. What had driven the innocence from his wide eyes, replacing it with a guarded expression?

"I promise you that it is." Hael stood and met his embrace. "I used to watch the skies for your return."

Kai laughed. "Tending my wingabeast was the real draw, I suspected."

Hael smiled, and his eyes glittered in the firelight. "That's not true, if you didn't know. I made a hero of you."

"How long ago that seems." Kai cleared his throat, which had thickened. "I'm sorry I didn't recognize you."

"I don't blame you for that. I hardly know myself these days." Hael sank onto the log he'd occupied before.

Kai sat back down across the fire. "Tell me what you're really doing in this forest."

"Trying to discover what's happened to Mara. I separated her from Freaer's son and brought her to Cobbleford. I can't help but worry about her, though. I asked her to tie a bit of linen in her window to signal that all was well." Hael exhaled heavily. "She hasn't done so, not that night nor any night since. I've watched all the windows for any clue that she's alive. I've found none."

"Perhaps she forgot. Arriving in a new place can overwhelm a person."

"I impressed it on her mind. She should have remembered."

"Do you know the whereabouts of Lof Shraen Elcon or Lof Raelein Arillia?" Kai pressed him.

"Sorry, but no."

"I hoped to find them at Cobbleford Castle. We presented ourselves at the gatehouse this afternoon, only to be turned away. We'll go back tomorrow and hopefully find a more receptive guard on watch."

"I doubt the guards will let you in. The queen has made changes of late, or so I hear."

As Kai recalled, King Euryon had been slow to stand against Queen Inydde's demands. That had been long ago during Elcon's fateful visit when he'd fallen in love with Aewen. The queen had strongly influenced her husband then. How much more power had she taken since? He scowled. "We need to enter the castle, now more than ever."

"If all goes well, I'll stand inside it tomorrow." Hael rose. "I'll leave you now. I've a camp of my own, with a band of followers awaiting my return."

"How do you intend to enter the castle?" Kai demanded. Hael's claim galled him in the face of today's rejection.

"Never mind asking. I'm an outlaw these days." Hael turned back on the river bank. "I'll give you word, whatever I find."

15

INSIDE THE ABBEY

Lyneth bent to gather herbs for her basket from one of the square beds in the abbey garden. Caerla was teaching her to make healing concoctions. Lyneth found it gratifying that her tinctures, salves, and oils would ease the suffering of those who ailed within and without Cobbleford's gates. Today she needed to make a tincture from the leaf of peppermint and raspberry, chamomile petals, and dandelion root to soothe Arillia's nausea. Sickness took the Lof Raelein often of late. She'd grown pale and weary, given to sleeping in and retiring early at night.

Brother Robb, a plump man with a balding pate, strode toward her. His basket overflowed with vegetables, which he spent much of his time tending. He frowned at her but nodded in passing.

Lyneth smiled at him. "I enjoyed last night's stew."

Brother Robb's frown deepened. "Food is for sustenance." He strode away from her and reaching a stout door, pushed it open. He vanished into the kitchen, no doubt to cook another nourishing meal.

Lyneth continued to the next garden bed, her boots crunching in the crushed rock that covered the ground. Rain had fallen in the night, leaving bright droplets in the hearts of the chamomile flowers. She shook the blossoms free of moisture and dropped them in her basket.

"Psst!" An odd hissing sound distracted her from her task. Glancing over her shoulder, she saw nothing. Lyneth moved to the next bed, where raspberry blossoms frothed in delicate sprays beneath pleated leaves of glossy green.

The sound came again, louder this time.

Lyneth paused from cutting raspberry leaves, turned her head, and almost cried out.

Searcher stood in the shadows of one of the pillars that supported the covered corridor wrapped around the outside of the abbey.

She hurried to him. "What are you doing here?" She kept her voice low, but her words echoed down the corridor, mocking her caution.

Searcher winced, but a smile glittered in his eyes. "I hoped when I found you for a softer welcome."

She couldn't quite meet his eyes. "You were looking for me?"

"Well yes, for you and Mara, to learn how you fare. You didn't signal that you were safe."

"I couldn't. The Lof Raena disappeared the night we arrived at Cobbleford."

"What happened to her?" Searcher's question sent echoes scurrying. He pulled her out of the corridor and into the shade of a strongwood tree at the edge of the garden. The trunk ran straight to a junction of branches that formed a seat she might have climbed in her early days. The tree's whorled leaves swirled and swished in the breeze to sing a hushed melody.

"Queen Inydde locked her in the tower, I'm told," she murmured.

"That doesn't surprise me. The queen's misdeeds

are well known."

"Softly." Lyneth gripped his arm and glanced about in alarm. "Speaking ill of the queen within the castle walls is not wise."

"Nor is keeping silent about injustices, but I'll heed your warning. I must help Mara."

"Caerla, prioress of the abbey, freed her and brought her to shelter in the abbey last night."

"That's at least part of the task. Will you bring Mara to me?"

"Now? She's asleep, I believe, and Caerla said not to disturb her slumber."

"It's urgent, I promise you."

Lyneth hated to disobey the prioress, but it was hard to think of duty when Searcher gazed at her with his amber eyes. She bit her lip. What harm could there be in letting the Lof Raena decide for herself whether to speak with him? "All right, If she will come, I'll bring her."

The lines of strain in his face eased. "Thank you, sweet Lyneth."

"You care for her very much," she said and waited for his response.

Searcher looked past her toward the abbey. "I've known and loved Mara for a long time." He brought his attention back to her. "Hurry, if you would. I need to leave soon."

She hurried off without inquiring into his means of entering or leaving the castle grounds. The less she knew about that, the better. That he had come into the castle with a price on his head revealed the depth of his love for Mara.

ɑ⅃

Her knock at the Lof Raena's door echoed hollowly. Lyneth glanced down the corridor behind her, trying to come up with an excuse to give the prioress for her intrusion. Caerla did not come around the corner, and Lyneth let out her breath on a sigh. She turned to knock again.

"Who is it?" the Lof Raena called through the door, sounding wide awake.

"Lyneth, bearing a message."

The door creaked open and Mara looked out. Bathed and dressed in a simple tunic, she appeared more docile than she had in Nadya's colorful skirts. "What does my step-mother want?"

Lyneth shook her head. "The Lof Raelein did not send me."

"Who did?"

"Another you know well."

Mara gazed at her with a puzzled expression. "Tell me who."

"He's been known to ride a stag." Lyneth didn't want to speak Searcher's name out loud in the corridor.

Understanding dawned on Mara's face. "What message does he give?"

"One he hopes to deliver himself. He awaits you in the garden."

Mara's eyes widened. "He's here? Take me to him at once."

Lyneth retraced her steps, leading the Lof Raena to the garden, which seemed much the same as when she'd left it. The sun had climbed a little higher in the sky, maybe, and the birds sang more strongly. She stumbled to a stop. Something else had changed.

No one stood under the strongwood tree.

She swept a glance over the garden then turned to the Lof Raena, ready to tell her that Searcher had vanished.

"Psst!" The hiss came from above, within the tree.

Lyneth started toward it and caught sight of a booted foot. Searcher had climbed into the tree's natural seat and sat sideways with his knees up and his back to one of the branches. She held back to let the Lof Raena continue without her.

Mara turned back to her. "Stay close, if you would, and warn us if anyone nears."

The Lof Raena had given her a task she'd intended to perform anyway. Lyneth gathered herbs into the basket she'd almost forgotten she carried. Stolen glimpses showed Searcher jumping down from the tree, taking Mara's hands, lowering his head to murmur near her ear. An ache twisted in Lyneth's stomach, and she pulled her gaze away from the pair by the tree. She didn't want to feel the pangs of jealousy, especially not for an outlaw. Her job was to remain vigilant for anyone walking along the outside corridor or rounding the path from the chapel. "Thank you, Lyneth," Mara said from behind her.

"Of course, Lof Raena." Lyneth turned around and looked about. The garden gave no sign of Searcher.

"He's gone." Mara spoke softly.

Lyneth did her best to convince herself that she didn't care that he'd left without saying goodbye.

"He warned me that I'm not safe at Cobbleford, not even in the abbey, with the queen against me. He offered to smuggle me out and suggests that I leave with him in two days' time."

Lyneth had taken all the herbs she needed for the Lof Raelein's tincture but snipped a rose blossom to dry for tea. "Will you?"

"I'm not sure what to do. I should be here when my father arrives, and Caerla tells me that I'm safe at the abbey, that the royal family accepts its self-rule." Mara shook her head. "I'm not sure, though. The queen hates me, or at least she loathes what I represent. What would you do in my place?"

"It isn't for me to advise you, Lof Raena."

"Even if I ask?"

"My knowledge of the queen's mindset is inferior to yours."

"Granted, but what about Searcher? Would you trust him?"

"He seems to have your safety at heart." A bright butterfly floated above the garden bed, drawing Lyneth's eye. "I believe he loves you."

"I'm certain of that, although I wish he didn't." Mara touched a hand to her brow, as if her head pained her. "I doubt he would release me once he freed me."

"Where would you go, Lof Raena? I would think you'd welcome his protection." "That's the trouble. I have a duty to Faeraven that he might try to prevent me from fulfilling."

"I've known you only a short while, Lof Raena, but I don't think Searcher or anyone else could hold you back for long."

❧

"I, Kai of Whellein, guardian of Rivenn, come to you in the name of Lof Shraen Elcon of Faeraven." Seated on his wingabeast, Kai waited with Aerlic on

Argalent in front of the gatehouse.

"Oh, really?" The guard asked in a sarcastic voice. "And have you brought the Sword and the Sceptor with you?" He guffawed, his laughter joined by others, probably guards out of sight behind the wall.

Kai touched Sword Rivenn's hilt but left the weapon sheathed. "I demand to speak to King Euryon."

"The king cannot be disturbed this day." The guard scratched his bearded chin. "Go away."

"We'll only come back tomorrow," Kai warned.

"He'll be busy then too."

"When will he not be busy?" Aerlic shielded his eyes.

"Oh, the other one speaks, does he?" the guard chuckled.

"Name the day." Kai cut into his merriment.

"I think that you will be very old by then."

"I will relay your treatment of me to the Lof Shraen." Kai turned Flecht away from the gatehouse.

Aerlic, his face reddened, rode abreast of Kai. "This guard put the one yesterday to shame."

Kai gave no answer but crossed the bridge that arched over the river while pondering what to do next. The only solution that made any sense was to breach the castle somehow. His plan would have to be foolproof. If he and Aerlic wound up in Cobbleford's dungeon, they could help no one.

Flecht stepped off the bridge, and Kai turned his head westward on the path along the river. He would broach the idea to Aerlic when they returned to camp.

The creaking wood and clanking metal behind them announced the raising of the castle's portcullis. Kai glanced backward across the river. A wagon trundled through on the road, crammed with stone masons singing a working ditty with gusto. The portcullis creaked down again, and the song ended as the castle gates banged shut.

Aerlic sighed. "Oh, to be a stoneworker, or to travel into the castle with them."

"They'd have no reason to help us. Besides, with our long eyes and pale hair, we could never disguise ourselves as Elder." Kai continued the journey in a darker mood. He'd raised his own hopes with thoughts of sneaking into the castle. However, as he'd explained to Aerlic, that option wasn't available to them. They could dye their hair, but the shape and color of their eyes would betray them.

No pheasant roasted on the fire this night. Kai chewed stale waybread while staring into the flames. Across from him, Aerlic poked at the fire unnecessarily. Kai's mind ran in feverish circles that brought him no relief. The journey had brought them to a dead end, a place he knew far too well. He closed his eyes, aware of the fire's warmth on his skin, the sizzle of resin, and the redolence of wood smoke. *Lof Yuel, help me. I don't know how to go on from here.*

He laid down to sleep with more serenity but no solutions. Slumber took a long time claiming him. No sooner had he fallen asleep than Aerlic roused him for his watch. Now weariness tugged at him, making the long vigil a misery. Yellow-eyed beasts ringed them about and would have attacked if not for their fear of the fire. The skill of long training kept him awake, but if it had not, the growls that carried through the night would have allowed for no slumber.

The sky lightened from inky black to pewter, and then the sun's early rays slanted in to gild the gray expanse. The clouds blushed and the horizon bloomed with deeper color. It would be time to wake Aerlic soon.

"I thought I might find you still here." Hael's quiet voice reached him from outside the firelight. The beasts had thankfully fled with the dawn. Hael strode into camp and took a seat on the log opposite Kai. "You've passed a bad night, it's clear from your face."

Kai threw a twig into the fire. "You're awake early. Is that by choice?"

Hael laughed softly. "Do you imagine that a guilty conscience troubles my sleep?"

"I didn't mean to imply that."

"You would be wrong if you had. I am an innocent man condemned to live an outlaw's life."

"If that's true, I'll help you clear your name."

"That can be done only where truth is cherished." Hael gave him a guileless look. "This is not such a kingdom."

Kai had witnessed the beginning of Westerland's slow slide into corruption when he'd visited with Elcon long ago. He shook his head. "A kingdom cannot survive without truth."

Hael's eyes narrowed. "Perhaps you can help me in another way,"

"Name it and I will tell you if it's possible."

"What if I told you that Mara is alive but in need of rescuing?"

Kai searched his face for any sign of deception. "How would you know this?"

"I spoke with her yesterday morn. She narrowly escaped the queen's captivity and now resides in the abbey by a slender thread. Nothing can harm her in that sanctuary, provided Inydde chooses to honor tradition."

Kai frowned. "That seems unlikely."

"My thought, exactly."

CR

Mara glanced at Arillia across the table in the prioress's meeting chamber. "The King turned down my request for help."

"Euryon's response makes little sense. Did you explain that Freaer is certain to invade Westerland?"

Mara tapped a fingernail on the side of the cup Caerla had filled with tea. "Our conversation didn't take that turn. I hoped to make that clear to him, but I'm not certain he'll see reason."

Arillia smirked. "Euryon is used to thinking in ways that are hard for him to give up."

"I wish I could talk to him again."

"I doubt Inydde would allow you to enter the castle again." Arillia stood and paced to the window. She looked out for a long time, then turned with light spilling around her. "What do you think, Caerla? Would the king come to us here?"

Caerla paused with the knife she'd used to cut bread suspended in her hand. "Possibly, if my mother had no knowledge of his visit."

Arillia perched on the bench across from Mara. "Could you arrange such a thing?"

Caerla set down the knife and sank onto the bench beside Mara. "As you've both noticed, my father is not easy to sway."

Arillia leaned forward. "For Westerland's sake and for Faeraven's, we must try."

Caerla glanced at Mara, and then back to Arillia. "I will consider it."

Arillia rose. "Whatever your reason for helping us, I'll be grateful. Now, if you'll excuse me, I need to lie down in my chambers."

Lyneth, seated by the hearth, jumped to her feet. "Lof Raelein, you look so pale. Let me take your arm."

"Are you ill?" Mara asked.

"Pray don't fuss." Arillia pulled away from her servant. "I'm merely sleepy. The days have been warm of late."

Looking chastised, Lyneth stepped away from Arillia.

Mara retreated into silence.

"Perhaps it is something more." Caerla spoke hesitantly.

Arillia firmed her jaw. "All I need is rest. Come, Lyneth, and play the lute Brother Robb gave you."

"I'm not very good at it," Lyneth protested.

"It soothes me regardless."

The door burst open before they reached it.

A gasp escaped Mara, and she flinched.

Queen Inydde stood in the opening. Her dark blue eyes glared at Mara. Chin jutted, she strode into the chamber. Arillia fell back before her, and Lyneth moved protectively to her side. The queen halted her march in front of Caerla. "Why do you shelter these Kindren?"

Caerla rose and faced the queen. "They needed refuge."

Inydde's face worked. "I won't have it, do you hear me?"

"Mother—"

"You will address me as queen."

"Very well, your majesty." Caerla bowed. She stood to her full height, which matched the queen's. "And you may call me prioress."

Inydde's nostrils flared. Her hand came up as if she might slap Caerla but fisted and dropped to her side. "Send them away."

"That's not a decision you command." Caerla countered her mother. "The realm must not interfere with the abbey."

"We will see about that." Inydde turned on Mara. "Don't think you can escape me."

"Must you rail at your own granddaughter?" Arillia demanded.

The queen glared at Mara. "This urchin is no granddaughter of mine."

"Who have you become?" Arillia's voice broke the stand-off. "The Queen Inydde I once met would not have said such a hurtful thing."

Inydde rounded on her. "Don't pretend we are anything but strangers."

Arillia's eyes widened then narrowed. "My mistake."

Inydde turned on Caerla. "Have them out by tomorrow or live to regret it." She turned on her heel and left as abruptly as she had arrived.

Mara wrapped her arms around herself, trying to stop her trembling. It went against the grain to cower before anyone, but Inydde managed to strike to the heart somehow. The queen stood tall, but Mara's reaction had more to do with Inydde's harsh spirit and strong mind than her physical stature.

"I'm sorry." Caerla spoke softly, her tone soothing. "I knew my mother would object to your staying here, but I thought she would do so in private."

Arillia lowered herself to one of the benches by the hearth. "I'm sorry that our presence causes problems."

Caerla heaved a sigh. "Any trouble the queen stirs lies at her door, not yours."

Mara folded her arms across herself. "Perhaps we should go."

"And bow to her bullying?" Caerla made a sound very like a snort. "The queen knows of the ancient agreement that prevents the throne from interfering with the church. Failing to uphold it would bring shame to the royal household."

Arillia shook her head. "How much might she surrender to protect the family honor?"

"She gave up her daughter for it." Caerla spoke quietly, but her words vibrated so intensely she might have shouted them.

"My mother," Mara breathed.

Caerla's boots tapped the stone floor and stopped behind Mara. She rested her hands on Mara's shoulders. "I've always regretted the way Aewen and I parted. I thought only of myself in those days. I gave her no compassion. It took my sister's death to show me my selfishness. I can't change what happened to Aewen in the past, but I can help protect the future for Aewen's child."

Arillia arched a brow. "Does that mean you'll invite the king to speak to us?"

"I'll do it for Mara's sake, and also for Aewen's. My sister wouldn't have wanted Freaer's forces to invade Westerland. That would harm the poor, whom she cherished. Defeat would end our way of life forever."

16

ESCAPE AND CAPTIVITY

"I've come to say goodbye." Mara kept her voice low, although no one had followed her through the corridors to the Lof Raelein's chambers.

Lyneth let her in, fastened the door, and retreated to her room.

Arillia stood up from the bench by the fire. "What do you mean?"

Mara clasped her hands. "There's no point in my staying here. The king refused my request for help. Kai, who directed us here, has vanished. The queen will stop at nothing, I'm certain, to imprison me again. And I would rather not pit my aunt against her mother."

Arillia frowned. "What good will it do for you to leave if I remain? Inydde made it clear she wants us both gone."

"You are not the embarrassment to her that I am. If I go, she might relent where you're concerned."

"I don't know. I remind her of Elcon, and that makes her think of Aewen. I doubt she'd risk provoking the abbey to rid herself of me, though."

"You'd be better off waiting for my father to join you here, and Kai may yet come."

"Don't worry. I have no intention of traipsing into the wild lands ever again. I'm not entirely sure you should either, although I understand what needs to be done. What about your father? When Elcon arrives, he'll look for you here."

"We don't know how long will pass before that happens. Meanwhile, the Kindren scatter while Freaer's forces strengthen." Mara shook her head. "I know what my father would do if he could. As Heir of Faeraven, I must stand in for him."

"Elcon spoke of his wishes before I left him, but it seems too cruel a burden for a maiden's slender shoulders. What do you know of war?"

"Nothing at all, but then my task is not to fight but to gather the Kindren willing to defend Faeraven."

"Challenging Freaer without the Elder nations would be suicide."

"Which is why I hope you can sway King Euryon. Whether or not he helps us, we must act. If we do nothing, death will arrive on swift feet."

Arillia paced to the window and looked out. The morning bathed her form in gentle light, lending her an otherworldly appearance. A silence stretched between them. Mara twisted her hands together in an old nervous habit but forced herself to stop.

Arillia turned at last. "All right, but you can't go alone."

"I hope to take Dorann with me."

"Good idea. You'll need a protector. Once you leave the castle, the queen may try to attack you, and other dangers lurk in the wild lands. If you see signs of warriors, you'll have to turn back."

Mara drew a relieved breath. She would rather travel with Dorann than Hael. The tracker would understand her mission and could help her find survivors from Torindan hiding in the wild lands.

"Provided the way remains clear, Dorann can lead me to my father. I'd like to ask his advice on what to do."

"Elcon is hiding in a hut, if he hasn't abandoned it already to come here. You might meet on the road."

"If my father arrives without seeing me, tell him that I've gone to gather the remnant from Torindan hiding in the wild lands."

"What good will that do if only a handful have survived?"

"I can send messengers from among them. Calling for the loyal ravens to rally around Faeraven's banner will give them hope. The Kindren have been in short supply of that since Torindan's fall."

"They may die for that hope. If the Elder won't help us, I doubt Faeraven can rise on its own."

"The Rose of Rivenn will fly above the Kindren while they fight, with or without the Elder. May you succeed where I have failed and win the king's support."

"I'll do my best."

Mara frowned. "My aunt might object to my leaving."

Arillia nodded. "I won't mention your departure right away."

"That would be best, although I wish I could tell her goodbye."

"I'll do it for you." Arillia came to stand before her. "Be careful, Syl Marinda. If you see signs that warriors from Pilaer are on the march, turn back."

"I will."

Arillia touched her shoulder and proffered a quiet smile. "May Lof Yuel keep you."

Mara laid her hand briefly over her step-mother's. "And you." She started for the door but turned back before she reached it. "I'll need help preparing for the journey. Would you be willing to lend Lyneth to me?"

"Certainly. She can go with you now. Stop and inform Dorann that he's to escort you to your father."

Mara knocked on the servant's door with a sense of relief. She'd hurt Hael terribly when she'd run away from the inn without a word. She couldn't do the same thing to him a second time but talking with him while her emotions were so raw would be difficult.

Lyneth could inform him that she wasn't coming.

Ↄↄ

Lyneth left the garden path and strode across the grass to the strongwood tree.

Hael sat in the seat of the tree's intersecting branches. He tilted his head. "Why have you come instead of Mara?"

"I bring a message to you from the Lof Raena." She spoke with mixed emotions, certain he wouldn't like what she had to tell him. During the short while since she had met him, she'd already learned that he preferred to do a job himself rather than trust another to perform it.

He dropped before her with a thud and leaned closer than her composure could manage. "And?"

Lyneth swallowed. "The Lof Raena chooses not to come."

He glared at her. "Did she say why?"

"She thanks you for warning her to leave the castle," Lyneth went on. "However, she prefers to travel with a Kindren guard."

He scowled. "Why didn't she deliver this news

herself?"

"Perhaps" —Lyneth hesitated, selecting her words with care— "she feared your reaction."

Hael's eyes widened and his eyebrows shot upward. "Do I come across as angry?" he snapped.

"Perhaps a little."

He searched her face, then shook his head. "I'm sorry to have given you that impression."

Quick sympathy warmed her, and she touched his arm. "You've suffered many things, I think."

"I have, but never would I take anything out on a maiden."

"I believe you," The knowledge strengthened her voice.

He captured her hand and carried it to his lips. "Thank you."

She looked up at him, lost in his gaze.

"Sweet Lyneth." He lowered his head and brushed her forehead with his lips. "Careful how you look at a man or you'll collect broken hearts."

Lyneth pulled away from him. "A life of service allows no room for matters of the heart."

"But you would make a fine wife."

"I am the Lof Raelein's servant."

"How long are you bound to her?" Curiosity crept into his voice.

"Until she releases me from my word."

"But that could be a lifetime."

"Why are we even discussing this? Lingering with me in the garden is not safe."

He chuckled. "Of that I'm well aware." He pulled her into his arms and lifted her chin. "I've a taste for danger."

"Stop this!" She struggled to free herself.

He released her. "I'm sorry to upset you."

"You don't look it, not the least bit." She glared at him, but a smile tugged her mouth and would not be quelled.

His smile stole her breath. "You've found me out."

"You should leave the castle at once." She put up a hand to push against his chest but clutched his jerkin instead.

He lowered his head and covered her lips with his.

By the time she recovered her wits, the desire to repel him had fled. She turned into his arms.

Only a few days ago, she'd watched him gazing down at Mara in this very spot.

The stray thought rescued her from the brink of calamity. She shoved him away. "Spare me your pretty speeches, *Hael*. I know where your heart really lies." Her words had slipped out with more zeal than caution, but how dare he kiss her when he loved another?

He flinched. "Do you blame me for trying to forget Mara when she doesn't love me back?"

Footsteps alerted her, and she turned around. Brother Robb, with two guards keeping pace beside him, strode along the abbey's outer corridor. The knowing expression on his face and his quickening step warned her that he must have seen them from the abbey and summoned the nearest guards.

Hael gripped her upper arms and pulled her backward against him. "You'll have to come with me."

"I'm staying here with my mistress."

"And when asked who you were with, what would you say?"

Her mind went blank.

"Would you tell them that Mara sent you to me?"

"Of course not."

"You spoke my name just now," he said near her ear. "Where did you hear it?"

"The Lof Raena let it slip once. But don't worry. I won't give you away."

"They might give you little choice." He swung her into his arms. "Sorry Lyneth, but I can't take chances."

"What are you doing?" she cried in alarm.

"Saving you from a life of servitude." He broke into a run, carrying her along the path to the chapel. Lyneth threw her arms around his neck to save herself from falling. With the guards in pursuit, she couldn't bring herself to struggle. Slowing Hael down might secure him a place in Cobbleford's dungeon.

"Put me down," she gasped as they rounded the chapel, "I can run on my own."

"Why should I trust you?"

"If you intend to escape, you'll have to. The guards are nearly upon us."

CR

Hael lowered Lyneth onto her feet. She swayed, but then gained her balance. He captured her hand and drew her along beside him. A knife flew past, glinting in the morning sun. He wove a zigzag path, in case others followed. Why did Lyneth remain with him?

The guards shouted behind them, and others answered. He slowed and made out archers just ahead on the inner wall. Veering would carry them out of range but reaching the postern gate would take longer. The guards might arrive before they did.

He swung wide anyway. Lyneth might seem

delicate, but she ran like a deer pursued by a pack of wolves. If she continued her present pace, they'd reach the gate first. Their feet pounded the ground, and their huffing breaths sounded louder than the calls behind them. The outer wall loomed ahead, stone upon stone towering into the sky.

Lyneth cried out, stumbled, and fell. He found her clasping her ankle while a snake slithered down a hole behind her.

Hael scooped her into his arms and kept running. The episode had cost them time and carrying her would slow him. The wooden planks of the postern door hove into view, gapped slightly as his stonemason friend had left it. Hael curved toward the door, his side vision picking up the guard almost upon them. He glanced down at Lyneth. "Can you walk on that ankle?"

"I think so. I only twisted it."

"Good." He lowered her and pulled his dagger. "Try to stay clear of the fighting. If you see a clearing, go through the door."

"All right."

He glanced at her in surprise, but then the guard swung his sword. Hael arched away from the blade.

The guard came back the opposite direction.

The shouts grew louder.

Hael ducked and ran in with a desperate thrust at the armor covering his opponent's foot. The guard screamed and went down. Hael swerved to search for Lyneth. He found her pressed against the wall beside the door, watching him with wide eyes. "Sorry you had to see that." He took her hand, pulled her through the doorway, and ran a zigzag course across the sward and into the forest. Arrows pelted the ground at their feet, shot by guards on the wall. Hael set his jaw, irritated on Lyneth's behalf. The guards should have held their fire for her sake.

He guided her through wetlands braided by river channels and stopped only when he judged they had won free of pursuers. Within the concealing branches of a weilo, he supported her while she clung to him, breathing in gasps. He sheltered her in his arms, taken by an overwhelming desire to shield her from every evil. "Why did you come with me?" he asked when his breathing eased. "You could have run the other way while I was fighting at the door."

"You'd convinced me I shouldn't."

He frowned. "How?"

"I could see you were right. The guards would give me no rest. I'd either betray you and the Lof Raena or suffer whatever they put me through. And for what? The Lof Raelein will never trust me again."

"For what it's worth, I'm sorry." Why had he given into the urge to console himself with a beautiful maiden after Mara's rejection? He'd made Lyneth into a fugitive like him.

ॐ

Rand put a calming hand on the neck of his horse. He'd captured his mount from those left behind by Pilaer's warriors. Black as pitch, the creature would not stand out should they travel by moonlight. Night would find them before long, and the half-light of late afternoon turned the keirken grove ahead on the road to Cobbleford into a place of mist and shadows.

On the back of a black wingabeast, Craelin rode at

the front of the advance guard. Eathnor and Sheiltel, a pale-haired guardian who rarely spoke, shielded Elcon on his wingabeast from either side. Rand traveled with several other guardians on horseback to bring up the rear guard. From this vantage point, he had watched Elcon holding his own throughout the day, although every so often the Lof Shraen swayed in the saddle, a reminder of the toll this journey exacted from him.

Craelin halted, and the entire column ground to a stop. He rode back to Elcon. "Lof Shraen, I'm in favor of turning aside to make camp."

"What, here?" Elcon glanced about. "We'd be out in the open."

"I'd suggest staying under tree cover, but in the wild lands such advice changes. I'd rather go through that keirken grove in broad daylight."

Elcon's wingabeast danced, and he reined the creature in. "What makes you mistrust it?"

Craelin squinted in the direction of the grove. "I'm not certain, to tell you the truth."

"You'll have to give more of a reason with the possibility of Pilaer's warriors following and an urgent need to reach Cobbleford."

"Begging your pardon, Lof Shraen," Eathnor said, "but I feel it too."

Guardians in the advance guard began to mumble.

"Silence!" Elcon turned to Craelin. "You've inspired misgivings for no reason."

Craelin glanced away. "I'm sorry, Lof Shraen, but I thought you should know.".

"I would normally give your hesitations sway, but not this time. Keep your wits about you but continue."

Rand frowned. He didn't like this place, and neither did his horse, but the Lof Shraen made a point worth taking. The keirken grove might host its share of wraiths, but the warriors of Pilaer were fearsome creatures of flesh and blood. Much as he loathed the idea of passing beneath the dark, twisting keirken branches at this time of day, waiting might make matters worse.

Craelin nodded without argument. "As you wish, Lof Shraen." He rode back into the lead. "Fall in!"

Darforth, the guardian between Rand and the right edge of the guard, muttered beneath his breath. Rand urged his horse forward. Darforth kept pace beside him, skittering glances about.

The grove closed in, bringing a sudden chill. Rand's horse shied at nothing. Many of the others had trouble controlling their mounts. Humming the lullaby Rand's mother had sung in his early days made his horse lift his ears. Rand might have soothed the frightened creature, but his own dismay had grown. He guided his mount along the road, even while his own gaze strayed into the shadows.

Darforth's muttering returned and strengthened until his fervent prayer for Lof Yuel's deliverance became clear.

Sheiltel's horse snorted and sidestepped. The tow-headed guardian subdued the terrified creature with difficulty.

Elcon turned in the saddle and glared at Darforth. "You're frightening the horses."

Darforth's prayer became considerably more subdued.

A gust swept into the grove and rushed through the trees, setting the leaves whispering. The sound lingered so long it couldn't have been natural. The hilt of Rand's sword felt solid against his palm, although it could not help him against this kind of foe. A shimmering maiden emerged from beneath a tree but dissolved the next instant. Haggard faces peered from the shadows and turned away.

Darforth had stopped praying. He turned aside from the road and into the grove.

"What are you doing?" Rand called after him. "Come back!"

The guardian continued unchecked

Craelin's horse reared and pawed the air. "To your swords," he shouted.

Sheiltel no longer protected Elcon's flank. Rand drew his weapon and plunged his horse toward the breach. A mist sprang around him. He could no longer see Elcon or the others. He sensed the Feiann, a silent people who spoke with their minds.

The shimmering maiden walked out of the mist and took hold of his bridle. A smile lit her face. *You are not with them.*

"How can you know anything about me?"

Her smile widened. *I know all about you, Randolph of Pilaer. Come down and walk with me.*

The yearning to obey that came over him could only be an enchantment.

With the ease of long practice, he retreated into the small, still place within himself where Lof Yuel waited.

The shimmering maiden faded to nothing, and the mist dissipated.

Rand cast about, searching. His horse stood in roughly the same place. The keirken grove looked the same, although the shadows had lengthened. Only one thing had changed. The others had vanished.

17

SECRET TUNNEL

Mara caught her breath. The pounding at her door came again. What could have happened? She hurried to answer, but some instinct warned her at the last instant before opening the door. She laid her palm on its worn surface. "Who's there?"

"Open in the name of the queen!" A deep voice vibrated the air.

Mara shrank backwards. Why did this have to happen so close to her escape from the Abbey?

The pounding came again, louder, making the bar across the door shake in its rests.

"Open, I say."

"I cannot at present. I'm afraid." Mara found her voice. "I'm not presentable."

Scrapings sounded within the wall behind her. The abbey's rats seemed determined to make an appearance at the worst time possible. She glanced behind her and started.

A secret passage had opened in the wall. Caerla and Dorann stood within it.

Her aunt put a finger to her lips and gestured for her to join them.

"Pray clothe yourself. The queen desires your presence forthwith."

"Give me a little while," Mara called. She snatched

her cloak from its hook and moved swiftly into the passageway. Caerla closed the door, and it scraped back into place. Her aunt lifted a lanthorn high. "Hurry," she whispered. "The guards will guess about the tunnel when they break down the door and find you gone."

Mara hurried after the lanthorn light, which constantly receded before her. Dorann had moved into rear guard position, and she could hear his boots thudding behind her. Thumping sounds followed them, probably made by the guards searching for her escape route.

Light shone beyond the circle cast by the lanthorn. Caerla climbed a ladder and turned back to offer Mara her hand. "Quick as a mouse with you."

Mara climbed the ladder and stood blinking in the sudden light. Her vision cleared to show her two wingabeasts, saddled and laden for a journey. Dorann went to gather their reins. Mara turned to Caerla." Thank you for your help." She hadn't thought Caerla would understand her leaving, but her aunt had surprised her.

"Turns out I was right to give you that particular chamber. I thought the tunnel might come in handy."

"You seemed so certain that the queen couldn't reach me at the abbey."

"I was, mostly, but that was before the castle gates were breached by that outlaw and Lyneth ran off."

"What's happened? I don't understand."

"Neither do I, but there's no time to discuss it."

With footfalls echoing behind them in the tunnel, Mara took her point. She held back, however. "What of Arillia?"

"She's safe. I hid her in a place the queen will

never search."

"And you?"

Caerla smiled. "Don't worry about me, child. I am better than I have been in a long time."

"But the guards—"

"They won't hurt the king's daughter. Now go, unless you'd like to keep that interview with the queen."

Mara gave her a quick hug and mounted the silver wingabeast that Dorann held for her. He climbed onto his Blue, and they started off beneath the green boughs of the kaba trees.

C3

Dying sunlight tumbled into the river in the place where the water spread wide across cobblestones. Red swept the sky and stained the line of rocks that marched above the shallows in a line that reached the opposite shore. On the first stone of this natural bridge, Lyneth lifted her foot, ready to step to the next. The water sliding beneath her foot created a dizzying sense of movement. She made it to the next rock but put her other foot down in the water. The current pulled at her, and she flailed to avoid going in entirely, then pulled her dripping foot onto the rock. Hael's long stride had carried him partway across. He turned, impossibly balanced on the tip of a stepping stone, while she caught up to him. He led them across, a little way down the grassy bank, and into the forest where mist snagged in tree branches. Or was that smoke? She caught the acrid stench of burning and the crackle of fire.

She hung back, but Hael strode forward. A voice she recognized spoke, and she hurried after him. In a small camp beneath the trees, Kai and one of Torindan's archers sat on fallen logs across a fire. She pushed past Hael. "Kai, it's good to find you safe. The Lof Raelein will be pleased." She would not be present to witness Arillia's joy, a realization that brought tears to her eyes.

"Lyneth," Kai stood, a startled expression on his face. "You look chilled. Won't you warm yourself?"

"Thank you." Shivering, and with her skirts and boots wet, she went to the fire. Its warmth reached her at once, and she sighed.

Kai returned to his seat on the log and tilted a glance toward Hael. "Where is Mara?"

Hael dropped onto the log beside Kai. "She didn't want to leave Cobbleford, at least not with me."

Aerlic glanced up from waxing his bowstring. "But she will with someone else?"

"A Kindren guard escorts her," Lyneth supplied the answer.

"Eathnor and Dorann?" Kai asked.

She shook her head. "Dorann only. Eathnor guards the Lof Shraen."

"Where is Elcon?" Kai snapped out the question.

"Somewhere in the wild lands." Lyneth watched steam curl from her skirts. "He sheltered in a hut, but he may be on the road to Cobbleford now."

"We should leave at first light," Hael tossed a twig into the fire.

"Agreed," Kai said. "We can follow the Lof Raena's trail, provided the weather remains clear."

"And assuming the gate guards allowed her to leave the castle." Hael tossed a twig into the fire.

Kai shot a glance his direction. "Do you think they would not?"

Hael shrugged. "The queen controls the gates these days."

"And Lyneth?" Kai spoke in a soft voice. "Why did she come away from the castle with you?"

Hael's gaze caught Lyneth's. "Events forced her to leave Cobbleford."

"I can't go back." Lyneth blinked away moisture, pierced by her own words. She'd always prided herself on living an honorable life. Had she suffered a lapse of judgment? Hael had given her little choice but to go with him at the outset, but after that she'd taken matters into her own hands. She sighed. For good or ill, she'd made her choice and must abide by it.

Hael stood. "I'll return to my camp and bring my companions back early."

Kai eyed him. "These friends of yours are outlaws, I presume?"

"They're some of the best trackers you'll find in this forest."

"Tell them to stay on the right side of the law," Kai warned. "Anything less, and we'll travel separately. Meanwhile, Lyneth must entrust herself to my protection."

Sleep eluded Lyneth until long after the glowing eyes gathered at the edge of the firelight. How she hated that about the wild lands, but it was now her portion. She could go home to her family but would return in disgrace. She had broken her promise to the Lof Raelein by leaving her service, and she wasn't ready to face her parents' disapproval.

Slumber took her on a shiftless vigil filled with troublesome dreams.

A hand fell on her shoulder, startling her out of sleep. Her heart thudded, and she stared wildly about. She couldn't name her location.

"Wake now." Hael's whisper lured her back from the edge of nightmare. She sat, blinking in the early light. He watched her, his throat moving as he swallowed, then turned away. An urge stirred within Lyneth to call him back. She scolded herself, determined not to let her fascination with Hael confuse her thinking any longer. A way to ignore him must exist. If only she could find it.

Trader and Barret, quickly introduced, came from the outlaw camp and joined them. Garbed in rough clothing and riding shaggy horses, they almost seemed part of the forest. Kai and Aerlic had already broken camp. Hael lifted her onto his horse and mounted behind her. They rode toward the castle.

Hael left Lyneth beneath a weilo that trailed its tresses into the river at a small distance from the bridge. She waited, thus hidden, while her companions searched for Mara's trail. They returned with slumped shoulders and defeat written in their expressions. She joined them on the upstream side of the weilo, standing where no one looking out from the bridge would see her.

Kai ran his hand over his face. "Now what?"

"We should check the postern gate," Aerlic suggested.

Hael shook his head. "That would waste time. After the guards chased me through, they would have secured the breach."

"Mara must still be inside the abbey," Kai burst out.

"There's another explanation," Lyneth said.

"Once, to calm the Lof Raelein, Caerla mentioned an escape tunnel from the abbey." All eyes turned to her. "Sometimes the prioress would forget my presence and speak of things she might otherwise have kept hidden."

"That is a servant's curse and privilege." Kai glanced at Hael. "Where would an escape tunnel come out, I wonder?"

Hael smiled. "That's easy to guess."

Kai arched a brow. "Oh?"

"Anyone escaping the abbey would want to go away from the castle gates."

❦

Inydde glared at her husband, who had no more of a clue of how to rule their kingdom than the wooden lions carved into his throne. She stamped her foot on the thick rug beneath her. "Will you not listen to me?"

"I don't understand." Euryon, gripping the sill of his outer chamber window, spoke with his back to her. "Days before this when you told me Syl Marinda had gone, you expressed no concerns of any nature."

Inydde frowned. She'd thought him too far gone with drink to remember anything she'd said that night. "I've given it more thought since then. We can't afford to have her roaming the countryside." She paced, warming to her subject. "She would remind the people of old tales that bring shame to our family."

He turned and pinned her with his gaze. "What would you have me do?"

She quelled her impatience and summoned a calmer tone of voice. "Will you not send guards to bring Syl Marinda back?"

"Let the poor child go on her way, Inydde. She is our flesh and blood, whether you own it or not."

"I'll not acknowledge a half-caste Kindren as my granddaughter."

"May I ask why you told me Syl Marinda had chosen to leave even while she remained at Cobbleford?"

Euryon's narrowed eyes betrayed that he suspected something. She'd have to be more careful. "I only just learned of her continued presence at the castle. Merwith sheltered her. That kitchen maid needs to be taken in hand."

"Has she crossed you in some way?" Euryon asked in an overly casual tone.

"The gate guards tell me she interfered with them on more than one occasion."

"Do you concern yourself with matters of security these days, Inydde?"

She shrugged. "It was a chance remark I heard in passing." Yes, she'd better watch what she said. She'd hate for anything to happen to Euryon. She should have poisoned his wine long ago. It made no sense that she hadn't, except that she'd grown used to having him around. She'd driven him from their marriage bed after Caerla's birth, having given him two sons and two daughters. That would have to be enough. Besides her determination not to ruin her figure by bearing more children, his consumption of wine had made him mildly repugnant. And yet…she could remember how, in his younger days, the sight of her husband had made her giddy.

A great deal of time had gone by since then. Their sons had grown into fine men. They'd lost both daughters, however. One had given in to her carnal nature, and the other to the fears that consumed her. Whatever Caerla protested, she had chosen to take the veil to avoid being passed over for marriage. It wouldn't have happened due to the family wealth and prestige, although finding a suitor had proven difficult. It was too bad that Rafe, Prince of Darksea, had taken Aewen's betrayal so hard. Caerla's reckless nature had been more suited to his adventurous spirit. She might have tolerated his domineering ways better than the paltry creature he'd married. From all accounts, the woman had walked about like a shade and died in her childbed a mercifully short while after marrying him.

Inydde pushed away her unproductive thoughts. She couldn't afford to allow Euryon the upper hand, but she'd always hidden her intentions behind a pretext of submission. What did it matter? He didn't have the backbone to stand up to her anyway. She drew herself to full height and cast away caution. "If you won't send guards to bring the brat back, I will."

18

AEWEN'S CHAMBER

Caerla faced the guards running out from the tunnel.

The captain reached her first. His sword glinted in the sunlight, pointed at her even while his dark gaze traveled beyond her. "Where has the Kindren princess gone?"

"Go back to your post, Ramnor," Caerla answered. "She is not here."

He sheathed his sword but stood immovable while the rest of his men surrounded her. "I must insist that you come with me."

She drew herself to her full height, which did not come close to matching his. "Will you constrain a daughter of the royal House of Cobbleford and the abbey's prioress, to go anywhere with you?"

He shifted his gaze away from hers. "I speak at the queen's demand."

"Oh, really?" Caerla didn't have to feign her indignation. "Take me first to my father."

"Captain Ramnor." One of the older guards shouldered forward. "Consider well your answer."

"Hold your tongue or I'll cut it out of your head," Ramnor snapped. "You will come with us, Prioress."

Caerla tamped down on the desire to refuse. Ramnor forgot himself, but her mother had fostered his attitude. Since the queen wanted to talk, Caerla might as well give her an earful. One of the guards took her arm, but she pulled free with a glare at him. "I am able to walk without escort." She matched her deeds to her words and started past the captain toward the tunnel.

He caught up to her but stopped short of taking her arm. It cheered her to know that her mother's influence did not hold absolute among the guards. Stone walls closed in, and her boots thumped against the beaten floor of the tunnel while the musty scent of damp earth clogged her nostrils. She left the daylight behind with a feeling of contentment. She'd made a way of escape for her sister's daughter. She could rest in that knowledge. When Aewen had most needed her help, Caerla had allowed infatuation with Rafe to overrule her common sense. Looking back, she could only wonder at Rafe's appeal to her younger self. Rejection by the brutish, loud, and unkind prince of Darksea had spared her a thousand heartaches. If only she could have explained that to Aewen and apologized for hurting her. She sighed. There was no point fretting over the past. Resolving to leave her guilt behind, she picked up her pace. The sooner she put this charade of an inquisition with her mother behind her, the better. She had work that mattered to do. Aewen could never again comfort Cobbleford's poor, but Caerla could do it in her stead.

After reaching the chamber Mara had vacated, the guards escorted Caerla out of the abbey and into the castle. In the queen's parlor, Ramnor nodded to Caerla. "As you requested, here is the culprit who helped the Kindren princess escape."

"Thank you, Captain Ramnor. You'll be rewarded. Now, leave us." Inydde circled Caerla while the guards withdrew.

"Why have the guards brought me to you?" Caerla demanded. "They should have taken me to the king instead."

Mother shook her head. "You have a rebellious streak, like your sister before you."`

"Don't speak against Aewen to me."

"You defend her now, but I recall how readily you once condemned her."

"I didn't know better." Caerla defended herself, but with a sinking feeling. When Mother took this tack, the conversation never went well.

"Oh, is that how you excuse your behavior?" Her mother looked down at her. "I at least had the honesty to inform her of my distaste. You, on the other hand, pretended to love her."

Caerla folded her arms. "I did love Aewen."

"Don't pretend that's true. You sent her away without a goodbye." Her mother's voice rubbed Caerla's emotions raw. "Why not admit the truth? The only person you care about is you."

"Stop it!" Caerla cried, only just preventing herself from covering her ears like a child. "You don't know the first thing about what I think and feel."

"Then tell me. Why did you help Syl Marinda escape Cobbleford?"

"It wasn't the castle she ran from, but your cruelty." Goaded by her mother's chiding, Caerla lashed out with a harsher tone than a prioress should use. "I was happy to help her."

Mother's eyes narrowed to sapphire slits. "You would do well to remind yourself that a prioress is not immune to a queen's displeasure."

Caerla curled her hands into fists at her side.

"Must I remind you that the abbey and the crown remain separate?"

Mother's nostrils flared with anger. "The agreement that makes them so can change at my will. I've a mind to—"

The door flew open and thumped against the wall.

Caerla started, but the tension that went through her eased at the sight of her father. Garbed in the simple garments he wore when relaxing in his chambers, he stood scowling in the doorway. "What's the meaning of this?"

Mother tossed her head. "Your daughter needs taking in hand."

He strode into the chamber and banged the door shut. "I am told the guards compelled my daughter to this chamber by an order you gave."

"Who said that?" Mother asked.

"Never mind." He glanced at Caerla. "Is it true?"

"The guards obeyed my command." Mother spoke before Caerla could answer. "However, Caerla's disobedience was the force that brought her to my chambers in want of discipline."

"What has she done to warrant that?"

Mother arched her eyebrows. "I'm surprised that your informant didn't mention it."

"Perhaps I want to hear it from your lips." Father spoke in a voice laced with emotions Caerla couldn't identify.

"Very well. Your daughter has taken it upon herself to help Syl Marinda escape."

He displayed no surprise. "We have different opinions on whether she should be allowed her freedom."

She paced closer to him. "You are a soft fool."

He lifted his head." However you feel about my opinion, Inydde, it is the one that matters in this kingdom. You will do well to remember that."

She stared at him, her mouth working and her face red. "To make that true, you'd have to stay out of your cups." She turned and slammed from the room.

Father heaved a heavy sigh. "I'm sorry you witnessed that."

Caerla took the steps that carried her to him and laid her head on his chest. "Don't worry about me."

He tucked her under his arm. "Try not to cross your mother."

Her chin came up. "Should I have let her imprison Aewen's child?"

"What do you mean?"

"Mara never left Cobbleford. Mother locked her in the same tower where she'd kept Aewen. She's angry with me because I prevented her from recapturing Mara."

The veins stood out on her father's neck. "Thank you for telling me."

Caerla laid a gentle hand on her father's sleeve. "Mother is not well, I'm afraid, and she seems to be worsening."

He patted her hand. "Seeing Aewen's child would naturally upset her. That's all."

Caerla shook her head. "No, it's more than that. I've seen it happening over time. Send her to the abbey for care."

"I know you mean well, daughter, but the queen would never allow that."

Caerla wanted to bang her fist in frustration. Why did her father so often bow to Mother's wishes? "You may have to intercede to help her."

The light of hope that shone from her father's face warmed Caerla to quick sympathy, but then his expression went flat. "I'll consider it."

Caerla recognized that saying more might erase any good she'd done. "Meanwhile, pray come with me. There's someone wanting to talk to you."

CR

Arillia's hand itched to throw open the shutters, but she refrained. Someone might notice her standing at the window and report her presence in the castle to the queen. Dwelling in a voluntary confinement was far preferable to being cast into a prison of another kind. Why she should be held accountable for the actions of her servant, she didn't know. Lyneth, not her, had run away with an interloper. She frowned. Who had Lyneth's companion been? She had given no hint that such a plan lay in her future. Lyneth had always been such a sweet maiden. It was hard to think she might be different than she'd appeared.

Pacing from the window to the bed then back again gave Arillia something to do. She hadn't spent a full day in hiding but already ached to escape the suffocating chamber. Caerla had given her a basket of needlework, but she couldn't settle her mind to it. All she could think about was the former occupant of this chamber. Aewen had slept in that very bed behind the blue velvet hangings. She'd warmed herself at the marble hearth carved with Westerland's lions and gazed at her reflection in the mirror glass. Her hand had touched the carved wood of the chairs, and her feet the rugs of woven wool. It seemed strange to breathe the air in this room when Aewen never would again.

Arillia put a hand to her forehead and closed her eyes, willing the images away. It seemed a cruel joke that Caerla would choose to hide her here, but her logic had been sound. This was the only chamber in the castle that the queen would not enter. Inydde had made it abundantly clear that she wished to forget the daughter who had brought shame to her. It must gall her that Euryon treasured Aewen's memory and kept her bedchamber as she had left it. She could picture him moving through the chamber, touching a window hanging, picking up a comb his daughter had once used, and gazing at nothing. Did it comfort him to come here or help him release his grief? She knew from the miscarriages she had suffered that the pain of losing a child never faded completely.

Elcon had felt that way about Syl Marinda, she realized in a way she hadn't before. Staying in this chamber brought Aewen to life as a person and not a rival. Arillia had accused Elcon of not laying his first wife's memory to rest, but she needed to do the same thing. Tears tracked down her cheeks, genuine sorrow for the life that had been cut short and for a mother denied the chance to see her baby daughter grow into a maiden.

A key grated at the door. Arillia hid behind the bed hangings.

The door hissed open on well-oiled hinges. Footsteps walked into the chamber. The door clicked shut. "Lof Raelein?" Caerla called softly.

Arillia let out her breath. She wiped tears from her face with a shaking hand, then stepped from her hiding place. "This chamber has me on edge." She stared at King Euryon, who stood beside Caerla with a stricken look on his face. "Your Majesty." She put a hand to her throat and waited for what he would say.

He came forward. "Lof Raelein, I'm pleased to renew our acquaintance, but I regret the circumstances under which we meet."

Arillia stared at the hand he extended, and then placed her own in its warm grasp.

"You have found the accommodations comfortable?" He darted glances about, as if checking that she hadn't moved anything.

"Yes, although I regret intruding upon chambers so special to you."

His gaze returned to her. "I find your safety equally important."

Arillia sighed. "Thank you for setting my mind at ease. I feared you might punish me for the actions of my servant."

"Is that what this is about?" He swung a glance at Caerla, who nodded. He squared his shoulders. "I regret that hiding you has become necessary, Lof Raelein. I will take steps to correct the situation. Meanwhile, you must remain here."

Would Euryon confront the queen who had long cowed him? Arillia lowered her gaze to hide her surprise. "I am in your hands."

"My daughter mentioned that you wished to speak with me."

"Yes, King." Arillia chose her words with care, wary of alienating her newfound ally. "Torindan is in ruins."

"So I understand. I'm sorry such a fate has befallen the High Hold of Faeraven."

She nodded. "I hope it will not also happen here."

"If Cobbleford is attacked, the garrison will defend the castle."

The set of Euryon's jaw communicated the inflexibility Syl Marinda had mentioned, but Arillia tried anyway. "How can one kingdom stand against the combined forces of Pilaer? Westerland needs help as much as Faeraven."

He shook his head. "I'm sorry to mention this, Lof Raelein, but from what I have heard, Faeraven may no longer exist."

Part 3
19

Mara reined in her wingabeast and peered down the road, which stretched endlessly without a sign of human life. If any refugees from Torindan had escaped the warriors, she had yet to come across them. She gusted a sigh.

Dorann drew up beside her. "What's troubling you, Lof Raena?"

She lifted a shoulder. "Maybe this attempt is ill-advised."

"We've only been searching for a couple of days."

"What if no one escaped?" Mara confessed her deepest fear in a rush. "I'll have dragged us both into danger for nothing."

Dorann shook his head. "We'd be in danger no matter what, with the wild lands to survive in or else Norwood, which Freaer's forces have overrun. To the west lie Elder kingdoms that receive Kindren with suspicion at best, and the mountains make a formidable barrier in the east."

"Thank you." She spoke in a dry tone. "Knowing all that makes me feel better."

He smiled. "Wait a little longer, Lof Raena, before

giving up."

"I thought only to change strategy, but I'll take your advice."

She started off again with the tracker beside her. They rode through dappled shadow that would have been pleasant enough if her route hadn't returned her to the place she'd fled. It had not escaped her attention that they could face warriors who would like nothing better than to capture her.

Dorann had put the situation in perspective. What else could she do but keep her promise to her father? She would unite Faeraven or die trying.

Euryon headed the Council of Elder that united the kingdoms, but perhaps she should have bypassed him and appealed to the other Elder kings for help. The thought died at birth. After seeing her father's authority challenged, she would not do such a cruel thing to her grandfather. A glimmer of feeling had passed between her and Westerland's king, like a butterfly emerging to dry its wings in the sun. She regretted its loss, for the bond had touched the child without a mother who still ached within her.

Mustering her courage, she pressed onward. Her wingabeast's hooves clopped the beaten earth in a steady rhythm while its head nodded in time. The early summer sun kissed her skin, and the fresh air bathed her lungs. The piquant aroma of kaba leaves blended at times with the scent of water, the richness of hummus, or the moist smell of stone. They clattered over a bridge above a cascade that pounded the rocks and sprayed mist into the air.

Dorann reined his horse. "Shall we rest, Lof Raena?"

She stopped beside him. "I can't think of a better

place."

They turned aside onto a faint trail that led into a tiny clearing near the pool at the base of the cascade. Mara dismounted and stretched while Dorann watered the wingabeasts. She found a boulder to perch upon out of sight from the bridge, and its warmth spread through her like a blessing. Dorann joined her, bringing elk jerky and waybread. Tired of these staples, she ate enough to soothe her hunger but no more. Mam had worked her hard at the inn but fed her well. The meals at Torindan had been altogether fine, but she preferred simpler fare. How she longed for potatoes swimming in gravy, bruin stew on a bread trencher, and spiced apples. Homesickness for the inn washed over her, and she brushed away tears.

"Now you're weeping," Dorann protested.

He spoke with such masculine horror at the prospect of a weeping maiden that Mara couldn't help but smile. She pulled in a shuddering breath. "I wish I could go home to the inn."

"Ah, yes. And where is that located?"

"In Norwood near the Whitefeather River."

He tilted his head. "You do recall that going there would not be wise."

"Of course I do," she snapped. "That's beside the point."

Dorann ventured no more observations. The tracker had already spoken more than usual.

Mara watched the water splashing into the pool while she wrestled for control of her emotions. When she'd succeeded, she turned back to the tracker. "I'm sorry for being so touchy."

"Don't think of it further." He tossed away a blade of grass he'd been chewing and stood. "If you're ready?"

She smiled and took the hand he extended.

Hoofbeats echoed from above.

Mara followed the tracker into the shade under the trees at the edge of the clearing. The hooves rang sharply on the bridge and thumped along the road, then faded into silence.

"Wait here," Dorann mouthed.

Mara nodded, and he left her. The hair at her nape bristled. She peered about, suddenly aware that she stood alone in the kaba forest.

A branch creaked above her, but she didn't dare look. Had that sound been an indrawn breath? She turned, ready to run.

A person dropped to the ground in front of her with such ease that he barely made a thud. She drew in a breath to scream, but then released it on a sigh. "Shouldn't you be tied up in the outlaw camp?"

Rand laughed. "Such a greeting you give me. I escaped, thanks to you."

"You're welcome. I hated seeing them treat you like a dog."

"All but Trader."

Her respect for the wanderer grew. "How did you find me?"

"By accident, if you must know, while headed for Cobbleford."

"But we hid—"

"The wingabeasts gave you away. I could see them in the clearing from the bridge. I rode past and doubled back on foot. Quickly now, who rides with you?"

"Me," Dorann answered from the path. "Rand, it's good to see you alive and well." He came forward, and they shook hands.

Rand divided a glance between them. "Why aren't you both at Cobbleford?"

Mara frowned. "We overstayed our welcome."

"I'm sorry to hear that." Rand watched her with a sympathetic expression. "I know you hoped for more."

She looked away from him, blinking to clear the tears that started to her eyes. "We're searching for survivors from Torindan but so far haven't met any."

"That's not true." He pointed his two thumbs toward the leather jerkin covering his chest. "Here's one."

"I stand corrected, but we'll need more. I also hope to find my father, although we're not quite certain where he is."

Rand's smile faded. "I can tell you that. I had no choice but to leave him with the Feiann. If I'd lingered in the keirken grove, I would have joined them too."

She stared at him, trying to take in his meaning. "My father? The Feiann?"

"I'm sorry, Mara." He spoke in a softer voice. "I should have broken the news more gently. Your father and the guardians who rode with him have fallen prey to the Feiann. There were others there, too, but they turned away before I could see them clearly. Perhaps that is where the remnant from Torindan have gone."

"But this is terrible!" Mara refused to accept what had happened. "We must free them."

Rand looked away from her. "I know of no way to do that except by surrendering a life for a life."

CR

Mara drew her cloak closer and shifted nearer the watchfire. She normally made her bed back from the flames but within the protective circle of light. For a little while, she would contend with the smoke to gain warmth. Rand's face stood out, bathed in the warm light of the fire. She smiled to think that he'd come back to her, and that he watched over her now. His presence was enough to keep her awake, but something else disturbed her slumber.

She'd heard stories of the Feiann while growing up at the inn. Always, the tales painted the people native to Elderland as an unrelenting force with which no man could reckon. Those who succumbed to their illusions rarely saw freedom again. The few who did described long stretches of wasted time in which they'd dwelt in confusion.

Mara couldn't bear to think of such a fate for her father. The solution seemed obvious but too hard.

She slipped into a restless state between sleep and wakefulness. A chill crept over her, so subtle that she didn't recognize its threat until the first tentacles of darkness curved around her soul. She tried to pull away but the darkness gripped her so hard she could barely draw breath. The fetid smell of death filled her nostrils. With panic jabbering across her mind, she couldn't think or find the way of retreat she relied upon. She struggled to free herself, but that only entrapped her more hopelessly. She moaned.

"Mara, look at me," Rand called from above her.

She jerked her eyes open, met by the sight of his moonlit face. He held her gaze, and she felt the brush of his soul touch. She clung to it.

"Evil grows when you fight it." Rand's voice penetrated the fog surrounding her. "You know how to shield yourself."

Mara turned inward and found Lof Yuel waiting. The darkness slid away. She sat up with shudders wracking her body.

Rand pulled her into his arms and stroked her hair. "That wasn't pleasant."

She gave a shaky laugh at his understatement. "No."

He tilted her chin, and she lifted her face toward his.

"Is everything all right?" Dorann asked from across the fire.

Mara pushed away from Rand at the same instant he released her. "Yes," they answered together.

Dorann smiled. "I'm glad to hear it." He settled down again. "Sleep while you may, Mara. Day will break soon."

She took his hint and laid down. The rest of the night passed in dreams that came as a series of images. She stood at the edge of a cliff with a wilderwen roaring at her back. Her father lay on his funeral bier with the rose of Rivenn between his folded hands. Rand reached to her from the back of a wingabeast, but their clasped hands separated.

Mara awoke more refreshed than she should have after the night she'd spent. She lifted her face to the morning sun and breathed in the crispness of a new day. She would miss such simplicity, if the Feiann allowed her to remember it at all. The confusion of the night had fled, and she made up her mind.

She found Rand packing for the day's journey and placed a hand on his arm. "When we reach the keirken grove—" She broke off, unable to continue with a lump swelling her throat.

Rand went still.

Tears gathered in her eyes. She dashed them away, but they returned. She heaved a breath and forced the words out. "I'll surrender myself to free my father."

CR

Kai picked up a stone and turned it over, revealing its charred side. "They made camp here."

Hael watched him from beside Lyneth, with Aerlic and the other outlaws ranged about them. "We can't be far behind."

Kai hefted the stone. "It's still warm." He released the rock, which landed with a thud. "If Lof Yuel smiles upon us, we should catch them soon."

"I'll be glad to see the end of this chase," Aerlic attested.

Kai led his wingabeast up the scant trail to the road, where he could mount without being brushed off by low-hanging branches. From the thrashing sounds behind him, the others followed.

The thump of a hoof on the road warned him to stop before breaking clear of the tree cover. The underbrush parted, and Kai found himself staring at four of Cobbleford's guards. Surprise rendered him speechless, but he had no need to cry out, for the scrape of Hael's knife told him that the outlaw had seen the guards. More of the contingent waited on the road, including a tall man with dark hair and eyes who wore the insignia of a captain. He sat astride a sleek horse.

"Here's two Kindren, Cap'n!" A red-cheeked guard holding a sword bellowed. "And some outlaws to go with 'em." He divided a glare between Kai and those following him. "Drop your weapons and come out slowly if you want to keep your hides."

"You'll have to come for us!" Hael sang out before anyone could obey. Kai hadn't fully understood until now how traveling with an outlaw could create problems. A glance behind revealed Trader and Barret with bows ready.

"Happy to do so." The ruddy guard grinned. He rode to the side and a line of archers nocked arrows to their bowstrings.

"Wait!" Kai called. "I need to consult with my companions."

The ruddy guard gestured his mocking agreement.

Kai turned around and glared at Hael. "Have you lost all reason? The guards outnumber us three to one, in case you haven't noticed."

Hael's eyes gleamed. "I don't know about you, but I'd rather take an arrow than rot in Cobbleford's dungeon under the queen's tender mercies."

"Why trade what might prove temporary sorrow for the permanence of the grave?"

Hael's jaw tightened. "I'll not surrender to any man."

"Is your pride at stake, then? You'll lose it quickly while in your death throws." Kai glanced at Lyneth, staring back at him with wide eyes, and wished he hadn't had to speak so frankly. "I assume you're not in favor of this lunacy."

"I'd rather remain alive," she answered in breathless tones.

Kai nodded to Aerlic. "What about you?"

"As always, Kai, you have my loyalty. I've never regretted following you."

Kai faced forward to address the captain of the guard. "We seem to have a fundamental disagreement on how to proceed."

The captain turned his horse toward the line of guards. "Hold your fire!" He wheeled back around. "I normally wouldn't trouble to save a Kindren, but the queen may have questions for you. Surrender your weapons and step away from those outlaws so we can pick them off."

Kai laid down Sword Rivenn beside his dagger. He'd failed in his duty to keep the great sword safe.

"That's a pretty piece of cutlery," the ruddy guard crowed. He reached for the sword with eager hands.

"Bring it to me," the captain commanded. "The queen will want to claim such a weapon."

While the guard obeyed, Aerlic came forward and laid down his bow. He stepped back to stand beside Kai. The clatter of weapons being laid on the ground sounded behind Kai, and he glanced behind to discover the outlaws divesting themselves. His gaze caught Hael's.

The guards surrounded Kai, tied his hands in front of him and left a length of cord with which to pull him along. Flecht and Argalent screamed and reared with their wings batting but did not escape the lassos flung by the guards. The horses received similar treatment.

The captain sent his horse, with its prancing gait, forward and looked down on the ruddy guard. "Arctar, take a handful of men and deliver the prisoners to Cobbleford."

"Happy to." Arctar's face spread in his annoying smile. "They can run all the way, then cool their heels in the dungeon while they await the queen's pleasure."

"Give this into the queen's hand." He tossed

Sword Rivenn by its hilt, and Arctar caught the weapon. "Tell her that I'll bring the Kindren princess forthwith."

◈

Mara dismounted from her wingabeast, which had taken to fidgeting, and gazed across the forest. The bluff above the site they'd chosen for tonight's camp gave onto views in all directions. The shores of Maer Ibris glinted in the last rays of the sun beyond the green canopy in the west. A slash through the forest north of them betrayed the course of the road from Cobbleford. To the east, lofty mountains reared their heads. A small distance southward, the keirken grove floated like an island in the mist. Mara stared at the dark trees as if they might give some clue to the secrets they hid.

Rand joined her and dismounted to stand beside her. "We shouldn't linger up here. The fact that we can see so well should alert us to the fact that others might spot us as easily."

"You're right, but I hate to leave. The sun still shines up here, but the forest already forms night shadows." She nodded to the keirken grove. "Tomorrow we'll reach it."

"I'm not convinced we should take you there."

"Can't you see? My father's freedom matters more than mine. He is Lof Shraen and should lead Faeraven, not me. Under my father's guidance, Freaer might be defeated, whereas I have no idea how to attain such a goal."

"I'm not entirely sure what trading a life for a life

means to the Feiann. I overheard that in my early days and shouldn't have passed it along as fact. The Feiann could kill rather than keep you, or maybe trick you into remaining with them without giving up your father."

"Don't try to talk me out of this. If I don't try, my father may be lost forever."

He sighed. "I understand wanting to help a parent—I would have laid my own life down to free my mother – but this isn't a good idea. We don't know what will happen, and there's no one to tell us."

Mara clasped her arms around herself. "Don't you think I've already thought through every possibility? I'm sorry, Rand, but for the chance of saving my father and possibly Faeraven, I'm willing to accept the dangers."

He gave a sad smile. "Perhaps there are risks for both of us."

"I don't want you or Dorann to come into the grove with me. There's no point in endangering you."

"That's not what I meant."

The raggedness of his voice alarmed her, and she turned to ask him to explain.

He caught her against him, his kiss chasing the question from her lips. Taken off balance, Mara held onto him. He smelled of the forest and tasted of the berries they'd grazed along the road. Her hands crept up his chest and around his neck. His skin warmed her hands, and she pulled him closer to better seal his mouth to hers. She'd never behaved this way before, and her mind registered shock even as her senses overpowered her common sense. He broke the contact, breathing heavily. "I promised myself I wouldn't do that again. It's—unwise."

"Is kissing me so odious?" she asked in a tone of

indignation, although she agreed with his assessment.

He groaned and took her back into his arms, giving a thorough answer to her question.

She summoned the strength of mind to step away. "You'll make me regret my decision."

He stroked her hair. "Your father wouldn't want you to surrender yourself for him."

She knew the truth of that but couldn't let it sway her.

20

A Life for a Life

Mara's heart pounded as she stared into the keirken grove in the morning light. No flicker of movement betrayed that anyone dwelt within the trees. If not for the reluctance of her wingabeast to move forward and her uneasiness at entering the grove, she would not mark this place as more than another section of the road.

Rand rode beside her with his jaw set, and Dorann made up their rear guard.

She'd caught the tracker's disapproving glances, but he'd made no attempt to change her mind. Perhaps he had figured out that any argument he made would not sway her. She reined in her wingabeast before the grove could close around her and turned to Rand. With his hair tousled and his chin unshaven, he had never looked more desirable. "I'll say goodbye to you here." Her voice wavered.

"That you will." He caught her wingabeast's bridle and glanced back to Dorann.

The tracker rode forward and took the other side of her wingabeast's bridle.

"What's this?" she cried.

"Do you think I would let harm come to you?" Rand asked. "Since you insist on completing this foolish errand, I'll go in your place." He ripped the reins from her grasp and passed them to Dorann.

"What are you doing?" she spluttered. "Let me go at once."

Rand's jaw tightened. "Not on my life would I allow you to come to harm while I walk free."

"Did you both hatch this scheme?" she asked, although the answer was obvious.

Rand dismounted and gave his reins into Dorann's hands. His gaze swept over Mara and lingered on her face. "I love you, Mara." He turned and walked away from her.

Mara pulled in a painful breath. "Wait!"

He continued toward the grove.

"I love you, too." She shouted the words she'd resisted saying.

He turned and his gaze burned into hers. "You're above my touch, Lof Raena."

"I was raised a serving wench."

He smiled. "You are a Lof Raena now." He started into the grove.

"Come back!" She wailed the words. Sacrificing herself would be less painful.

Rand neither broke his stride nor turned back to her.

Mara shifted her weight, ready to swing her leg over the wingabeast and run after him.

"Don't try it," Dorann warned. "I can run faster than you."

"Remember that I'm your Lof Raena. If you dared to stop me, I could have you arrested for treason."

"That's true." Dorann frowned, but then brightened. "I also serve the Lof Shraen, however. I know what he would want me to do."

She'd lost sight of Rand while arguing with

Dorann. Scanning the road yielded nothing. Rand had moved too far ahead.

"Lof Raena, we should wait in better cover." Without waiting for her reply, Dorann led the wingabeasts toward a stand of weilos at the edge of the wetlands.

Understanding his intent to hide where they could see anyone who emerged from the grove, she made no objection. The wind had gone out of her, leaving her no energy to stand up to dominating males. She blamed Rand for Dorann's sudden defection. The tracker knew his own mind but had never crossed her will before. Stricken by the thought that she sounded like Arillia in one of her moods, she resolved to forget Dorann's offense. It would be hard to arrest him with no guardians anyway.

Hooves clopped in the distance, and a company in the blue and gold of Westerland swung into view on the road from Cobbleford. A shout arose from the guards, and their horses broke into a run.

Mara's breath hitched. "They've seen us."

Dorann veered away from the weilos and set off across the wetlands. Mara leaned over her wingabeast's neck and held on throughout the shifting course. Arrows shot past on either side, but none came close. The reason for the tracker's weaving came clear.

They skirted the bank of a channel through the bog. The bank gave way, canting Mara's wingabeast sideways. Mara held onto the pommel as cold mud engulfed her leg to the thigh. The great wings batted, one splattering her with muddy water. The wingabeast lifted upward on its dry side, but this only tilted them further. The mud made a sucking sound and dragged at her skirts. Mara let out a cry.

"Hold on!" Dorann's shout penetrated her panic. Mara ground her teeth and made sure her feet remained in the stirrups. She retained her hold on the wingabeast's straining neck but also gripped its side with her knees. The terrified creature bucked and heaved, then went still, panting.

The hoofbeats pounded nearer, shaking the mud.

"Hold onto me." Dorann reached for her.

Mara tried to latch onto his arms, but the wingabeast's tilt made it impossible. "It's no use."

"I'll try to move closer."

"There's no time! Save yourself."

Dorann's expression gave his opinion of that idea. He drove his wingabeast closer to the edge and reached out again.

Mara gripped his arms.

The tracker clasped her forearms and exerted steady pressure.

The bog held onto her like a living thing.

Mara moaned at the strain.

With a sucking sound, the mud released her.

Dorann caught her and swung her to the ground. "Hurry! You can ride Rand's wingabeast."

She held back. "What about mine?"

"We'll have to leave her. She can't fly with that wet wing."

"I can't abandon her in the bog."

"Don't worry about her dying. The guards won't pass up a chance to claim one of Torindan's wingabeasts."

The Westerland horses huffed as they neared.

"Lof Raena, would you please hurry?" Dorann spoke with admirable calm.

The leader of the guards stopped well back from

the bank. "Halt in the name of Queen Inydde."

CR

Rand put one foot before the other and walked away from the maiden he loved. He'd meant every word he'd uttered, including that she was out of his reach. It would be better for Mara if he didn't return. He wouldn't wish such a fate on himself, however, and hoped for a better outcome.

His footsteps crunched on branches that had fallen across the way with none to clear them. Light streamed into the leafy bower from above and fell in beams that shifted as if spirits dwelt within them. He tamped down on such imaginings, needing no extra reasons for wanting to flee. The place where Elcon and his guardians had vanished came into view. Rand made it his destination. Perhaps he would find a clue to their whereabouts that he'd missed before, something that might save him from his dreadful purpose. He alone had escaped the fate of his companions the other time he'd come here. It seemed somehow fitting that he should return.

He'd tried to help after discovering Elcon and his guards missing, an impossible task under the circumstances. After almost succumbing to the Feiann, he'd put distance between himself and the grove. He'd set off for Cobbleford, where he'd hoped to find Kai. Coming across Mara had been a blessed coincidence, although it had brought him back here.

The shimmering maiden he remembered stepped out from one of the light beams and floated toward him. Mist swirled, closing them in together.

You came back to offer a life for a life? She laughed, the tinny sound grating his nerves.

"I wish to surrender myself in exchange for Elcon's freedom, but you seem already to know that."

She smiled. *Don't be angry that I read your mind. It is the way of all Feiann.*

"Your *way* intrudes on others."

Which is better? To hide lies or expose truth? The Feiann do not shelter unspoken secrets as you do, son of Freaer.

"How do you know my father?"

The Dark Lord is known by us.

"That's no answer," he shot back.

It is an answer, but not the one you seek. You wonder whether we belong to the Dark Lord.

"Well?"

"We exist apart from him, but we often serve him.*

Rand shook his head as if that might clear his confusion. The sooner he ended this interview, the better. He peered into the mist surrounding him. "Where is Elcon?"

"The Lof Shraen of Faeraven is not well. We have made him comfortable, but we don't expect him to live."

"Take me to him." Rand challenged her.

She shook her head. *That is not possible. I have tried twice to bring you into our world, but you will not come. Instead, you vanish from sight into a hidden place within your soul."

The temptation to give in wove around Rand with invisible threads. He broke free of the spider web they formed, unwilling to surrender.

She lifted a shoulder. *You do not make a suitable candidate.*

He would be glad about that, except that it left Elcon in the hands of the Feiann. "Who would?" he asked against his better judgment. He shouldn't linger with her.

She slid her arms around his neck and lifted her beautiful face to gaze into his eyes. "The person who will not yield to the desires of the flesh. Among those who have tried to prove themselves, we have not found one."

He tried to back away, but she held him fast with a strength greater than her frame. Her eyes glittered, and she lifted her lips to hover a breath from his.

He brought an image of Mara to his mind and the tingle of desire the Feiann woman had stirred left him. "Let me go."

She frowned, but then smiled. The planes of her face softened and blended, changing into Mara's. He stared at her, searching for the flaw in her deception, and found none. *Kiss me, Rand.* Mara's voice whispered in his mind.

He cupped her head and tangled his fingers in her hair.

The lips so close to his own, smiled.

He pulled her head backward, away from his. "You make of yourself a figure of shadow and light and dare to take Mara's shape? She is so much more than you."

His tormenter stepped away from him and morphed again, this time into a hideous crone.

He winced. "Is that your true appearance?"

Do you blame me for putting on the semblance of youth and beauty when I have neither? I am as old as time. She put her hands over her haggard face. *Leave me.*

"Release the Lof Shraen, and I will go."

She smiled, showing gapped teeth. *Elcon wishes to remain.*

"He wouldn't, if you hadn't crippled his soul."

Fury gouged lines in her face. "You will go, never to return, or die where you stand."

Rand backed, turned, and ran without stopping until he broke free of the shadows into the light. A black-haired Elder stepped into Rand's path as he left the shadows of keirken grove. "Wait."

Rand halted, his hand straying to his sword hilt. "Who are you and what do you want with me?"

"My name is Emmerich, and I'm headed for Cobbleford."

"I'm Rand of Rivenn." He named his adopted raven rather than Pilaer.

"Well met, Rand. Will you walk beside me for a while?"

He shook his head. "Not if you're going in that grove, thanks all the same."

Emmerich nodded. "You are wise to flee from evil."

"So you know that the Feiann dwell there but plan to go into it anyway?"

"My reason concerns Elcon."

Rand stared at Emmerich. Was he, too, a trick of the Feiann? Why else would he enter the keirken grove naming Elcon as his reason? Rand alone had escaped the day that Elcon and the others had succumbed, and he'd told no one save Mara and Dorann.

"You're wondering whether you can trust me."

That Emmerich spoke like a Feiann, with knowledge of his thoughts, did not reassure Rand. "I'll leave you to your journey and continue mine." He walked around Emmerich, keeping a wary eye on him all the while. The man did not carry a sword but might possess other weapons.

"Don't fear me, Rand." Emmerich remained where he stood but turned to watch him pass. "I have nothing to do with the Feiann."

"How do you know my thoughts, then?"

Emmerich smiled. "They aren't hard to read."

Rand nodded toward the keirken grove. "Stay away from there unless you want to join the Feiann."

"I haven't come for that purpose." Emmerich met Rand's gaze unflinchingly. "I've come to free those in their power."

Rand halted. "How do you know about Elcon?"

"He called out to me when it happened."

"But, how?"

"By a means much like the shil shael. Come into the keirken grove with me and you will see the Feiann banished and their captives freed."

Rand hesitated. He would dearly like to witness such a thing.

"Don't let fear hold you back."

Emmerich understood far too much. "All right." Rand turned back into the keirken grove, not entirely sure he hadn't taken leave of his wits. Why he should trust this stranger on short acquaintance made no sense. He only knew that he did.

The shadows beneath the trees seemed darker than before, but the light penetrating the canopy shone brighter. A breeze skipped at their feet and lifted the leaves in its path, its freshness driving away the fetid breath of decay.

Emmerich stopped in the place Elcon had disappeared. "Elvina, come out."

The shimmering maiden formed in the road before him. *Why do you summon me, Lord of Light?*

"You know the reason."

Don't take away all the souls I own.

"I will free those who wish it."

She sighed. *Most won't. They prefer the pleasures of their own minds to your truth.*

"We will see."

She glared at Rand. *Why do you bring that one back with you?*

"He has chosen to walk beside me, and that is reason enough."

I promised to harm him if he returned. You will have to pay the price to prevent it.

"Willingly, and for all those in need of deliverance."

Her eyes gleamed. *You will suffer all the more. I will see to it.*

"So be it."

"Wait!" Rand cried. "What are you doing?"

Emmerich gave him a sad smile. "What you could not."

Come then. We will begin.

"Agreed." Emmerich placed his hand in hers.

"No!" Rand bellowed. "I won't let you do this."

"Why do you object? You were willing to surrender yourself."

"I didn't understand what that meant."

Elvina scowled at Rand. *He's a lot of trouble. Are you sure you want to pay his fee?*

"I am."

"That is your choice." Elvina waved a hand, and mist crowded around them. She led Emmerich off the road and beneath the trees. Rand followed behind them with misgivings. Shimmering figures ran out of the mist and circled them, more of the Feiann who inhabited the grove. Others watched from the shadows, and he recognized faces of guardians he had known. The light had gone from their eyes, and they scowled with mistrust.

Having fallen behind, Rand hurried to catch up. Emmerich now stood on a wide stump with his clothing removed and a sheet wound about him. Those watching howled with laughter. They hurled insults at him. Some pelted him with stones. Through it all, Emmerich stood silent, his head bowed.

Rand's thoughts swarmed. He tensed, ready to storm through the crowd and rescue Emmerich. Surely he could defeat these insubstantial people who refused to speak, fought with their minds, and hid in mists. Even as he sought for ways to intervene, he knew the futility of doing so. Emmerich had made his choice.

Elvina held up a hand, and waited for the crowd to quiet. *Few are willing to pay for a life with a life, and only one who has ever presented himself possesses the necessary virtue.*

Rand frowned. He had been willing, but the second requirement had eliminated him. The dark deeds he'd committed stared at him. He'd destroyed innocent animals during his warrior training to satisfy the bloodlust of spectators, never mind that he'd been pressured to do so. He'd accepted the mission to take Mara's life without questioning whether he should. His father had richly deserved death when he'd attempted to assassinate him, but that judgment had not been his to execute. The fact that his brother's death had been an accident did not eradicate his guilt for holding the sword that killed him. He could argue that as Freaer's illegitimate son, he'd had little chance of leading a blameless life, but these choices had been his to make.

We can find no flaw in Emmerich, known to the Elder as the DawnKing of Prophecy, called Shraen Brael in the Kindren tongue. His death will atone for all the souls held captive here and across the entire world. Bring the captives.

Rand started forward with his hand to his sword, knowing only that Elvina had spoken of Emmerich's death. He had to do something.

A man with dark hair and a sword of light blocked his way. *Go no farther.*

"Let me pass," Rand warned the Feiann guardian.

A maiden with flowing hair joined the man. *This is the one Elvina could not beguile.* She gave him a brilliant smile. *I've a mind to try.*

You'd be wasting your time with that mark on his forehead, the guard answered. "The One who sees, knows, and loves all has set him apart.*

"What are you talking about?" Rand demanded. "There's no mark on my forehead."

The Feiann guard jerked his head to the west. *Go and find the Pool of Truth, if you want to know—*

Thumping sounds drowned out the rest of his words. Elcon, Craelin, and the other guardians Rand had traveled with stood among a group of ragged Kindren he didn't know. They had formed two lines with a passage between them. Feiann moved among them, placing clubs made of branches in their hands. These they thumped on the ground. Flanked by guards, Emmerich walked toward them.

"No." Rand uttered the word barely above a whisper. With a sense of horror crawling over him, he stumbled toward the captives.

Halt. The guard appeared before him. From the waist down his body wavered like a reflection in water, but the sword he pointed at Rand's chest seemed solid enough. *Take another step and you will feel the heat of a Feiann blade.*

Emmerich walked into the passage between the captives. A blow caught him across the stomach, and he doubled over. Another slammed into his face, and blood spurted from his nose.

"What are you doing?" Rand drew his blade and stumbled forward. "Stop this!" The guard swung his sword, which slashed into Rand. He dropped to his knees, groaning while fire consumed him from within. He stared in disbelief at his side, neither bleeding nor showing a wound.

The guard stood over him. *Take that as a warning blow. The next will hurt far worse.*

Emmerich had fallen, and the captives descended on him, landing blow after blow without mercy.

"What have you done to make them attack their rescuer?" Rand squeezed out the question between painful breaths.

The guard smiled. *Do you like the irony? It only took a small deception to hide the truth from them. They don't know what they're doing but believe they protect themselves from a threat.*

Emmerich lay still as blows continued to rain on him. Rand winced. No mortal could have withstood such an assault. The captives dropped their clubs and stared at Emmerich's body with confusion. The gruesome scene vanished behind a veil of tears. Rand swallowed hard. "Release the body to me for burial." It was the least he could do for the man who had taken his place.

The guard gave a nod. *Elvina may agree to that, although there may be a cost.*

"Don't try to deceive me, Feiann. How can any fee remain?" Rand watched Elcon drop his club and stare at the blood on his hands. "Emmerich must surely have paid every one."

21

DEATH AND LIFE

A guard opened the queen's parlor door before Mara, and two others pushed her into the chamber. She didn't resist, having learned on the journey back to Cobbleford that such attempts only brought pain. Any hope that her connection to the royal family would shield her from mistreatment had fled. With her hands tied in front of her and her feet bound, she'd been thrown over a horse's saddle and lashed down.

Dorann had suffered worse, having been made to keep up with the horse guards all the way to Cobbleford Castle. The guards had separated her from the tracker at the gatehouse. She put a finger to the cut on the side of her mouth, which she had earned by protesting Dorann's removal to the dungeon.

The guards retreated to wait beside the door while Queen Inydde arose from a carved and gilded chair padded in gold velvet. "You've returned to us after all, haven't you?" Her hair coiffed in braids about her head and clad in a rose velvet tunic with a golden chain at her waist, she matched the elegance of the chamber that housed her. Tapestries in vibrant colors hung on walls paneled in kaba wood. The warm reddish tone of the wood stood in contrast to her graying black hair and erect posture.

Refusing to be cowed by the queen or her

surroundings, Mara met the icy stare directed at her. "Not by choice."

"Your agreement was not a requirement." The queen swept her sapphire gaze over Mara. "What have you been doing? Rolling in the mud?"

She must have spoken to Mara's mother in the same tone of voice when her hair wanted brushing. "My wingabeast suffered a mishap in the marsh."

"You're a mess, much like your mother when she wandered afield." Inydde's forehead puckered. "That's where she began to go wrong. Spending time among the peasants made her strange."

"Don't say anything against my mother to me," Mara snapped, past caring how Inydde might respond. All her muscles ached, and she felt every bit of mud on her skin. She needed a bath and the chance to comb the snarls from her hair. After that, she would very much like to sleep somewhere comfortable without being locked inside a chamber. Sadly, she doubted any of that would happen.

The queen pressed forward and stared into her eyes. "Your mother deserved what she received."

"That's a horrible thing to say. No natural mother would speak so ill of her child."

"What do you know of anything?" Inydde strode about as she ranted, her nostrils flaring. "You've never borne a child, I'll warrant. Aewen became a grief to my bones. She shamed our family in front of the Elder nations."

"Can you never forgive my mother in her youth?" Mara spoke softly, moved to unexpected pity for this broken woman. "Surely now that she is in her grave, she can hurt you no longer."

"Ah, but that's not true." Inydde halted before her.

"She still haunts me at night in my dreams. And now she sends you to reproach me."

"Queen Inydde..." Mara paused, choosing her words with care. "I fear your soul has lost its way. Has no one suggested such a thing to you?"

"Who would dare but Aewen's daughter?" Inydde shook as she laughed. "I should thank you for reminding me why you must be locked away forever."

Mara stared at her. "I've done nothing to earn such a thing."

Inydde retreated to her chair and picked up a drinking horn. "Your resemblance to your mother is reason enough." She waved a hand. "Take her to the tower."

A guard came up beside Mara and grasped her upper arms. She glanced into the face of Merwith's brother and read sympathy. "Come along," he murmured.

She pulled away. "Will you really cast me back into that wretched tower?" She appealed more to him than to Inydde.

Merwith's brother gazed at her with sorrow in his eyes but did not speak.

The door burst open and crashed against the wall. Guards with swords drawn strode into the chamber. King Euryon followed behind them. "Members of the castle guard whom the queen has summoned, you will remove yourself from this chamber immediately or suffer the consequences." Queen Inydde stood to her feet. "What's the meaning of this intrusion? Captain Ramnor!"

"Move at your peril, Ramnor. I hereby remove you from duty as captain of the guard and name Delfort your replacement." Euryon glared at the queen.

A brief skirmish ended with Captain Ramnor and several others withdrawing from the chamber at the point of swords, including one belonging to Merwith's brother, who had traded sides as the fighting began.

Euryon flung his arm in a dismissive gesture. "Take them to the dungeon." Inydde swept toward her husband. "I see no reason for such drastic action."

The king's jaw tightened. "You will not interfere with my decision. I've allowed you to have your way for too long." He held out an arm to Mara. "Come, child."

Mara held back in indecision. When had his change of heart come about?

"She's as willful as her mother."

"Don't speak ill of the dead, Inydde." Euryon took a step toward Mara. "There's no need to fear me, Syl Marinda."

Mara went to her grandfather, and his arms closed around her.

"You were always a soft fool." Inydde watched them with a look of loathing, having completely lost her elegant veneer.

"Will you despise all tender feeling?" Euryon looked away from her. "Guards, seize the queen."

"Have you lost your wits?" Inydde demanded in an outraged tone, but fear edged her voice.

The guards stared at their king with surprised faces. "Seize the queen." He repeated with emphasis. "You will answer for any failure to execute my command."

Merwith's brother strode forward, followed by several others. Inydde shrank as they neared her. "Don't be ridiculous."

"You have lied about Syl Marinda's whereabouts

while keeping her imprisoned, and you now stand in direct disobedience to your king's wish to allow her to leave Cobbleford Castle unchallenged." King Euryon turned to Delfort. "Bring in the prioress."

The door to the chamber opened, and Caerla walked toward her father.

Inydde's eyes narrowed. "What does our daughter have to do with this?"

"Silence!" Euyon's face went red. "I could throw you into the dungeon for treason, but I've chosen to grant mercy. You will remain in confinement within the abbey under the custody of Pioress Caerla until I decide otherwise."

Dismay settled on both the queen's and Caerla's faces. Caerla bowed her head to the king. "I am at your service, Your Majesty."

Inydde gave voice to her frustration all the way down the corridor.

"Take care of your mother, Caerla." Euryon murmured.

Caerla lowered her gaze. "I doubt it will be easy, but I promise to do my best." She glanced toward Mara. "Shall I make up your room at the abbey?"

"My granddaughter will remain at the castle as my guest." Euryon turned to Mara with a hesitant look on his face. "That is, if you choose to honor me with your company."

"Thank you, Grandfather." Mara smiled. "I'll stay until I've rested. I wish it could be longer, but I have an errand to complete. I must beg freedom for my guide, Dorann. The queen's guards cast him into the dungeon when we arrived."

"He shall be released," her grandfather promised. "Also, let me know if I can help with your errand."

Mara looked at him in surprise. "What, may I ask—" She hesitated, unsure how to continue.

"You're wondering what caused my change of heart."

She nodded, grateful he had voiced her question.

"I won't deny that I've made my share of mistakes in this life." He shook his head. "The one I regret most was not being stronger with Inydde. If I hadn't given in so much, Aewen might still draw breath."

"You can't know whether that's true."

"I don't know that it isn't. Learning that Inydde planned to harm you forced me to decide whether I wanted to make the same mistake again. My actions make the answer clear."

ɔ⃝

Kai closed his eyes and leaned his head back against the cold stone wall of the dungeon cell he shared with Aerlic and the outlaws. Lyneth had not been cast into the dungeon, but he didn't know how she fared. His world had shrunk to the dull routine of waking and sleeping, with occasional meals of disgusting gruel and water the only relief from eternal boredom.

Kai summoned Shae's image, not gazing at him with sad eyes as he'd seen her last. Instead he pictured her seated on a rock at the edge of the river combing her hair with no hint of beguilement in her posture. She'd utterly captivated him. Thoughts of Shae helped push the darkness from his mind. He held to them and to his faith in Lof Yuel. The High One would not forsake them while they dwelt in this forgotten place.

Hael paced behind him. "We should never have laid down our weapons." Regret laced his voice. "Look where it's landed us."

Kai dragged himself into the present with reluctance. "Better here than the grave."

"I hope you're right about that." one of the outlaws remarked. Hael's footsteps stopped behind Kai. "Right now there doesn't seem to be much difference between the two."

Kai turned to face him. "I'll admit that being penned up like this this isn't easy, but where breath survives, so can hope."

Hael's lips quirked. "Has anyone ever told you how annoying your optimism can be? The sorry truth is that precious few ever leave Cobbleford's dungeon unless they find that grave you'd like to cheat." Hael went back to pacing.

Kai looked out again at the unchanging view of the corridor ranked by cells. He shut his eyes and recalled the touch of Shae's hand at his waist while he'd carried her on his wingabeast. They'd ridden well together, balancing for the wingabeast's shifts and for one another. The old longing to hold her rose within him, and he set aside his memories before sorrow could overwhelm him.

A door rasped open and clanked shut. Through the bars of the cell, Kai could see Dorann walking toward him down the corridor, flanked by guards carrying torches. Kai shielded his eyes from the torchlight and backed away. The key grated in the lock, and the opening widened enough for them to shove the tracker inside.

"Here's another Kindren to join your party." One of the guards guffawed. The door banged into place amid jeering laughter. The torchlight moved away.

Kai bent over Dorann, who had fallen. "Are you all right?"

"A bit winded—" Dorann panted. "I can't recommend…keeping up with horses."

"The *dogs*!" Aerlic cried. "Did they make you do that? Here, lean against the wall. I'd bring you water but our supply is gone."

"They poured some…over me."

Kai touched Dorann's soaked head. "That would cool you, at least."

Dorann mumbled something incoherent and fell silent.

Kai felt the pulse at the tracker's throat. "He's asleep, I think."

Aerlic crouched beside him. "I'll watch over him."

Kai straightened, leaving the archer to protect Dorann from rats. He'd relieve him from the duty later. No doubt, the tracker wouldn't wake any time soon.

The guards came for Dorann while he still slept. A bucket of cold water changed that situation.

Kai, already shivering in the dank cell, tried to avoid being dampened further, an impossible task in close confinement.

One of the guards dragged Dorann to his feet and propelled him through the cell door. "You're to be freed by order of the king."

"What about my friends?" Dorann looked over his shoulder. "They don't belong in a dungeon."

"They don't deserve their freedom. I doubt you do either. Now move along before the king changes his mind."

Kai regained his wits enough to call after the tracker. "And what of Mara?"

"She's here at the castle." Dorann's answer floated back. "I don't know where they took her."

"Quiet, you," a gruff voice warned. The door clanked shut.

Kai blew out a breath. "What do you suppose happened? Why would they put Dorann in the dungeon only to free him the same day?"

Aerlic came to stand beside Kai. "It's puzzling,"

Hael joined them on Kai's other side. "Could it have anything to do with Mara?"

Kai considered the idea. "It's possible she's influenced her grandfather."

"I would once have said that couldn't happen." Hael shrugged. "Now I'm not so sure."

∞

Rand rode through the driving rain, ignoring the wetness that lashed his face and the droplets tracing a cold path down his neck. He crested a rise, and after checking the hollow below for movement, glanced back to the silent bundle draped across the horse he led. The Feiann had released Emmerich's washed and perfumed body to him. They'd wrapped Emmerich in white cloths, presumably to prevent decay long enough for his burial to take place.

Most of the freed captives had seemed aimless to Rand, soulless even, their eyes hollow from the atrocities they had witnessed after Torindan's fall. He'd watched guilt creep over their faces at the realization of what they had done in the keirken grove. All except a few of them had ridden off after paying their respects to Emmerich in the briefest manner possible. They might have been deceived into killing the DawnKing, but his lifeless body must reproach them nonetheless. Elcon had been among the few who had lingered. Watching him weep for Emmerich had been hard to bear.

Rand sent his horse into the hollow and up the other side. He might have asked for help, but he wouldn't have to dig a grave. The Feiann had directed him to a cave small enough to seal off with large stones. Taking advice from a Feiann struck Rand as risky at best, but he wanted to spare Emmerich's body from desecration by wolves or other wild animals. Preventing Emmerich's death had been out of his reach, but this much lay within his power.

He looked behind him into the hollow from the other side, still watching for movement. His experience in the keirken grove had made him jumpy. He would welcome the chance to join Elcon, who had continued on toward Cobbleford. Rand could do that soon, provided that the Feiann hadn't tricked him.

He entered a short canyon that opened to a valley with cliffs rising on all sides. Golden trees bowed before the wind that tore at him. A stream ran across rocks in a shallow bed between mossy banks. The open meadows on either hand would be pleasant in fair weather but on a blustery day offered little shelter for a sojourner. From the description given him, the cave lay at the far end of the valley. Squinting, Rand made out above a hedge of wild roses a dark indent in the rocky face of the cliff. Could that be the top of a cave entrance? The faint trails crossing the valley testified that if any ventured here, they were few in number. He knew from tales shared around campfires that most people feared this place. Stories abounded of those who had lost their wits and dashed themselves against the boulders after gazing upon their reflections in the Pool of Truth. That infamous landmark, hazed with rain, lay beneath the cliff he sought. He'd made up his mind not to look into the pool. Some things should remain hidden.

He crossed the valley against the buffeting wind and with little complaint from the horse he rode. If they survived this ordeal, he would reward the hapless creature with a bag of oats. He reached the pool and quickly averted his gaze from its waters, although the temptation to turn his head nearly overpowered him. He'd found it easier to avoid the Feiann. The truth, it would seem, held more allure than deception.

Rand reined in at the base of the cliff and peered into the cave. Carrying Emmerich up that shoulder of rock would not prove difficult. Sealing the entrance would be easy since plenty of rock debris lay scattered beneath the wild roses nearly covering the cave's mouth. Rand dismounted and began the task before him, never resting until Emmerich lay still and pale, his arms folded across his chest, in his makeshift tomb. His bruised face and broken nose told the story of violent death. Rand bowed his head and wept. He had known Emmerich only a short time but watching him die had broken him.

On impulse, he plucked a handful of wild roses and laid them on Emmerich's chest. What would become of the Kindren now that they had killed the DawnKing of Prophecy, sent by Lof Yuel to save all Elderland? Rand didn't know. He pushed the question from his mind and began the work of closing up the cave, a process that took the rest of the day.

Leaving the valley by night would prevent the

possibility of glimpsing himself in the pool, but exhaustion dragged at him. The rain had not stopped, as if nature itself mourned. Rand laid down beneath a rocky overhang near the cliff where Emmerich's body rested. Sleep claimed him at once.

He opened his eyes to birds singing in the sunshine. Gazing across the rain-washed valley, he breathed the fresh air and mustered the will to leave. His fears had fled with the storm, replaced by a sweet yearning to linger beneath leafy bowers and soft grasses.

Hunger turned him toward his saddlebags to pull out elk jerky and waybread. When he had sated his hunger and thirst, he went after his horse, which had wandered while cropping the grasses. A butterfly clothed in the finest raiment skipped along before him at the edge of the shining pool, which no longer seemed terrifying. The journey from watching its bright wings and gazing into the pool came with the ease of breath.

The waters shimmered, breaking up the sky's reflection, and settled again.

A reflection gazed at Rand from the surface. He dropped to his knees, gasping, and bowed his head. He'd wanted to believe that good intentions could redeem him, but now he saw that would never be enough. He lifted his head, drawn to look once more despite his revulsion.

From the depths of the pool, Draeg's face stared back at him.

CR

Rand peered into the pool, held despite his urgent desire to look away. The ground trembled beneath him and went on shaking. The world darkened and a cold wind blew. A bird gave a sharp cry, breaking the reflected image's hold on Rand. He watched a whirlight's ungainly flight as the large white bird fled the valley. More winged creatures followed, dotting the sky, until only a lone vulture remained within his field of vision. Seated on a snag, the bird observed Rand's every move with bright eyes, then preened its feathers with a sharp beak before flapping into the sky.

"Rand."

He started. Distracted by the vulture, he'd noticed no footsteps. The voice that had called his name sounded impossibly familiar. How could this be?

He turned his head. "But you're dead. I buried you."

Emmerich smiled through his bruises. "Death can only hold those belonging to it."

Rand pulled in a painful breath. "I deserve to die, for my sins."

"You've been gazing into the pool. What has it shown you?"

"That I am no better than my wretched half-brother."

"Every grief breaks Lof Yuel's heart, which is why He counts them all the same. How can a broken heart be measured? However, an important difference separates you from Draeg. Your sorrow makes your redemption possible. I died to free more souls than those trapped by the Feiann."

Rand stared at him. "I thought you came to deliver Elderland from Freaer, not to save us from ourselves."

"If I do one, have I not done the other? Rise to

your feet, Rand. The vulture flew off because it will have no meal here today."

Rand obeyed and looked up at the cave in disbelief. "How did you move those rocks so quickly? It took me a long time to pile them."

"Which is harder, shifting a pile of rocks or rising from the dead?"

Rand shook his head. "I have no idea how you did either."

Emmerich smiled. "Go find Elcon. He's troubled in his mind and needs a friend."

"I doubt he thinks of me as one."

"That doesn't matter, although Elcon thinks better of you than he did before. He needs to reach Cobbleford Castle at once. War waits at Westerland's door."

"What about you? Won't you come and help?"

Emmerich shook his head. "The battles I fight are not of this world."

"But you once saved the Kindren during Freaer's siege of Torindan."

"The enemies I defeated that day were not flesh and blood. Go and tell Elcon that I've already given him what he needs to win Elderland. But first, look in the pool again."

Rand shuddered. "I'd rather not."

"Don't fear the truth. It has shown you the condition of your soul. Now see what trusting yourself to Lof Yuel can make of you."

Rand overcame his reluctance. The waters swirled, then smoothed. He caught his breath. Clear-eyed and noble, a king gazed back at him. A double-edged sword flashed in one hand, and a shield covered most of his armor. A crown rested on his head, its many jewels returning the light of the sun. He gazed in wonder at a blaze on his brow that matched a gash on Emmerich's forehead. "A Feiann guard spoke of a mark…"

"It protects you in the spiritual realm."

Rand squinted as his reflection. "What does it mean?"

"That I have claimed you."

22

IMPRISONMENT AND FREEDOM

Kai didn't wish Dorann back in the dungeon but seeing the tracker freed had made him feel more imprisoned. Being confined was mind-numbing at best. At worst, it gave him too much time to reflect. Stories from the past played out in his head. He could see again his mother weeping as he'd left his home in Whellein for Torindan to pledge fealty to Shraen Timraen. Salty tears had run down his face while he'd carried Shae as a babe to safety across the Plains of Rivenn after the ambush meant to kill her. He'd wept again after Shae, now grown, went through the Gate of Life to change places with Emmerich to allow him to enter Elderland. He sighed and shut out his uncomfortable memories. Imprisonment would be utterly unbearable without his companions to distract him, although living at close quarters in an overcrowded cell created its share of problems.

A squabble broke out among the outlaws. Sunk in his own thoughts, he'd missed the source of the conflict, but it would be one of many irritations. Someone might have stood too close or taken a favored spot. Lately, he'd noticed more arguments over words than physical discomfort.

Of the outlaws, he liked Trader best. The wanderer knew how to laugh, even in adversity. The rest of them, himself included, could learn from the wanderer's attitude.

"Stop this." Hael turned on Trader and Barret. "Being locked away is hard enough without having to put up with your quibbling. Or, if you must fight, take to your fists and be done with it."

Kai shuddered to think what might happen if they took his advice. He made out a shadowy figure with his hands wrapped around the bars in the cell across from them. Whoever stood there never spoke, and the dimness of the dungeon didn't allow a glimpse of the person's face. "Do you suppose Dorann will have mentioned our plight to Mara by now?" Hael asked.

Kai pulled his attention back into the tiny cell. "Knowing Dorann, he has unless something prevented him. She may not be able to help us, though."

"That's a fair assessment, but I hope she can. The lodging in this place leaves a lot to be desired, and our hosts are not attentive."

"You might not want them otherwise," Kai countered. "No attention can be preferable to the wrong kind."

Hael smiled. "You're right."

The ground beneath Kai's feet trembled.

Hael's smile slipped away. "Did you feel that?"

"Yes, but I wish I hadn't."

"The dragon sleeping beneath the castle has awoken," Barret pronounced darkly.

"Don't be daft." Trader grinned.

Barret gave him a wounded look. "It could be a dragon."

"More likely, it's a mortal foe." Hael entered the fray. "We'll have to look lively if Freaer's warriors are ramming down the gatehouse."

"If that were the case, we'd hear sounds of battle." Aerlic inserted logic into the conversation. "More likely it's an earthshake." The fact that he had spoken gave away his opinion of the event's importance. The archer, never one for talk, had retreated further into silence since entering the dungeon.

The vibration turned into waves that rolled beneath Kai's feet. "Whatever the cause, it's strengthening." He gripped the bars before him to keep from falling.

The door wrenched from his hand and flew open.

Barret's eyes widened. "What's this?"

"Not your dragon," Trader answered.

"All right, then what?" Barret demanded.

Trader shook his head. "I wish I knew."

"Never mind all that." Hael pushed between them. "Has it escaped your notice that the cell is open?"

Kai stepped out and scanned the corridor, where every door hung ajar. "It's not ours alone."

"All the more reason to make our escape before the guards come and shut us in again," Hael started forward. "I'm going anyway. Is anyone with me?"

Barret held back. "Maybe we shouldn't. What if it's a trick?"

Trader shook his head. "You can't mean that."

"Why not?" Barret stamped his foot. "We'll be worse off if we break the law."

Hael snorted. "I don't consider myself bound to Westerland."

Joining Kai and Hael, Aerlic frowned. "I don't recall being imprisoned on the basis of any law." Trader grimaced. "Sorry Barret. I If you want to stay behind, you'll have to do it alone."

"You coming or not?" Hael asked.

Barret stared at them with rounded eyes. "I'll not do anything that will land me in trouble." He caught hold of the door and shut himself in.

Kai turned down the corridor with the others keeping pace. Other prisoners spilled into the corridor, but some made the same choice as Barret and looked out with sad faces from behind the bars they hid behind.

◌

Lyneth stared at the door, which, although locked, had popped open. She jumped to her feet and moved toward it slowly. The earthshake must have caused this. She picked up her pace, anxious to escape the queen's imprisonment. If she could make it to the abbey without being recaptured, she would throw herself on Caerla's mercy.

The queen's maid emerged from the tower stairs carrying a bucket of water, an empty chamber pot, and a loaf of bread. Her startled gaze went from the open door to Lyneth. "What are you about?"

"Nothing." Lyneth backed away from her. "The door opened on its own."

The servant looked at her with narrowed her eyes. "I doubt that."

"It's true, I promise you."

"The bar's completely out of its rest. What could make such a thing happen?"

"Did you not feel the tower shake? Perhaps its movement loosened it."

The servant shook her head. "I don't see how."

She swept into the chamber and maneuvered the door shut behind her. The bucket slopped water as it thumped against the floor. "Here's your portion for the day." The servant gave the bread into Lyneth's hands. "Mind you make it last. I'll not climb those stairs more than once a day." She traded the clean chamber pot for the one standing in the corner. "Earthshakes or no, this had better remain closed." The door thudded against its frame, followed by the thunk of the bar dropping into place.

Lyneth sat on the bed with a sigh. Escaping would have involved overpowering the servant, and she didn't want to add that offense to the marks against her. She leaned her head against the wall and closed her eyes while the servant's muffled footsteps retreated then became a memory. Her stomach churned at the thought of remaining locked away here, although she was grateful to have been spared the dungeon. Why Queen Inydde had chosen to imprison her so softly she didn't know. Perhaps some latent sense of decency had come over her. More likely, the queen intended to put her to some nefarious use. Lyneth's presence, after what she'd done, could bring shame to Arillia. Tears touched her cheeks. She had failed her mistress terribly.

Lyneth laid on the bed and pulled her knees to her chest, her habit whenever troubled. This time the familiar position failed to soothe the ache within her. "Lof Yuel," she whispered. "I've brought this imprisonment on myself, and there's no reason you should give me a second chance." She hauled in a breath. "Yet that is what I ask."

She drifted into a sleep world peopled by vague figures and eyes that watched from the darkness.

Footsteps thumped on the tower stairs, rousing her. She sat up and stared at the door, swinging inward by itself.

Hael stood in the doorway with Kai, Aerlic, and Trader behind him. Hael's eyes gleamed. "Will you join us, Milady?"

She restrained the urge to launch herself into his arms. "How did you find me?" She took it in stride that he'd escaped the dungeon. Of course he had.

"A few discreet inquiries revealed your prison. The queen's been locking people in this tower for a while now." He extended his hand to her. "Are you coming?"

Lyneth hesitated, overwhelmed by the second chance she'd asked for arriving so quickly and in the form of Hael. She was tired of running, and she'd accept the life of a fugitive if she went with him. And yet, remaining gave her no future. Besides, when he looked at her that way, she knew her path.

She rose from the bed and took the steps that carried her to his side.

CஃR

Caerla paused with her needle suspended above the cloth, then put down her needlework and went to the door separating her from the queen. "Mother, please stop that pounding. You must know that I can do nothing that would involve disobedience to my father, the king."

"Would you support the judgment of a tyrant?" Her mother's outraged cry vibrated through the wood.

Caerla would rather it had not come to this, but

Mother had brought judgment down on her own head. "You must take up your objections with the king." She turned away and picked up her needlework. In truth, Father was not innocent either. He had long refused to address the troubles brewing under his roof while seeking solace in the bottle.

She tied a knot, snipped the end of the silken strand, and threaded her needle with another length of blue floss. She hadn't seen Father take a drink since sending Mother to the abbey. Perhaps he'd realized his error.

Mother stopped pounding the door, thankfully, but then muffled sobs drifted from her chamber.

Caerla sighed. She should leave her mother alone to give her time to think, but an impulse of mercy sent her to the connecting door. She rested her forehead on the cool jamb, remembering how her mother had cradled her as a child when she'd fallen and scraped her knee. That had been before sickness twisted her mind. A lullaby Mother had sung to soothe her when night shadows turned into monsters sprang to Caerla's lips. In her quavering, imperfect tones, she gave it voice.

"Fly little dove, pretty dove, fly.
Where will you land if not in the tree?
Wing little bird, pretty bird, wing.
Rest your head and sleep near me."
Her mother's sobs quieted.

Caerla finished her song and tiptoed away from the door.

It wasn't much of a beginning, but she and Mother could go on from here.

CR

Rand reached Elcon's camp, if that term could dignify the site where the ragtag group of guardians and refugees would lie down, mostly in their cloaks. The fire lighting the sky gave way to flames in the circle of stones not far from the flimsy covering strung over a bedroll that awaited the Lof Shraen. Elcon sat warming himself beside Craelin on a log near the fire.

Rand submitted to the scrutiny of the guard who greeted him, turned out his horse, and approached the fire. Before his encounter with Emmerich, he might have slunk into the shadows to avoid notice. He wouldn't allow himself to hide this time, not when he had a message from Emmerich. He bowed to Elcon.

Elcon inclined his head. "You must join us."

"Thank you." Rand seated himself on the log.

Elcon studied him. "You've suffered a difficult journey."

Rand thought back to the lone ride through the wild lands. On more than one occasion, the hair on the back of his neck had bristled. Once, when sleep dragged him under, he'd roused to find were-beasts creeping near. After that, he'd been more concerned with keeping his watchfire burning than sleeping. With exhaustion overwhelming him, thoughts of Mara were at times the only thing that kept him going. "I have."

Craelin nodded a greeting. "Was it—successful?" .

Rand knew what the first guardian asked, but the question struck him as ironic. He had failed in what he'd set out to do, but that was no defeat. "I buried Emmerich in a cave within the Vale of Truth."

Elcon nodded. "I'm glad to think of him resting there."

Rand paused, searching for words. "He's not."

Craelin peered at him. "What do you mean?"

"Emmerich lives." Giving up on eloquence, Rand blurted out the simple truth.

Elcon shook his head. "How can this be?"

Craelin narrowed his eyes. "We saw him die."

"He did die, yes." Rand nodded.

"You must have seen a wraith." Elcon peered into the shadows at the edge of camp as if expecting a spirit to materialize.

"I touched him. Emmerich lives, I promise you."

"Where is he, then?" Craelin demanded. "Why isn't he with you?"

"He chose not to come but sent a message for the Lof Shraen."

"Why would Emmerich entrust such a communication to you, son of Freaer?"

Craelin's voice reminded Rand of the mocking tones Draeg had used when he'd called him Misbegotten. He shrugged. "I have no reason to lie."

Elcon turned to him. "What is this message?"

"He's already given all you need to win Elderland."

Elcon smiled. "It sounds like something Emmerich would say."

"Why wouldn't he speak for himself?" Craelin pressed his lips together as if stopping himself from saying more.

Rand could understand the first guardian's hostility toward him, but it grated all the same. He shrugged. "I can't explain that, and I don't know how he rose from the dead. Believe me or not, he did."

❧

Mara sat up in darkness. *Where was she?*

Soft fabric brushed her hand, and she curled her fingers around the bedhangings. She tugged them back. Faint light filtered into the chamber around the shutters covering tall windows.

She had looked out those windows onto the Cobbleford River while talking to her grandfather. He'd told her stories about her mother in childhood, and she'd answered his questions about life at Torindan. They'd made a beginning, although it would take time to adopt one another properly. She would feel better if her grandmother had wanted her too, but Queen Inydde's problems went far beyond whether to accept her granddaughter.

Mara stretched out on the feathered tick and spread a hand over the counterpane. Her mother had slept in this bed as the child Grandfather had described. He'd brought Mara here after that horrible episode in the queen's parlor. Arillia had been in residence but had vacated the chamber on her behalf. For all Mara knew, she had been eager to relinquish any claim to it. Sleeping in a chamber that had belonged to her husband's first wife could only feel awkward. Arillia had hidden here, as Grandfather had explained, but the need for that posed no further threat.

He'd meant of course that her grandmother was no longer a threat. Confined in the abbey, the queen remained under Caerla's supervision and in Brother Robb's care. The priest, Arillia had informed her, excelled at helping those whose minds lost their way. Since Queen Inydde seemed to suffer such a state, Mara hoped she would benefit.

Mara slipped out of bed quietly to avoid waking the servant sleeping in the maid quarters, whom Grandfather had assigned to her. She dressed herself in a simple tunic, lit the fire laid in the outer chamber's hearth, and sat down on a cushioned chair to comb her own hair.

A tap came at the door, and she went to answer.

Caerla waited in the corridor. Garbed in a simple tunic and with her hair beneath a wimple, she seemed tense but tightly composed. "I'm glad to find you awake early."

"Come inside." Mara stepped back.

Caerla entered the chamber and turned back to her. "Father told me where to find you. Are you pleased to stay in Aewen's chambers?"

"I find them comforting, but I'll have to relinquish them tomorrow."

Caerla's gaze swept her face. "I hoped you wouldn't leave again."

"Won't you warm yourself by the fire?"

"Thank you." Caerla went to stand before the hearth. "The mornings are chilly as yet."

"How does the queen fare?"

"She is angry at her confinement."

Mara knew that feeling well. "I hope it will not be overlong."

"Do you?" Caerla slanted a glance at her. "I'd have thought you'd want her locked up indefinitely."

"Only until she finds healing, if she may."

"Judging by her reaction to living at the abbey, her cooperation may take a while."

"Poor Aunt Caerla. That can't be comfortable for you."

Caerla shrugged. "I'm called to a dutiful life, not

an easy one. That reminds me. I've brought news."

"Oh?"

"I've taken in refugees from Torindan and also from the law. They have connections to you, so they say."

Mara lifted her eyebrows. "To me? What are their names?"

"Kai, Aerlic, Hael, and Trader. I'm also sheltering Lyneth."

Mara sank into a chair. "I know them all."

"Come visit the abbey and help me sort out how best to help them."

Mara nodded. "I know why Kai and Aerlic are here, but I thought the others would have kept far from the castle."

"They had no choice but to return, by the queen's orders. They sought asylum after escaping imprisonment."

"And have they found it?"

Caerla shook her head. "I can't award it to them. Asylum is meant for political prisoners, not for those who break Westerland's laws. Each of them stands guilty of that."

"What else can be done for them?"

"The king could pardon them." Caerla tited her head. "Since you know them so well, perhaps you should be the one to ask."

Mara nodded. "I'll try my best. Did Lyneth tell you why she ran away?"

"No, only that she regrets doing so."

"That doesn't surprise me. She didn't strike me as willful." Mara shook her hair back. "I wish there was a way to restore her to service."

"I'll talk to the Lof Raelein. I know that she misses

Lyneth. You have such lovely hair, thick and black like your mother's. May I brush it for you?"

Caerla's offer rendered Mara speechless, but she managed to nod and give her aunt the brush.

"Your mother used to do this for me." Caerla stroked the brush down her hair, the bristles massaging her scalp. "I don't recall returning the favor. My own needs were more important to me then, but I've taught myself to think of others also."

"That is a better way to live altogether."

"Aewen would have agreed with you." Caerla rested a hand on her shoulder. "Sometimes you remind me so much of your mother that it takes my breath away."

Mara placed her hand over her aunt's. "I hope I may soon return for a longer visit." She had other wishes also, but she didn't voice them. Why remind Caerla of the fragile balance of power within Elderland and the possibility that the scale might tip the wrong way?

After seeing her aunt from the chamber, she called upon her maid to help her dress for an audience with the king. With her hair braided and wearing red silk and a vest of green brocade patterned with leaves and laced with gold, she sent her servant with a message to her grandfather. He responded at once and instructed her to meet him in his chambers.

The guard admitted Mara right away, a far cry from the reception she'd received the first time she'd tried to speak to her grandfather. The guard showed her into the king's meeting room, where her grandfather was seated. He stood but waited to speak until the door clicked shut, leaving them alone together. "What matter has placed that frown upon your face, my granddaughter?"

"I've come to beg you for mercy on behalf of my friends who were taken prisoner."

"I've heard that there are Kindren in the dungeon. Sit down and tell me their story."

Mara explained the circumstances in which Kai and the others had found themselves, as relayed to her by Caerla.

Euryon held up a hand. "What did you call this Kindren?"

"Kai of Whellein."

"I remember Kai. Who are his companions?"

"There's an archer named Aerlic—"

"Yes, yes, I know him too. They were in the dungeon?"

She nodded. "All save Lyneth, Arillia's servant. She was in the tower."

"What was their crime?"

She shook her head. "None, except being Kindren."

"Well, then. There's no pardon needed. They may go free, but send Kai to me. There's a sword the Kindren will want back."

She hesitated. "Thank you, Grandfather. One more thing — the others are known outlaws. However, the leader was falsely accused of theft in Norwood, and I believe the others' stories are similar."

"In Norwood, you say?" Her grandfather sent her a sideways glance. "That's nothing to do with Westerland, now is it?"

"I don't suppose so," Mara agreed.

"As long as those outlaws are no longer on the castle grounds by tomorrow, I'll have nothing to say."

"Thank you. I'll make sure they understand."

Her grandfather cleared his throat. "I have another matter to discuss with you."

"What is it?"

"A messenger delivered unsettling news last night. Pilaer's forces press from Norwood into the north of Westerland."

"I'm sorry to hear it. That is why I must leave Cobbleford—to find my father and to gather the Kindren who escaped Torindan. Messengers can summon help from the shraens loyal to Faeraven."

"You may ride under the guardianship of Westerland. Also, I have called the Council of Elders to Cobbleford to discuss uniting with the Kindren." He shook his head. "I was wrong to suggest that our nations don't need one another. You must bring the Kindren you find here. We have bounty enough to strengthen them."

"You are very kind."

"I haven't always been so. I shouldn't have said that Faeraven was already gone. Where there is life, hope may survive."

23

SECOND CHANCES

Mara stared into the distance, hardly believing her eyes. Guardians garbed in the green and gold of Rivenn rode her direction, and farther back in the column waved the high king's banner. She turned to Kai, riding beside her. "Do you see my father's standard?

He smiled. "It's good to know that the Lof Shraen lives."

Mara urged her wingabeast faster, eager to join her father.

The guardians halted and pulled off the road.

Kai and Hael caught up and flanked her wingabeast on either side.

"Slow down, Princess." Hael smiled at her. "You'll want to wait until you know you're welcome."

Mara frowned. "Why have they stopped?"

"They could be concerned that we're riding with Cobbleford's guards." Kai offered an explanation.

Hael nodded. "That's the problem. They don't know what to expect."

Kai halted their advance. "Wait here." He gazed at Mara pointedly. "Aerlic and I will approach them."

Mara watched with frustration as the two rode off.

Hael whistled. "I know the look on your face. Glad I'm not the target of it."

"I don't see why I have to wait."

"You can't blame Kai for watching out for you. From what I understand, it's his job."

She lifted a shoulder. "My father charged him with my safety, but then circumstances separated us. Now he seems determined to make up for lost time."

"Whatever his reasons, you'll have to bide your time until he returns."

His words were all the more annoying because they were true. She made a face at him, a childhood habit.

Hael laughed. "While I have your attention, I want to thank you for speaking up for me with the king. You kept me from going back to the dungeon."

"I was glad to do it. You don't belong in that place."

"I'd like to belong somewhere."

She nodded. "I understand." She had felt that way once. The realization that she no longer did made no sense with Torindan in ruins. For her, belonging must be more about family than having a place to call home.

The column of guardians started moving again, with Kai and Aerlic beside Craelin at their head. For Kai's sake and to Hael's amusement, Mara repressed the urge to ride out to meet them. The column slowed as it neared. She started out toward the high king's banner, riding past the guardians. One face stood out to her, and she slowed. "Rand?"

His eyes devoured her but he dipped his head and remained in line.

How could she have forgotten his promise to her father? Rand had pledged to stay away from her. Now that she didn't need to depend on him for survival, he obviously intended to keep his word. She reached for him with the soul touch, but he turned away. Another soul brushed hers, infusing her with strength. She caught her breath, recognizing her father's soul touch. He was very near.

The column ground to a halt, but she continued until she reached the high king's banner. "Let me through to my father." She summoned her most commanding voice for the guards surrounding him.

"Step aside and let me greet my daughter." Her father's cry pierced Mara's heart.

The guards riding at his flank dropped back, opening an avenue for her.

"Syl Marinda." Her father, astride a wingabeast, gave her a weary smile. Thinner than before and with a look of strain in his face, he sat unsteadily in the saddle.

"I'm glad to find you alive and well, Father." She couldn't help the catch in her voice.

"I could say the same about you, my daughter. You'll have to tell me all about your journey to Cobbleford. I hope it wasn't as eventful as mine."

"Where did all these guardians gather? When Dorann and I searched before, we could find none."

"That's a long story, and one best told beside a fire."

"Yes, of course. You must rest. But first, I think we should send messengers to the loyal shraens and request they join us in Cobbleford."

He stared at her. "Don't tell me—"

"King Euryon has agreed to stand with us and has summoned the Council of Elders to discuss the situation."

"We'll raise an army to bolster our cause. I consulted with Craelin after Pilaer's warriors attacked our camp. We sent out messengers instructing the shraens to prepare for battle. The Kindren would have fought Freaer without help from the Elder."

"I'm glad we don't have to."

Kai approached them. "Pray forgive me for interrupting, Lof Shraen, but I have an item in my possession that belongs to you." He drew his sword from its sheath.

Several guardians started forward, but Elcon waved them back. "It's all right."

Kai extended the hilt to Elcon. "The Scepter of Faeraven and the Circlet of Elder were lost at Torindan, but I claimed Sword Rivenn in your name."

Elcon accepted the sword and raised it. Jewels in its hilt caught the light, and the luster of its blade proclaimed its value. "In this sword find birth, life, and death." He recited the ancient words spoken by every ruler of Faeraven since the alliance began.

Cheers went up from the Kindren within hearing distance. Swallowing against tears, Mara joined in their chanting. "Faeraven will rise!"

∳

Lyneth gazed onto the abbey's herb garden from the window in her chamber. Brother Robb, his portly figure garbed in brown robes, bent above one of the beds, a gathering basket over his arm. She didn't look forward to facing his scrutiny when they chanced to meet, assuming Caerla allowed her to remain.

A flock of flitlings chirped in the trees that pressed against the outer castle wall. The tiny birds chased one another from branch to branch. They seemed such happy creatures.

She might have to go back to her parents' household in disgrace, and that was cause to weep. Her parents had raised her to be well-bred, discreet, and modest. Her behavior in recent days had been none of those things. The only explanation for her lapse in judgment was that she'd fallen in love with Hael, although that provided no excuse for foolishness. She could admit the truth now that she would never see Hael again. His interest in her had coincided with saving his own skin, apparently. He'd been eager to leave her in the very place he'd stolen her away from, but he'd accomplished his reason for carrying off, to remove her from service to Arillia. The king had been quick to enlist Hael and his outlaws in Elderland's forces and had granted them full pardons. The outlaws and Kindren trackers knew the wild lands best and could fight in ways the garrison knew nothing about. They would need their best skills against Pilaer's vast forces.

She sighed. Even if Hael survived the coming war, she doubted he would look for her again.

Caerla's knock sounded on the door.

Lyneth turned away from the sunlight pouring through the window and went to let her in.

Caerla carried a tray with a bowl of stew and a portion of bread. "You didn't come to the kitchen last night or this morning, so I thought you might welcome some food."

Lyneth averted her gaze. "I haven't been hungry." In truth, she could barely choke down nourishment.

Caerla raised an eyebrow. "A maiden of your youth should have a better appetite."

Moisture sprang to her eyes. "I try to eat, really I

do."

Caerla placed the tray upon a side table. "You must force yourself, child. Giving in to sorrow will only destroy you."

Lyneth's tears fell onto her cheeks. "I can't help what I feel."

Caerla patted her shoulder. "I know you grieve, but you must call upon your inner strength to keep body and soul together."

She pulled in a painful breath. "I've destroyed my life."

"I once believed that about mine." Caerla dropped into the room's single bench, which rested beside the hearth. "It's a lie. No life is too far gone for restoration. I am proof of that."

Lyneth sat beside her on the bench and folded her hands in her lap. "Then tell me what to do."

Caerla's arm went around her shoulders. "When you have sinned against another, you must ask forgiveness."

"What if Arillia will not give it?"

"You can't let that possibility stop you. No one can decide for another how to react, but we each choose how to live in this world."

Caerla's words made sense, although Lyneth dreaded doing as she suggested. She nodded anyway. "I'm willing to relieve any pain I've caused the Lof Raelein."

Caerla smiled. "Have a bite to eat, wash your face, and make yourself presentable. I've an idea the Lof Raelein will speak to you right away." She stood and went to the door. "You've made a worthy decision."

Lyneth gave her a weak smile. Maybe her life could work out after all

CR

Arillia repressed her first instinct of mercy at the sight of Lyneth, trembling and pale beside Caerla. A Lof Raelein did not react with sentiment. She had every right to expect loyalty from her servants. The fact that Lyneth had not given it was reason enough to dismiss her.

"Lof Raelein, I can only beg your forgiveness." The words wrenched from Lyneth.

She suspected a story lurked behind what had happened, and hearing Lyneth out would provide it. "Very well. I will listen to what you say."

"I let myself be beguiled by an outlaw and failed in my duties to you. There was no excuse for my actions, and no reason you should allow me to continue in your service."

Arillia had expected excuses perhaps, weeping, or even anger — not this composure and remorse. The stray thought that she would do well to glean from her maidservant's example flitted annoyingly across her mind. "It is well that you take responsibility for dishonoring yourself and betraying my confidence."

Lyneth bowed her head in silent acceptance.

Arillia edged a little closer to forgiveness. "Won't you take a seat?"

"Thank you, Milady, but I do not deserve to sit in your presence."

"Even when I suggest it?" Arillia asked in a steely voice. "I'll not have a display of false humility."

Lyneth raised her head. "I apologize for offending you, Lof Raelein, but my repentance is not insincere."

"Pray seat yourself." Arillia extended the invitation a second time.

Lyneth sank into the chair nearest her.

Caerla moved behind the maiden and gave Arillia a pleading look.

Arillia relented a little more. "Explain to me what happened." She sat down on a carved and cushioned chair across from Lyneth. "How did you meet this outlaw?"

"I came across Hael in the wild lands. I doubt I'd have survived without his help. He escorted me with the Lof Raena to Cobbleford."

"Did he violate you?" The question had to be asked, although Arillia had no taste for it.

Lyneth shook her head. "It wasn't like that. Hael was kind and seemed to care about me."

"Why did you run away with him?" Arillia well knew how kindness could turn a maiden's head, but she kept her tone hard.

"Brother Robb saw us talking in the garden, and I didn't want to explain about Hael to him. That, and I feared I might be forced to betray Hael in some way." She shook her head. "I let my emotions blind me to the consequences."

Arillia understood how the heart could yearn for forbidden love. When Elcon had returned with Aewen from Westerland, she had felt similar stirrings. Yet she had chosen the path of honor, going so far as to embrace his new wife with her own heart breaking. "Your behavior shows a lamentable lack of decorum."

Lyneth nodded. "I cannot deny that. I went against the prudence my parents instilled in me."

Arillia's opinion shifted again. She knew Lyneth's household and their reputation for surpassing integrity. Lyneth's sorrow at besmirching it spoke well of her. One question remained, however. "How can I know you will not repeat this behavior?"

Lyneth's upper lip quivered. "Because I have known the pain of living outside your favor."

Arillia paced to the window and looked out blindly. How could she, who had suffered the humiliation of rejection, bestow it upon a remorseful servant? "Very well." She turned and faced Lyneth. "I will give you a second chance."

◯3

Arillia waited outside the door carved with twin lions. Why would the king summon her to his private chambers? Most of the Elder kings had dalliances, she'd heard, although Euryon's name had not come up in particular. On those few occasions she'd met him, he'd seemed devoted to his wife, perhaps too much so. Being strong-minded herself, Arillia did not object to a wife giving her opinions and even taking a share of the burden of rulership. However, Euryon had allowed Inydde so much sway that his own will had often bowed to hers. This had cost him the respect of his subjects, and his constant drinking had only made matters worse. All that had begun to change, but not enough for her to have faith in a private meeting with the king.

The door swung open, and she gasped. Elcon stood on the other side. Forgetting all dignity or the watching guards, she ran to her husband and flung her arms about him. He winced and shifted her away from his injured side, but then clasped her closely and kissed her hair, her eyelids, her mouth. She clung to him, clutching the linen of his tunic while tears slid down her face.

The door closed with a discreet click.

Arillia glanced around and discovered they were alone. "I thought you would never come. What delayed you?" A petulant note crept into her voice.

He grinned. "I hope you know that only matters of the greatest urgency would keep me away from you."

It was hard to act offended when he used that coaxing tone. "I hope we will see no more of those."

"If I had my way, I'd never leave you." He kissed her forehead. "Sacrifice is required of a lof shraen, however."

She pulled away from him. "What does that mean?"

"Faeraven must ride into battle soon, and I with it."

The room tilted. Arillia put out a hand to prevent her fall but clutched only air. The stone floor crashed into her.

"Arillia!" Elcon flung himself down beside her.

She swam to the surface of awareness. Hands were at her throat, loosening her collar. "Answer me if you can hear me." The voice seemed a long way away.

She forced her eyelids open.

Brother Robb bent over her.

"Where am I?"

"In your chamber, Lof Raelein."

"Where is my husband?"

Smiles wreathed his face. "In your outer chamber, anxiously awaiting news of your condition."

"You must tell him that I am well."

"I'll do that." Brother Robb turned toward the

door but looked back before reaching it. "Would you have me say anything about the babe you carry?"

She gave a breathless laugh. "Let me do that." She would tell Elcon, but at the proper time and not before. They'd lost so many infants, she had little confidence that her womb would hold onto this one. And if Elcon insisted on fighting while still wounded from the last battle, she would tell him nothing that could distract him.

Elcon came in at the door. "How do you fare?"

She smiled. "Well enough."

He crossed to the bed. "Have you been unwell of late?"

"No." Not unless one counted mornings spent fighting nausea and long days devoted to sleep.

"I wonder what made you faint."

"I'm sure it was the shock you gave me." She sat up, supported by his arm around her shoulders. "Couldn't you have given me one evening to keep you to myself?"

He stroked her hair. "I'm with you now."

She put a hand to her temple, where a headache throbbed. "It's not the same."

He enfolded her in his embrace. "We will reclaim our lives, Arillia, and restore Faeraven. The House of Rivenn will rise once more."

She placed a hand on his chest and felt his heart beating, strong and sure. "I make only one request."

He lowered his head until his mouth hovered a whisper's breadth from hers. "Name it."

"Return to me safely."

He closed the gap between their lips, and for a time she forgot about battles, warriors, and Faeraven itself.

CR

The ribbons Arillia tied on Elcon's arm fluttered brightly in the breeze. She'd selected red and gold, the colors of Rivenn's Rose, for her mark of favor.

He laughed, his eyes teasing. "What's this? A raelein who chooses her shraen rather than a guardian to fight in her name?"

She forced a smile to her lips, even while fear whispered that he would never return. "You will have to live with the shame." Elcon might protest, but she could tell that her choice of a champion pleased him. Despite her objections to his decision to ride into battle with the combined forces of Faeraven and the Elder nations, she'd resolved not to fight him. From this shift, supporting his choice hadn't taken much more effort.

He swept her into his arms and kissed her soundly, then lifted his head to gaze into her eyes. "I love you, Arillia."

She touched her forehead to his with a soft smile. "I know."

"Oh, yes?" He laughed and tilted her face upward with a finger under her chin. "I seem to have convinced you at last."

Tears swarmed her eyes. "I love you, too."

"And that's a cause for weeping? I must have more work to do."

She laughed more readily this time.

Elcon gave her a lingering kiss, and then stepped away. "See that you take care of yourself while I'm gone. No more fainting."

She smiled at his gentle bullying. "Goodbye, my

love."

He mounted his wingabeast and took his place near the middle of the long line of guardians and Elder troops. Westerland's banner flew in front of Rivenn's. She noticed Euryon, girt in armor, his two sons beside him, riding out to take their positions. Darksea's flag lay behind Rivenn's. Beyond that, she couldn't see.

Arillia turned to find Elcon's daughter at her elbow. "Did you miss sending your father off?"

"We said goodbye earlier. I thought you might want someone beside you while they march off to war."

"This can't be easy for you either."

The maiden's eyes were fixed on one of the fighters in Elcon's advance guard. Arillia shielded her own eyes against the sunlight. Garbed in leather armor and wearing a helm, his identity was hard to make out. "Who is that warrior behind Kai?"

"Randolph of Pilaer." Mara answered in an offhand tone that failed to hide her interest.

"I see," Arillia murmured, and she did indeed. The emotion showing on Syl Marinda's face was the kind that endured.

In the forefront of the column, the battle horn sent out its hollow cry, the sound going on as each contingent down the line picked it up. Boots thumped and hooves pounded. The march began.

24

HOMECOMING

Hael parted the leaves before him and peered down into Pilaer's camp. Disorder reigned, with bedding strewn about and ragged warriors fighting over supplies. He withdrew, moving high above the forest floor through the interconnecting branches of the kabas. He climbed down the tree and joined Dorann, who had stationed himself behind a boulder to watch over the road.

"Well?" Dorann asked, low.

"Conditions are favorable for a surrender."

Dorann blew out a breath. "Finally."

They stayed low as they crept toward the camp shared by the combined forces of the Elder and Kindren, some distance away. Hael kept an eye out for spies from Pilaer, although from what he'd seen, the warriors wouldn't send any. Hael and Dorann reached their destination without mishap. Hael gave his report to Delfort, captain of Cobbleford's garrison, with a sense of relief.

"That's good news," Delfort said with feeling. "We've worked hard for this."

"We have." It had taken a series of battles, but they'd driven back Pilaer's armies to the edge of the forest near Torindan.

Delfort clasped his shoulder. "We couldn't have

advanced this far without the help of your contingent. Your methods might be unconventional, but they work."

"We were glad to contribute to the effort." They'd earned their pardons, anyway. Together with Dorann and his brother Eathnor, Hael and his outlaw band had hidden traps to be sprung at a careless footstep, kept watch in places the other guardians didn't know about or couldn't reach, and maneuvered through the forest on missions like this one.

Delfort smiled. "The stew wasn't gone, last I saw. Go and feed yourselves."

Hael moved off toward the fire, grateful for a rest. He settled beside Dorann with a steaming mug of stew. Eathnor, Trader, and Barret soon joined them. Trader sat on the log across from Hael and Dorann. "It's good to find you safely returned."

"I'll agree to that." Hael toasted with his stew. He glanced about him and lowered his voice. "I've a feeling this nightmare will soon end." *What will I do then?* The question tugged at his mind. He'd signed on to serve the king for the duration of the present conflict. Once that ended, he and the other outlaws would be free to pursue an honest existence, by agreement with the king. Hael had every intention of living up to his promise, but he seemed to have a knack for stumbling into trouble.

A wife would settle him down, no doubt, except that he'd lost his heart to Lyneth, who seemed content to spend her entire life as the Lof Raelein's servant. He should check on her, though, in case her return hadn't gone well. He would hope that it hadn't, but Lyneth's happiness mattered more to him than his own.

He gave a wry smile at the realization that now

that Mara and Rand seemed to be ignoring one another, he no longer wanted to pursue her. Mara had been the maiden of his youthful dreams. He'd needed to meet Lyneth to discover that he loved Mara more as a friend. His love for Lyneth was something else entirely.

Hael finished his stew and went to sleep early. The word had gone out that they'd wake early to attack Pilaer's camp before dawn. He fell asleep at once.

"Time to rise." Dorann's voice intruded into his slumber.

Hael sat up and palmed his eyes, yawning. "I just closed my eyes."

Dorann laughed. "You were sleeping when I went to bed after sitting up by the fire with Trader. He tells riveting stories about life as a wanderer."

Hael smiled. "He has a bard's wit."

Dorann sobered. "We've quite a day ahead of us."

They reached the enemy camp before dawn and spread out to encircle it. At a blast from the battle horn, they began the attack.

Hael rushed in with the others, soon lost in the sound and fury of battle. They'd had the advantage of surprise, but Pilaer's warriors possessed the energy of desperation and the persistence and bloodthirst their vile training instilled in them. In the end, logistics won out. The Elder and Kindren forces were better supplied from Cobbleford than the warriors of Pilaer by what remained of Torindan's stores. One by one, Pilaer's warriors broke and ran.

The next days blurred into skirmishes, fleeing warriors, and endless days in the saddle. Pilaer's forces fought hard to keep Torindan, but failed to reinforce its breached defenses in time. They retreated into the canyonlands south of Torindan, leaving the castle to its dead.

Hael stood in the outer bailey of the ill-fated stronghold, where the bodies of the fallen had been picked clean by welkes or wolves. He'd known about Torindan's defeat but seeing the evidence twisted his gut. The High Hold of Faeraven, fabled center of learning, place of prayer, seat of the high king had been sacrificed on the altar of Freaer's ambition. If the Kindren's beacon of enlightenment could be destroyed for such a purpose, no one in Elderland was safe.

 લ

Rand pressed onward, ignoring his exhaustion. Traveling through the heat of the day in full armor wasn't easy, but he didn't blame Craelin for pushing relentlessly forward. Wearing an enemy down must always take a toll on the pursuers. Whenever they paused to drink, water bearers moved among them. This happened more frequently as the sun climbed into the bleached sky.

He had fought in several battles, and it never came easy. Why harming an enemy should afflict him but leave others unscathed he didn't know. He had felt this way since he could remember, grieving over dragonflies when Draeg pulled off their wings and left them to die. He'd considered it a weakness until his warrior training had taught him that having a penchant for mercy was a gift from Lof Yuel. The pain of it saved his humanity in the face of war.

Ahead in the column a banner with twin lions waved above King Euryon and his sons. Kai had told him the tale of Westerland's lions while they sat one night around the watchfire. He smiled at the memory. "The creatures can no longer be found in Elderland," Kai had said, "although some tales claim they still dwell in the south."

"That is possible without our knowing, isn't it?" He'd raised the question. "Neither Elder nor Kindren venture into Triboan these days.'

Kai had shrugged. "Believe what you will."

"Do you know the story of Westerland's lions?"

"That I do. Long ago, when lions still roamed the grasslands, one of the former kings of Westerland felled a female lion with his bow. He heard mewing from the cave behind the cat's lifeless body and discovered twin cubs sheltering there. It seemed a mark of favor from the High One. He carried the lions home to Cobbleford Castle and bestowed them on his twin sons. The lions grew along with the youths, who trained them to retrieve the game they hunted."

"That would come in handy, provided they didn't eat the quarry."

Kai smiled. "I'm sure they received their share. The king's sons moved into manhood, and the lions became their fiercest defenders in battle. Before the garns were beaten back into Triboan, the vile creatures roaned Elderland, attacking Kindren and Elder alike. While out hunting, the princes were attacked by garns. The guard surrounding them fell, all save one who rode to warn the king. The king's sons took refuge in a tree, while below them the lions kept the garns at bay. The king rode out with the garrison and drove away the garns. He found his sons alive."

"Did the lions survive?"

"Sadly, no. The sons grieved their protectors, and

the king decreed that the twin lions would from that day forward represent Westerland."

Rand's horse stumbled, wrenching him out of his thoughts and into the misery of the present circumstances. The memory had reminded him of the reasons he'd gone into battle. Despite the sorrow fighting caused him, he would defend Elderland.

Kai dropped back to ride alongside him. "Tell me, Rand, do you know of a weakness in Pilaer's defenses? Once we've driven the enemy back to Pilaer, we'll want to find one."

"There's a lever low in the wall to the right of the postern door," Rand answered without hesitation. "I've used it since my early days to escape into Weithen Faen and afterwards return to the castle. The last time I entered Pilaer by that means, though, the lever would barely budge due to rust."

"Does Freaer know of it?"

"I never saw a sign that anyone else did."

"Thank you." Kai sent his horse forward, returning to the lead.

The column marched on with mind-numbing constancy which made its sudden halt uncanny. Silence prevailed, followed by the voice of two battle horns in the forefront, one for each side. Pilaer's ululating war cry lifted, and the clash of metal amid shouts and screams announced that a new battle began.

CR

Euryon lifted his shield and braced himself for the blow that would come. The advance guard was no more. The call to retreat had been given. Warriors rode into the breach with warlances pointed, swords leveled, and battle axes ready. At his side his son Connor thrust his sword into an attacker. His oldest son Perthmon raised the battle cry of Westerland and interposed himself between his father and the rider aiming a lance at him. Euryon bellowed for his son to stop. Perthmon continued, angling his own lance.

Before the two adversaries could meet, the warrior flung his weapon. Euryon roared in fear and helpless rage. The tip came out Perthmon's back. Euryon watched in horror as his first-born son arched in pain. Perthmon fell and writhed on the ground.

Pierced through by the blade of grief, Euryon struck his son's murderer with his sword. His opponent's shield came up, but Euryon prevailed to unhorse him. The warrior fell to the blood-soaked ground. Euryon followed, his sword ready. He turned the warrior over to discover his head hanging at a strange angle. He released the dead warrior and pulled upright.

His stricken son lay staring at the sky. His chest did not move to draw air. Euryon knelt beside him, weeping.

Connor rode up, leading his horse. The banner bearer kept pace on a horse beside him. "Father, hurry!" His voice shook with his weeping.

Euryon closed Perthmon's eyes and broke the lance that had killed him. He bent to pick up his son's body.

"There's no time for such things," Connor called. "Don't ask me to lose both father and brother today."

"While I have breath I'll not leave a son of mine to rot in the field," Euryon growled. Connor stopped objecting, and jumped down to help Euryon haul Perthmon onto his horse.

"Quickly now," Connor shouted, "ride with me."

"Take my horse, Your Majesty," the banner bearer offered.

Euryon gave a shake of his head. "I'll not. Now more than ever, you must hold aloft the twin lions of Westerland."

Euryon mounted behind his living son with a heavy heart. He kept tight hold of his own horse's rein, lest he lose Perthmon's body.

Connor sent his horse southward, whacking his sword against those they passed. Euryon forced himself to remain vigilant. The Kindren's advance guard parted, and then closed protectively around them.

"Bring a horse for the king." Kai's shout went up and his gaze swept Perthmon's body. "I'm sorry, Euryon."

"My son died defending me."

"Pilaer must have mustered reinforcements." Elcon shook his head. "Why else would they turn back after we'd driven them this far?"

Euryon gave a sharp nod. "They'll be upon us before long, and you're vulnerable in this position. Westerland can't support you with our garrison in retreat."

Elcon nodded. "Kai, send Craelin to me."

One of the guardians brought a warhorse, and Euryon dismounted.

With a bloodcurdling cry, warriors broke from a stand of keirkens and raced toward them in a flank attack.

❧

Rand drew his sword and braced himself for battle.

Craelin shouted orders that heralds carried down the line.

Kai's wingabeast slid to a stop before them. "Craelin sends word, Lof Shraen. You must take your inner guard and withdraw with King Euryon behind Darksea's front."

Elcon paced. "How can I withdraw the king's banner when those who remain may die?"

"And you with them, if you won't go. Surely you know you are a desirable target. Where will the courage of Faeraven be with the banner gone? Or do you prefer that your daughter take it up in your absence?"

Elcon grimaced. "That maiden would, I'd warrant."

"She has her father's spirit." Kai nodded toward the first guardian of Rivenn. "Craelin will call for retreat once you're safe."

"All right, you've convinced me."

Rand turned with the others who had been named to ride closest to the Lof Shraen. Craelin had fought his appointment, but Elcon had insisted. Rand didn't know if that meant the Lof Shraen liked him or wanted to keep him close because he didn't trust him. They formed a tight knot around Elcon and pointed their mounts southward.

Rand had faced death so many times that he could react to this situation with clarity of thought. The Kindren of Rivenn had grown a little lazy perhaps and left their flank more thinly guarded while pursuing

Pilaer from the front. Guardians on horseback raced to form a living barrier between Elcon and the warriors running toward them from the side. There wasn't enough time to rectify the problem, by Rand's estimate. Unless something changed, which didn't seem likely with Westerland's forces now in full retreat, he'd have to fight with the odds against him.

The warriors slammed into the guardians shielding Elcon and his inner guard with such viciousness Rand flinched. The guardians of Rivenn would not have trained to fight against the base methods of Pilaer's warriors but held their own with the zeal of a cornered prey. They might stand if the forces given to the side attack didn't outnumber the guardians in flank position.

The distance Elcon needed to withdraw was not vast, but as their outer defenses gave way, Rand unsheathed his sword. Warriors broke through, the hooves of their horses drumming the sod as they bore down on the inner guard. Rand deflected the first blow aimed at him, managing to knock the rider from his horse. The warrior chased after his mount, but the terrified creature shrilled and bolted. Rand's attention diverted to thwarting a battle axe aimed at his middle. He looked back to find the rider impaled by a warlance and lying with his blood soaking the ground.

A blood-curdling cry led to thundering of hooves as Darksea's forces charged.

Distracted by this sight, Rand turned to face a new combatant too slowly but brought his shield up to deflect a thrust of the blade. The effort sent painful vibrations up his arm. His reaction slowed, he brought up the shield in time to turn but not deflect the blade. The flat of the sword whacked him in the back and laid him out against his horse. He gasped and held on, fighting to breathe. The reins whipped from his grasp. He waited, helpless, for the killing blow to come.

"I'll not end your wretched life, Misbegotten," Dabron, another of Draeg's friends, roared. "That would deny your father the privilege."

Rand's horse started forward as blackness swallowed him.

℞

Caerla gripped the hangings in her chamber window. Brother Robb had come around the chapel with more speed than usual and now leaned on the corner of the stone building, laboring for breath. His hunched-over posture warned her that something had happened. She hurried outside and met him partway down the abbey's external corridor. "What's wrong?"

He gripped her arm. "Come inside and I'll tell you."

His behavior alarmed her all the more. "Tell me what has happened!"

Brother Robb patted her back. "There's no news that isn't better for a cup of tea."

With this maddening statement he exerted gentle pressure, guiding her toward the abbey.

"I don't want tea." Recovering her senses, she pulled away from him. "I want to know what the matter is."

He frowned. "It pains me to present you with sorrowful news, Your Serenity."

She pictured her father lying dead. "Is the king all right?"

"He has returned from battle uninjured."

"Then what's the trouble?"

Brother Rob's face sagged. "Your brothers rode into battle with your father."

Suspicion crept over her. "Has this anything to do with them?"

His sorrowful expression gave away the answer.

Caerla turned and ran, not stopping until she reached the keep. She entered through the side door and called to the first guard she saw. "Where may the king be found?"

"He's in the throne room." The guard opened his mouth as if about to speak.

Caerla left him, not certain she could bear what he might say. Her boots thudded down the long corridor to the throne room. She skidded to a halt, catching herself against the door frame. She put a fist to her mouth.

A bier rested upon the throne dais, draped with linen but as yet undecorated. Upon it lay Perthmon with his hands folded across his chest above the linen draping him. His waxen skin and utter lifelessness left his condition in no doubt. Her father stood behind the bier. His head, which had been bowed, lifted. "Caerla, I meant to tell you before you saw him. You shouldn't have found out like this."

She sought for the cause of her brother's death but could not find one. "How did he die?"

"Defending me in battle."

Caerla stared at Perthmon, willing him to move, to breathe, to put the lie to this nightmare. "How can my brother be dead? He was so full of life." Tears choked her, and she gave way to grief.

Her father held her while she sobbed, then looked

down into her face. "I'm sorry I couldn't save him, Caerla."

"And what of my other brother?" She glanced about. "Has he returned with you?"

"Connor chose to remain. His presence keeps the banner of Westerland flying above the garrison."

She nodded, then pulled in a shuddering breath. "Who will tell Mother?"

"That duty is mine. How has she fared at the abbey? I've given her time for her anger to cool before attempting a visit."

"She's angry but adjusting."

"I must tell her at once." He touched her shoulder. "Will you keep watch over your brother while I go to her?"

Caerla nodded, although several guards lined the walls, ready to defend the corpse. Her father's request had nothing to do with the fleshly shell Perthmon had left behind. Her voice was not practiced, but she would sing for her brother the mael lido, the death song said to guide those newly arrived into the World Beyond into Lof Yuel's arms.

༼༽

Euryon braced himself outside Inydde's chamber while Brother Robb unbolted the door. He stepped into the room with misgivings.

"You snake!" Inydde rose from her chair and hurtled toward him. "How dare you darken my door?"

Brother Robb stepped between them. "The king honors you with his presence."

Glaring at the priest, she drew a hasty breath.

"Thank you, Brother Robb. Please wait outside." With a hand at his shoulder, Elcon guided the priest out of harm's way. "Your anger belongs to me, Inydde."

Her gaze snapped to him. "Because you are king, you can lock up your wife whenever she displeases you. If the world were otherwise, and a queen could put her foolish, drunken husband away, I'd have done so long ago."

The door clicked closed behind Brother Robb.

"I deserve that." Euryon gazed at his wife, struck by the yearning to comfort her. "I've given up spirits."

Her mouth dropped open, and she stared at him.

Her reaction did not flatter him, he decided. "I've been blind to the fool I made of myself. Can you forgive me?"

She lifted her head. "I will consider your request, once you have freed me."

He sighed. "Your king locked you up. I spoke as your husband, who grieves your confinement with you."

"Spare me this nonsense. King or husband, you could free me in an instant."

"Inydde, you are not well. I can't in good conscious release you until Brother Robb tells me that you have been delivered from your ailment."

"Will you mark me afflicted when I am not?"

"I and many others have drawn the same conclusion from your behavior. I'm trying to help you."

She eyed him with mistrust written on her face.

He ran a hand down his cheek. "We can talk about this another time. I came on another matter, one that I'm afraid will cause you sorrow."

"More than being shut away like a criminal?" She spat the question.

He nodded, searching for words to begin.

Her self-possession crumbled, and she stepped closer. "What else caused you to seek me?"

"Our son—" he croaked out the words but could speak no further.

Inydde's eyes widened. She clutched her throat with a shaking hand. "Tell me."

"Perthmon fell in battle." He pulled in air. "He didn't live."

"No!" Her wail throbbed through the air. She grasped his arm with both hands. "Take me to my son at once."

"All right." He had anticipated her demand in advance. In truth, denying her would have broken his own heart. What harm could there be in allowing a mother this last vigil over her son?

25

PERIL IN PILAER

Mara winced as her maidservant tugged her hair into braids. She leaned close and murmured near Mara's ear. "The king arrived home this morn."

"Why so soon?" Mara blinked away tears and composed herself to endure the grooming session. "The war can't be over yet."

"It's not." Frowning, the servant met Mara's gaze in the mirror glass. "He brought his dead son home."

Mara closed her eyes at the pain her grandfather must feel. She had not met either of her uncles save briefly the night before the march from Cobbleford began, but something of sorrow touched her as well. What a shame to barely know a kinsman now gone forever. That her family had broken on both her parent's sides created the longing in her to belong. With sudden clarity, she recognized that she needed to visit the inn. She could understand her father's anger at Mam and Da, but hopefully he would understand that she couldn't turn her back on them completely. They had raised her, and she would always love them, despite their sins. If she delayed to appease her father, it might be too late, as it had been with the uncle she'd never known.

Her maidservant tied her final braid, thankfully. Mara turned to her. "Help me dress quickly. I must go to my grandfather. Do you know where he may be?"

"In the throne room, Milady." The servant moved to obey.

A short while later, dressed and groomed, Mara walked down the long corridor toward the throne room. The doors stood strangely ajar and a beautiful song rode the air.

"Fly little dove, pretty dove, fly.

Where will you land if not in the tree?

Wing little bird, pretty bird, wing.

Rest your head and sleep near me."

Mara drew closer to the opening and had to wipe away tears. Caerla stood beside the funeral bier, singing the plaintive lullaby. Mara hesitated with her hand on the door. Such sorrow seemed private. Caerla's song ended, and she bent over her brother, weeping.

Mara pushed open the door. Two guards stationed beside it turned their heads and nodded. She crossed the chamber to stand silently beside her aunt. Curiosity guided her gaze to her uncle's face. In repose, he showed more of a likeness to her than he had while living. The discovery brought a pang, but she wouldn't feign sorrow. Her mother had loved her brother and would have grieved him, and that was enough to hold her here. She put an arm around Caerla's shoulders, and her aunt turned into her embrace. Mara held her while she cried, not counting the passage of time.

"I wish you could have known Perthmon." Caerla sniffed and dried her eyes. "I'm sure you would have enjoyed one another."

Mara nodded. She was beginning to understand how much she had lost.

The main double doors thrust open and her

grandfather strode into the chamber with the queen on his arm. Unprepared for such a sight, Mara cowered behind Caerla.

"Don't fear," her aunt whispered.

Mara tried to take her advice.

"You have no right to be here!" The queen shouted. "It's your fault that my son is dead."

"Stop carrying on, Inydde." Grandfather held onto her arm. "You're frightening Syl Marinda."

Caerla rose to her full height, which wasn't very tall but seemed impressive nevertheless. "How can you say such a thing, Mother?"

"Silence!" Inydde thundered. She put her hands to her head. "You're confusing me."

Pushing her fear aside, Mara walked toward the queen. "I'll go, but I want you to know how sorry I am for what you suffer." The words of forgiveness were hard to speak, but she said them anyway. Mara moved off, leaving her grandmother staring after her with a bewildered expression.

ᘓ

The combined forces of Elderland had driven back the warriors of Pilaer to the grasslands of Graelinn, Rand could tell from the landmarks they passed along the way. He would draw strength from this victory, no matter how much his captivity dampened his delight. Dabron made sure he suffered but stopped short of torturing him to the point of death. When they reached Pilaer, Freaer would finish the job, Dabron never failed to remind him, and Rand had no reason to doubt him. His father had long despised him, and since Draeg had died at his hand, would have no reason for a change of heart. Neither his father nor Dabron cared that Draeg had died while trying to kill him, and that he'd been defending himself against certain death. Draeg's welfare had always mattered more at Pilaer than his own. In his father's eyes, Rand would never be anything but an illegitimate son unworthy of acknowledgment.

In the Pool of Truth, Emmerich had shown him differently. Rand would hold through the beatings and name-calling to the last image of himself he had seen.

The retreat through the fen of Weithein Faen began. By now the warriors had lost their will to conquer and instead fought to survive. Dabron came to Rand in the morning and pulled him to his feet by the slave collar around his neck. "Come along, Misbegotten. It's time to deliver you to Pilaer." He mounted his horse and rode toward the stronghold, forcing Rand to run to keep up or have his neck broken.

He arrived at Pilaer winded and thirsty. Dabron watered his horse at the well and took long gulps of water himself but offered Rand no relief. Jeers followed him along pathways and corridors until they stood outside Freaer's chamber. The guards opened the doors carved with Pilaer's dragons, and Dabron thrust Rand forward. Rand stumbled into the room where Freaer sat cross-legged on the ancient throne.

Amora, who had been half-reclining on the throne beside him with a maidservant fanning her, sat up. "Look what the servants dragged in," she chortled, the beauty of her face transforming into something ugly.

Freaer glared at her. "Why do you instruct me as if I cannot see or hear?"

She stared at Rand with fevered eyes. "Give my son's murderer to me."

"Silence!" Freaer roared.

Amora leaned back on her throne without shifting her attention from Rand.

"Lof Shraen," Dabron made his bow. "I bring you grave news."

"Continue." Freaer spoke in a calm voice but gripped the hand rests above carvings of rampant gryphons.

"The Elder and Kindren forces have joined to drive us back. Some have broken ranks and deserted."

"How do you dare bring me such news rather than rallying my forces and fighting to the death?" Freaer's face went red. "Guards, arrest this coward."

"Wait, Lof Shraen, I beg you." Dabron cried. "I have not abandoned the battle but came away to bring you the prisoner I captured."

Freaer inclined his head, and the guards hovering behind Dabron moved away from him. "Bring him to me."

Rand started forward, hoping to prevent a jerk on his collar, but it came anyway. He stopped before the throne and met his father's gaze.

Freaer swept a glance over him. "You're wearing Rivenn's armor, I see."

Rand held his tongue, knowing that anything he said would not save him.

Freaer turned to Amora. "What would you have me do with him?"

She smiled. "Kill him in a way that displays the strength of your rule to your forces."

"How shall I accomplish this feat?"

She scrambled to her feet, circled Rand with

glinting eyes, and stopped before him. "Throw him from the balcony into a vat of boiling oil."

"Granted."

 CR

The jeers of the crowd that had gathered beneath Freaer's balcony came to Rand as if from a dream. Exhaustion and emotion had caught up with him, bringing confusion to addle his thinking. He had never felt more helpless. The guards had bound his feet together at the ankles and wrapped a rope around him, trapping his arms against his sides. They'd displayed him to the crowd on a stool in one of the embrasures between the raised merlins in the parapet wall enclosing the balcony. He'd had to stand in this position all the while guards set up a metal vat of oil on stone supports with a fire laid beneath it. Now flames licked the sides of the vat and the oil had started to bubble.

Freaer came out onto the balcony holding Amora's hand. He bent his golden head to hers. "You can have the joy of pushing him over. Go ahead. The guards can help you."

Amora pressed forward while Freaer stepped back. She minced toward Rand with a look of delight on her face.

He sent up a final prayer and waited for her to reach him.

The guards moved in behind her.

She had reached the embrasure beside his when the guards rushed her. Terror filled her eyes. The guards seized her, and thrust her over the parapet. Her scream sliced the air. She splashed into the vat and shrieked.

Rand forced his gaze away from the vat of oil.

Amora's shriek cut off abruptly.

The crowd's cheer vanished into the roar of flames as the spilled oil caught fire.

"Why did you kill her?" Rand asked in horror when the noise died down. He'd never liked Amora, but she shouldn't have died a gruesome death.

Freaer shrugged. "I'd had enough. She's shown a penchant for challenging me since Draeg died."

"Perhaps she laid his death at your door. Do you suppose it belongs there?"

Freaer scowled. "Don't tempt me to devise a slower, more painful mode of death for you."

A ruckus went up as the first of Pilaer's retreating warriors arrived at the gatehouse.

"Kindren forces are coming!" the shout rose from below, and the crowd scattered.

Freaer's guards rushed to the edge of the balcony and looked across Weithen Faen to the armies driving Pilaer's warriors before them.

"They'll kill us all," one cried.

"Cut out his tongue," Freaer ordered.

Several of the guards stared at him, but then turned to help hold down the hapless victim. Another produced a dagger. The screech that followed curdled Rand's stomach.

When the guards had finished their awful task, Freaer nodded toward Rand. "Cast him over."

Dabron grinned and stepped forward.

Rand reached out to Mara with a final soul touch, holding nothing of the love he felt for her back, then hid himself to spare her his death throws.

ᚢ

Sword drawn, Elcon led Kai and Aerlic into Pilaer's throne room. He advanced into the chamber, which stood empty, on silent feet. Raised voices on the balcony suggested why the doors had been unbarred and unattended.

He'd led the secret foray into Pilaer through its postern door over Craelin's objections. Elcon had ended the debate by reminding Craelin which of them ruled the other. He respected the first guardian of Rivenn, but sometimes Craelin acted like a mother bruin safeguarding her cub. To give Craelin his due, a shraen should not risk himself in this way. Elcon wouldn't have done so, except that confronting the Contender within his lair would save bloodshed. Freaer could only be brought down by Sword Rivenn. The spirit sword possessed the unmatched ability to dispel magics and destroy darksome creatures. He had promised to defend Faeraven that long-ago day when the sword had passed from his mother's hand to his, and he meant to keep his word.

Putting on the armor taken from a fallen warrior had repelled him. With Pilaer's forces in disarray, Elcon and his companions had slipped through the warriors more readily than he'd anticipated. Elcon had heard his name cursed more than once, making him thankful for the disguise that hid him. He and his companions had taken the final stretch to the postern gate ahead of the retreating warriors, but then despaired of finding the lever Rand had mentioned until Aerlic's sharp eye spotted a gap in the mortar.

Footsteps started toward them.

Elcon pressed close to the wall beside the open doorway, grateful that the noise from the balcony would hide any sound they made.

The footsteps halted and Freaer's suffocating soul touch dropped over Elcon. He had fought Freaer before, but never at such close quarters. Battered by wave after wave of darkness, he felt himself drowning. Sword Rivenn's blade glowed with blue light, radiating energy into him.

Freaer's shil shael broke and ebbed away.

"To your weapons!" Elcon pushed away from the wall and led the charge onto the balcony.

Freaer had backed away from the doorway and stood watching him with a sword in his hand. His posture suggested a cornered wolf. Twelve guards stepped between him and Elcon's blade.

Kai and Aerlic came up beside Elcon, the archer with his bow drawn. The arrow he launched ripped through the air, and the first guard fell.

"Kill Elcon!" Freaer called from the embrasure where he'd retreated. "Guardians, defend your Lof Shraen."

Shouts and the thud of running feet answered him. The guards came at Elcon in a body, forcing him to counter multiple swords.

Kai defended Elcon and Aerlic both, fighting with the mastery that had elevated him within the guardians. The archer's bowstring twanged again and again, followed by thuds and moans. Elcon caught himself favoring the side Draeg had wounded and forced himself to stop. One of the guards must have noticed, for he came at Elcon's injured side with more zeal than wisdom. The guard misstepped, and Elcon dealt him a blow that ended his assaults. The episode had weakened Elcon, a fact he could no longer hide. This prompted further attempts on his wounded side.

The blades that slashed at Elcon lessened in number, but the pounding of boots told him that more hurtled toward them down Pilaer's corridors. "Bolt the doors!" Aerlic withdrew into the throne room, his running footsteps echoing.

In the archer's absence, the four remaining warriors bore down on Elcon with renewed vigor. Elcon felt himself lagging, and his concentration suffered.

Kai seemed to sense this, for he shifted to fight shoulder-to shoulder with him.

Doors banged shut in the throne room, and the bar thudded into place. Fists pounded on wood amid shouting, telling Elcon how close to peril they had come.

The archer returned and dispatched more guards.

Elcon turned, panting, having felled the final guard.

Aerlic stood with his bow aimed at Freaer.

The archer released the arrow, which shattered in flight.

Freaer lowered the hand he'd raised. "Your paltry weapons can't harm me."

Sword Rivenn glowed blue, and Elcon braced for an attack from the unseen.

Wraiths surrounded him, wailing. He backed away from them, but then remembered from his previous encounter that the wraiths of his own regrets couldn't hurt his body. He cut Sword Rivenn through the wraiths, even the one with Aewen's face, and they vanished.

Freaer had already pushed past him.

Kai pursued Freaer into the throne room. Blue light arced through the air, and Kai cried out as it met him. His sword spun from his hand, and he gripped his wrist, in obvious pain.

'Your blade can't stand up to magics,' Freaer taunted. He turned to lift the bar from the doors and admit more of Pilaer's warriors.

"Turn and fight," Elcon demanded, "or I'll drop you where you stand."

Freaer spun about and lunged at him with his blade. Sword Rivenn blazed with light, cutting whatever magics had accompanied the blow, and deflected his blade.

Freaer eyed his weapon. "You bring Rivenn's sword against me."

A thump shook the doors, and Elcon recognized the sound of a battering ram.

Freaer moved into fighting stance. "The spirit sword can kill me, but only if you deliver the blow."

"Then I must do so." Elcon thrust at him.

Freaer sidestepped and came around to strike the armor covering Elcon's wounded side. Elcon deflected a second blow, but without armor, he'd have taken the blade. He backed to give himself time to recover.

Freaer followed, pressing his advantage.

The battering ram thudded the doors, splintering wood. Kai and Aerlic moved into position beside the doors.

Elcon stopped retreating and held his own against Freaer. Their blades clashed, igniting sparks. They held together, and then broke apart, panting. Sweat ran into Elcon's eyes and he blinked to clear his blurred vision.

Freaer dove at him, stabbing with his blade.

Elcon arched backwards. This had to end. Summoning every ounce of will he possessed, he brought Sword Rivenn slashing upward. He stepped backward, the drag on his sword telling him he'd made impact.

With a strangled sound, Freaer fell. He clutched his stomach, and blood welled through his fingers from the hole in his surcoat. "You were bound to win, son of Rivenn," he ground out between gasping breaths.

Elcon stood over him. "Why did you send so many to their deaths if you knew that?"

Freaer's smile was almost pleasant. "Because they didn't." He closed his eyes, and his face went lax.

The doors crashed open and warriors from Pilaer broke into the chamber.

Elcon stood to face them. "Freaer is dead."

Those in the forefront stumbled to a stop, holding back the mumbling crowd.

"Is he really dead?" a gruff-voiced warrior questioned.

"I assure you that he is." Elcon answered.

"We're free!" another voice shouted. The call went up throughout the crowd. A few fights broke out, but Elcon judged the murmurings as more pleased than angry. In the end, no one challenged them.

"I'm glad to find you alive." Elcon turned as Rand joined him. "Where were you hiding?"

"In plain sight. The guard trying to throw me off the balcony let go of me when you arrived. I hit my head and blacked out until Kai revived me."

"Perhaps it was a mercy that saved you from fighting your father."

"I would have done so."

"I know that, Son of Rivenn. You've convinced me of your trustworthiness." Elcon smiled. "In case you wondered. the requirement to stay away from my daughter no longer exists."

26

HOMECOMING

Kai guided Flecht through the hole near the summit of Maeg Waer and onto the landing at the top of the stone stair that Shae had traveled long ago to reach Gilead Riann. The Gate of Life had opened in the wall at the other end of the natural bridge that spanned the abyss of Lohen Keil, the Well of Light. His present journey, he hoped, have a happier result.

Elcon's determination to cast Freaer's corpse into the Well of Light at the earliest opportunity had guided his choices. With Freaer dead, the need for secrecy vanished, leaving the welkes who roosted in this place the only drawback. Once the combined Kindren and Elder forces had taken possession of Pilaer, Elcon and those with him had obtained wingabeasts. They had timed their flight into the mountain for morning after the raptor birds left their roosts to hunt.

Aerlic joined him, then Elcon leading a wingabeast bearing Freaer's body wrapped in a shroud.

While gazing at the Gate of Death, Aerlic blew out a breath. "So this is what Lohen Keil looks like."

"That's right." Kai glanced at him. "You never made it here." He smiled, remembering the miracle that had restored Aerlic to life.

"I've been waiting for you," a familiar voice called

to them.

Kai started. How had he missed seeing Emmerich standing on the bridge?

"Bring Freaer to me." Emmerich's command rang out.

"Gladly." Elcon lifted his head. "The sooner I'm rid of watching over Freaer's body, the better. I can't get over the feeling that he'll wake at any instant."

"He'll remain asleep this day," Emmerich assured him. "But unless I cast him into the Well of Light, he will wake."

Elcon lifted Freaer from the wingabeast and carried his body to the bridge. Emmerich held out his arms to receive the corpse. He walked to the center of the natural bridge and stepped to the edge. The Flames of Virtue shot upward from the depths of the mountain and licked the bridge. "I consign you to the double death, Son of Perdition." He pushed Freaer over the edge. The flames roared and receded with the falling body. "Lof Yuel has delivered Elderland from your curse."

The words sang through Kai, bestowing peace. His sufferings he had endured brought freedom to others. He frowned—all save one. "What of Shae?" He spoke the question that weighted his mind.

ભ

The earthshakes had stopped, for which Shae was thankful. Something had shifted in the right direction. She left the sanctity of the garden for the corridor between worlds. It stretched endlessly with gates on either hand, tempting her to explore. She pulled back from the idea. What if she went through a door and couldn't find her way back again? She'd be cut off from Kai, Elcon, and her family at Whellein. Quite possibly, her absence might hinder Emmerich's return.

She sighed. The garden had perfect weather, beautiful flowers, and all the luscious fruit she wanted to eat. She'd trade it all for the chance to go home. Mother and Father would have aged by now, and more of her sisters would be wedded. She could have been made an aunt many times over by now. Her lost brother Daeven might have come home from sea. And best of all, she could embrace Kai again. She wouldn't hold him to his promise to wait for her. What if he'd found another maiden to love? He'd drawn interest enough from the feminine quarter. His preoccupation with duty providing an intriguing challenge.

Shae shook her head, dispelling the dream that had carried her away. Each time she allowed herself to be drawn into these thoughts, setting them aside became harder. The garden would soothe her. There she could trail her fingers in the silken water of the pool and imagine Kai beside her.

A light shone into the corridor as the gateway opened. She stared in wonder, hardly daring to believe what it meant, but she could see through its mists. Emmerich had grown from the youth she'd traded places with to the man on the other side of the gate. She hurried toward him, with laughter ready to burst forth.

Lit from above by a beam of light, he watched her approach with a look of approval. "Others live because of your faithfulness, Shae."

Her face warmed. "I'm glad."

He smiled. "Kai waits for you. Go to him."

Shae passed through the gate with little more than a ripple. Kai stood on the natural bridge spanning the drop at the heart of Maeg Waer. The look he gave her and the arms he extended told her all she needed to know. She ran forward into his arms, laughing even while tears dampened her cheeks. He held her so tightly, she had to pull away to breathe. She gazed up at him and touched his face. "You haven't aged."

He caught her hand and kissed it. "The result of a time trap. You, on the other hand, have ripened into a beauty. I count myself blessed to possess your favor."

She laughed. "You own more than that, Kai, as I'm sure you know. My heart belongs to you."

"You have mine as well." He lowered his head and kissed her.

She pushed him away for modesty's sake, for Elcon and Aerlic watched them. "I don't know how your family at Whellein will receive the news."

"Whatever their reactions, we'll deal with them together." He took her hand in his. "Agreed?"

She smiled at him. "Agreed."

೧೩

Mara stopped short on the dais steps. How had Rand gained an invitation to dine at the king's table, and why was he seated next to her father? Realizing that her stare gave away her thoughts, she lowered her gaze, and continued up the stairs.

Her father stood. "There you are, Syl Marinda. You must sit next to Rand."

Mara sent her father a startled glance. When had he started calling Rand by his nickname? She took the chair he'd indicated.

Rand turned to her. "It's good to see you, Mara."

Was it her imagination or had his voice warmed on her name? Also, why was he looking at her with such intensity? "I'm glad you're back safely from battle," she blurted out.

"As am I." He smiled at her so brightly her breath caught. "I'm pleased to sit beside you."

The first course arrived, sparing her a reply. Mara took small portions, since Merwith had mentioned the menu earlier. Grandfather had ordered a true feast to celebrate victory. They dined upon hare soup, brined stag, stuffed chicken, and veal before the servants cleared the leftovers away and brought in meat pies, vegetable dishes covered in sauce, pomegranate seeds and sugared plums, plus saffron eggs. More courses introduced other meats and fishes. They also sampled plums stewed in rose water, cheese slices, and fruit preserves wrapped in pastry.

"I can't eat another bite," Rand groaned at last.

Mara laughed, having relaxed in his presence during the feast. "I'll confess to feeling that way myself."

"Walk with me in the garden?" He couched his request in the softest of tones, making it difficult to refuse.

In truth, she didn't want to leave him, not while enjoying the afterglow of a shared table in joyous company. "All right." Protocol called for her maidservant to accompany her, but that would introduce a delay and seemed silly besides. She'd traveled with Rand alone in the wilderness without incident. Well, mostly, if she didn't count the times he'd kissed her.

The moon shone from the sky, nearly full. She frowned. "Is it waxing or waning, do you suppose?"

"Waning," he answered at once. "It was full two nights past when we arrived."

She ought to have known he could give the answer. "A lot has happened since then."

"That's true." He took her arm to guide her down one of the garden paths. They passed beneath strongwood trees dripping silvered leaves from gnarled branches. Mara breathed in the sweet fragrance of a night-blooming flower with white blossoms. She sighed. "Did you hear that the king has hired Hael and his band as trackers to supply his table?"

"That's good news for them."

"Arillia gave Hael permission to court Lyneth. If they want to wed, she'll release Lyneth from service."

He held a branch out of her way. "Are you happy about that?"

"Why wouldn't I be?" She glanced up at him without thinking and found his lips far too close to hers. She averted her gaze. "I hope they find happiness together."

They walked in companionable silence along the edge of a pond. Steps led down to a curving bank. Mara watched the moon's reflection in the glassy surface with a sense of contentment. The world would continue without being intruded upon by Freaer's evil.

"I thought you might wonder why your father invited you to sit with me." Rand spoke from behind her.

"I did."

He chuckled. "He's given up on keeping us apart." His hands warmed her shoulders. "I tried my best to keep away from you, but I couldn't do it."

"Circumstances thrust us together."

"It was more than that, Mara, and you know it."

Losing an inner battle, she turned to face him. "I do."

At his indrawn breath, she lifted her head to meet his kiss. He gave it briefly but soundly, then removed her from him. "I should take you back to your father, Lof Raena."

She laughed. "He's far too involved with Arillia to care about my spending time in the garden with you. I'm to have a half-sibling."

"Congratulations. What does that mean for you as Heir of Faeraven?"

"I don't know, but I'm willing to concede if that's best. I've developed a feeling for wandering, and I'd be hard pressed to do that as Lof Raelein of Faeraven. The decision is a distant one at this point."

He offered her his hand. "Come, Mara. I'll not sully your reputation by keeping you in the garden too long."

She smiled. "Hear me out, if you will, and then I'll go back willingly."

He tilted his head in a listening attitude. "Go on."

"Some days ago, I felt a soul touch I'm certain came from you."

He nodded. "I remember it."

Her cheeks warmed. "I distinctly recall the message you sent me."

"I told you that I love you." He spoke the words calmly, like a person resigned to the inevitable. Perhaps his struggle had been similar to hers.

She turned to him and let go of safety. "I love you too."

He gathered her in his arms. "Thank you." He lowered his head, and she lifted her face to his for a lingering kiss. Quiet joy pulsed through her and a feeling of completion. She had come home.

Thank you…

for purchasing this Harbourlight title. For other inspirational stories, please visit our on-line bookstore at www.pelicanbookgroup.com.

For questions or more information, contact us at customer@pelicanbookgroup.com.

Harbourlight Books
The Beacon in Christian Fiction™
an imprint of Pelican Book Group
www.pelicanbookgroup.com

Connect with Us
www.facebook.com/Pelicanbookgroup
www.twitter.com/pelicanbookgrp

To receive news and specials, subscribe to our bulletin
http://pelink.us/bulletin

May God's glory shine through
this inspirational work of fiction.

AMDG

You Can Help!

At Pelican Book Group it is our mission to entertain readers with fiction that uplifts the Gospel. It is our privilege to spend time with you awhile as you read our stories.

We believe you can help us to bring Christ into the lives of people across the globe. And you don't have to open your wallet or even leave your house!

Here are 3 simple things you can do to help us bring illuminating fiction™ to people everywhere.

1) If you enjoyed this book, write a positive review. Post it at online retailers and websites where readers gather. And share your review with us at reviews@pelicanbookgroup.com (this does give us permission to reprint your review in whole or in part.)

2) If you enjoyed this book, recommend it to a friend in person, at a book club or on social media.

3) If you have suggestions on how we can improve or expand our selection, let us know. We value your opinion. Use the contact form on our web site or e-mail us at customer@pelicanbookgroup.com

God Can Help!

Are you in need? The Almighty can do great things for you. Holy is His Name! He has mercy in every generation. He can lift up the lowly and accomplish all things. Reach out today.

Do not fear: I am with you; do not be anxious: I am your God. I will strengthen you, I will help you, I will uphold you with my victorious right hand.
~Isaiah 41:10 (NAB)

We pray daily, and we especially pray for everyone connected to Pelican Book Group—that includes you! If you have a specific need, we welcome the opportunity to pray for you. Share your needs or praise reports at http://pelink.us/pray4us

Free Book Offer

We're looking for booklovers like you to partner with us! Join our team of influencers today and periodically receive free eBooks and exclusive offers.

For more information
Visit http://pelicanbookgroup.com/booklovers

How About Free Audiobooks?

We're looking for audiobook lovers, too! Partner with us as an audiobook lover and periodically receive free audiobooks!

For more information
Visit
http://pelicanbookgroup.com/booklovers/freeaudio.html

or e-mail
booklovers@pelicanbookgroup.com